For a cop, Cruz Gregerson was amazingly kind and thoughtful.

She might even say gentle.

But Kelsey had always thought him a gentleman, from the first time he'd come here. It was only the knowledge of what he did for a living that had changed the way she looked at him.

And somehow that didn't seem quite fair. He was still the man whose visits she had looked forward to each year. He was still the man who took the same quiet pleasure in her home as she herself did. Did knowing he was a cop really change all that?

She wasn't sure, but she had the feeling that Cruz Gregerson was not only not what she'd thought a cop would be but, as a man, far more than she had ever expected.

Dear Reader,

With the coming of fall, the days—and nights—are getting cooler, but you can heat them up again with this month's selections from Silhouette Intimate Moments. Award winner Justine Davis is back with the latest installment in her popular TRINITY STREET WEST miniseries, *A Man To Trust*. Hero Cruz Gregerson proves himself to be just that—though it takes heroine Kelsey Hall a little time to see it. Add a pregnant runaway, a mighty cute kid and an opportunely appearing snake (yes, I said "snake"!), and you have a book to cherish forever.

With *Baby by Design*, award-winning Paula Detmer Riggs concludes her MATERNITY ROW trilogy. Pregnant-with-twins Raine Paxton certainly isn't expecting a visit from her ex-husband, Morgan—and neither one of them is expecting the sensuous fireworks that come next! Miniseries madness continues with *Roarke's Wife*, the latest in Beverly Barton's THE PROTECTORS, and Maggie Shayne's *Badlands Bad Boy*, the newest in THE TEXAS BRAND. Both of these miniseries will be going on for a while—and if you haven't discovered them already, you'll certainly want to come along for the ride. Then turn to Marie Ferrarella's *Serena McKee's Back in Town* for a reunion romance with heart-stopping impact. Finally there's Cheryl St.John's second book for the line, *The Truth About Toby*, a moving story about how dreams can literally come true.

Here at Intimate Moments, we pride ourselves on bringing you books that represent the best in romance fiction, so I hope you'll enjoy every one of this month's selections, then join us again next month, when the excitement—and the passion—continue.

Yours,

Leslie J. Wainger
Senior Editor and Editorial Coordinator

Please address questions and book requests to:
Silhouette Reader Service
U.S.: 3010 Walden Ave., P.O. Box 1325, Buffalo, NY 14269
Canadian: P.O. Box 609, Fort Erie, Ont. L2A 5X3

A MAN TO TRUST

JUSTINE DAVIS

Published by Silhouette Books

America's Publisher of Contemporary Romance

SILHOUETTE BOOKS

ISBN 0-373-07805-6

A MAN TO TRUST

Copyright © 1997 by Janice Davis Smith

This edition published by arrangement with Harlequin Books S.A.

® and TM are trademarks of Harlequin Books S.A., used under license.
Trademarks indicated with ® are registered in the United States Patent
and Trademark Office, the Canadian Trade Marks Office and in other
countries.

Printed in U.S.A.

Books by Justine Davis

Silhouette Intimate Moments

Hunter's Way #371
Loose Ends #391
Stevie's Chase #402
Suspicion's Gate #423
Cool Under Fire #444
Race Against Time #474
To Hold an Eagle #497
Target of Opportunity #506
One Last Chance #517
Wicked Secrets #555
Left at the Altar #596
Out of the Dark #638
The Morning Side of Dawn #674
*Lover Under Cover #698
*Leader of the Pack #728
*A Man To Trust #805

*Trinity Street West

Silhouette Desire

Angel for Hire #680
Upon the Storm #712
Found Father #772
Private Reasons #833
Errant Angel #924

Silhouette Books

Silhouette Summer Sizzlers 1994
"The Raider"

Fortune's Children

The Wrangler's Bride #10

JUSTINE DAVIS

lives in San Clemente, California. Her interests outside of writing are sailing, doing needlework, horseback riding and driving her restored 1967 Corvette roadster—top down, of course.

A policewoman, Justine says that years ago, a young man she worked with encouraged her to try for a promotion to a position that was, at that time, occupied only by men. "I succeeded, became wrapped up in my new job, and that man moved away, never, I thought, to be heard from again. Ten years later he appeared out of the woods of Washington State, saying he'd never forgotten me and would I please marry him? With that history, how could I write anything but romance?"

Chapter 1

Rabbit?

No, too big.

Raccoon?

No, too small.

Possum.

Cruz Gregerson yawned and rolled over, satisfied that he'd correctly labeled the small sound that had awakened him. He should move Sam into this room when she came home, he thought sleepily. Then she could listen to all the noise her menagerie made during the night.

He yawned again, knowing he didn't really mind. He would rather have her here, her every spare moment spent caring for her small zoo, than involved in some of the activities that seemed to occupy other kids. His daughter was preciously innocent of the uglier ways of the world, and for that he would gladly put up with the collection of wild creatures she tended.

Except for the snake.

He shivered—a reflexive reaction to an aversion so deep-seated he couldn't remember ever not having it. It was a damn good thing the camp let her take the slithery thing with her; feeding the furry ones was one thing, but he wasn't about to feed their smaller brethren to the beady-eyed reptile that made him shudder every time he looked at it. And it took every bit of restraint he had to watch her handle the beast. Just the sight of it curling around her slender arm made him shaky, but he still refused to let her handle it unless he was there. Sam's patient explanation that the black-and-white king— which she had named, appropriately enough, Slither—was a good snake had had no effect at all.

"Some big, brave cop you are," he muttered to himself. For Sam's sake, he'd tried to overcome the fear. He'd tried often enough to know that it was something he was going to live with for the rest of his life; if he couldn't do it for his beloved little girl, he couldn't do it for anyone.

But the two-foot-long creature had thankfully gone with Sam, curled docilely in a loosely woven cloth bag and placed in a small cage Cruz himself had checked the latches on at least a dozen times before allowing Samantha to put it in the truck for the trip up to the summer camp in the San Bernardino Mountains this morning.

And tomorrow morning he left for his own summer camp.

He smiled into the midnight darkness. And jumped when the shrill ring of the phone cut through the night.

They wouldn't, would they? Not when he was officially on vacation for two weeks, as of yesterday. No, they wouldn't. Even if something big had broken, Ryan would handle it, or Gage. The detectives of Trinity West were the best there were, and—

The second ring of the phone jarred away the last remnants of sleep. He reached for the receiver.

"Gregerson," he said, out of long-ingrained habit; late-night calls to detective sergeants were rarely of the social variety.

When no answer came across the line, he sat up. The last time he'd gotten a call like this, it had been Lacey Buckhart, Ryan's wife, and the start of the steamroller case that had brought the end of Trinity West's worst gang and the rebirth of the Buckharts' marriage.

"Hello?" he said into the silent telephone.

"Hello, Cruz."

Cruz blinked, startled. He hadn't heard that voice in a year, but it was unmistakable to him, just the same.

"Kelsey?" Lord, she sounded just as Lacey had that night, when she was shaken by the premonition that Ryan had been hurt. "What's wrong?"

"I... Nothing."

He refrained from stating the obvious, that she wouldn't be calling at midnight if it was nothing. "Kelsey—"

"I'm just calling to tell you...you can't come tomorrow."

"What?"

"I... We're closed."

Cruz ran a hand over his sleep-tousled hair. This didn't make any sense. He went to the Oak Tree Inn every year at the same time, but now, the night before he was to arrive, she called to cancel?

"Closed?" he asked.

"We're... We have a water leak."

Warning bells went off in Cruz's mind, several of them at once. An occupational hazard, he supposed, although he doubted anybody could miss the fact that Kelsey Hall was lying through her pretty little teeth. And it wasn't just the fact that he knew the small bed-and-breakfast inn had all-new plumbing—she had just opened it when he almost literally stumbled across it three years ago—it was also that Kelsey was one of the worst liars he'd ever heard, and in nine years as a cop, he'd heard plenty.

"Kelsey, what's wrong?"

"Nothing," she repeated. Too quickly. Too urgently. "I'm sorry, Cruz, I know this is horribly late notice."

"So," he said, keeping his tone even as he concentrated intently on the undertone in her voice, "the whole place is flooded? Even the rooms upstairs?"

"No, but...it's a mess."

"I'll help you clean it up."

"No! I... That is, I've got help. Thank you, but—"

"If it's that bad, you can use more, right?"

"That wouldn't be right, it's your vacation."

"And it's up to me how I spend it."

"Cruz, please, just don't come, all right?"

He was right. He knew he was.

Sometimes he hated being a cop. Sometimes he wished he could be like most people, accepting others at face value. But there was no off switch on a cop's tendency toward suspicion; the best he could do was try to control it.

But sometimes it shouted too loudly to be controlled.

"What's wrong, Kelsey?" he asked softly.

She said nothing. And as was often the case with Kelsey Hall, her silence spoke volumes. He'd often welcomed that silence when he was at the inn, when she left him alone to find what peace he could in the quiet setting she'd made so welcoming. But now it rang in his head, unstoppably, as it so often did, that gut-level suspicion that was so easily triggered by a flicker of an eye, sweat on a brow, or, like now, by the faintest of tremors in a usually calm voice.

And by the vivid memory of Kelsey Hall's shock when, just as he was leaving at the end of his stay last year, she'd discovered he was a cop.

He'd never intentionally hidden the fact, it was simply that this was his one time away from it, and the whole point was to try to leave the job behind, at least for a while. When it had come up in their casual conversation, he'd used the camouflage many cops used when they didn't want to discuss their jobs; he'd said he worked for the city of Marina Heights and let it go at that. And Kelsey never seemed to pry; Cruz hadn't quite been able to decide if she simply wasn't the curious sort of woman, or if she was just exercising the discretion of a good innkeeper.

But on that last day, when he was literally in his truck in the inn's driveway, his mind already back at the department, he'd let it slip, thinking it would hardly matter at that point, after three years of coming to Oak Tree.

And Kelsey had paled as if he'd confessed to a felony.

"Cruz..." she began on the phone now, then stopped.

He couldn't help it, that undertone was still there in her voice, and all he could think was that it wasn't that she didn't want anyone there, it was that she didn't want *him* there. She'd always genuinely welcomed him before, even laughingly christened him "First Guest," as if it were a royal title, after he found Oak Tree and she let him stay before she had even officially opened.

"You look at this place like I do," she'd told him then. "Like there's peace for you here." And she'd added teasingly that as long as he kept coming back, she would know she must be doing something right.

Apparently it was he who'd done something wrong. He'd let her know he was a cop. And it seemed it was the cop she wanted to keep away.

"You can come some other time, on the house," she said.

"No," he said, not exactly sure what he was saying no to—the simple fact that this was his only vacation without Sam, her request that he not come, or the odd urgency in her voice.

"I'm sorry, Cruz. Really. But I have to cancel."

She hung up, rather abruptly, as if to forestall his saying anything more.

He sat there for a moment, the receiver still in his hand. His thoughts were tumbling in that rapid-fire manner he'd become used to when his suspicions were aroused. He barely knew Kelsey; her reserve had kept their acquaintance just that, despite the fact that he found her quiet demeanor appealing, and the combination of dark auburn hair that flashed coppery highlights in the sun and vivid green eyes strikingly attractive. Not to mention her distinctly female shape, curved in all the right places, not the rail-thin, boyish figure so many women seemed to strive for these days.

In fact, when he first set eyes on her, that day she found him sitting beneath the lovely, shade-spreading California oak, he'd almost turned down her offer to be the first guest at Oak Tree. He'd felt the spark of interest when she immediately put her finger on exactly what had drawn him off the main highway to this place, the lure of quiet and peace and the sparkle of the Pacific in the distance; Oak Tree was close enough to the ocean to offer an enjoyable view, yet not so close that it was caught up in the bustle of coastal activity and the resultant fast and expensive life-style. He'd felt that spark and wanted to retreat; Kelsey Hall was intriguing enough to be dangerous to his hard-won peace of mind.

Now he hung up the phone and flipped on the bedside lamp, blinking at the sudden flare of light.

He remembered what had changed his mind that day, what had overridden his instinctive retreat from this woman who caused a reaction in him that he didn't want and certainly wasn't going to pursue. She had not only seemed to instinctively understand why he was there, but had been more than willing to leave him to seek the peace he found only in this one week out of his year, in this place that held no memories but pleasant ones, no connection at all to the life that had shattered around him. She seemed to know that he came here for a respite, and her calm serenity helped him find it; he even found himself striving to equal the tranquillity she exuded.

That was why her nervousness now set him so on edge. True, he hardly knew her; they'd barely gotten beyond casual conversation and perhaps one shared meal during his stays. He'd sensed that she had a private side she kept hidden— and, considering his own past, he could hardly fault her for that—but he'd by necessity become a quick, accurate judge of people, and he would swear on his badge that there was nothing underhanded involved. She just wasn't the type.

But he would also swear on that badge that there was something wrong. Kelsey was not a woman who was easily fazed, yet she had definitely been distressed.

Sam was already at camp, Kit was going to take care of the zoo—minus Slither—and he was already packed. The facts marched through his mind like a checklist, and he knew he was looking for a reason not to cancel his plans. He wondered why he didn't just admit the biggest reason of all: He *needed* this escape.

So why not just go? If he was wrong, if she was really knee-deep in water, he would just help out as he'd suggested. It wasn't that he needed to rest physically, it was the mental break he needed. And if she truly didn't need help, or he would be in the way, he could just keep going up the coast, until he found a likely place to spend the week.

But if he was right…

All the more reason, he told himself rather crisply. He liked Kelsey, and if she had a problem—he couldn't quite manage to believe she herself had gotten into some kind of trouble that would make her so anxious to keep a cop away—maybe he could help. Whatever the problem was, it was clearly disturbing her. And he felt an odd need to help her restore her serenity; he saw so few people truly at peace, he didn't like to see it shattered in one who had managed it.

He would have to change his approach, he supposed, since he usually kept pretty much to himself while at Oak Tree. He would probably have to probe a little to get her to open up to him, but he'd always been good at that. It was one of the reasons he was a good cop; people tended to trust him.

"Yeah," he muttered to himself as he sat up, rubbing at gritty eyes. "They trust you because they don't have a clue how screwed up you are."

He knew it was true; everybody always talked about how together he was, how he never shorted either his job or his young daughter, but he knew he wasn't anywhere near the superman they painted him. He knew that half the time he was flying blind, running on hunches and instinct, never really knowing if he was right or wrong, just hoping that he didn't make any major goofs.

On the job, it could get somebody killed. At home, it could screw up a little girl's entire life. A little girl he loved beyond measure. Sam was the best thing in his life. He'd been sort of neutral about kids when Ellie announced her pregnancy, but the moment he held that tiny bundle of humanity in his hands, he'd lost a part of his heart he'd never even known existed. He'd known then that he would never get it back, but he didn't want it back; it was Sam's, no matter where she went or what she did.

And every time he saw a kid in trouble, he thought of her, felt the fear every parent felt, only magnified a thousand times by the knowledge of the dark, ugly side of the world cops were privy to. It was why he didn't work the juvenile section; he knew he would go crazy. He didn't know how Gage Butler did it. Maybe not having kids of your own did make a difference. But he doubted it; Gage was as driven as any man he'd ever known, although Cruz didn't know why.

He lay back, knowing that somewhere beneath all the random thoughts, another level of his mind had been busy. It was how things worked, and he'd grown used to this process he couldn't really explain; it was what had helped him solve more than one tough case.

And it was what decided him now. It wasn't just that, as a cop, he was automatically suspicious of anyone who didn't want a cop around. It was that gut reaction to somebody in trouble, that reaction he couldn't seem to shake, couldn't bury beneath a layer of self-interested indifference as so many did.

Kelsey Hall had a problem, and he liked her just enough not to be able to walk away.

He sighed and rolled over, wondering what he was letting himself in for this time.

"Great," Kelsey muttered to herself. "Now you've really done it."

She stared at the phone, wishing she could take back the idiotic call she'd made. She sighed. She'd reacted impulsively, panicking when she looked at her calendar late last night, for the first time all day, and realized Cruz Gregerson was due to arrive tomorrow.

Cruz Gregerson, who had been her first guest, before she even opened Oak Tree, who had so clearly been drawn to this quiet, peaceful setting for the same reasons she had been, who had been back for a week every year since, who had spent hours sitting beneath the spreading oak that gave Oak Tree its name, quietly working on something in the small spiral notebook he always brought. Just looking at him had given her an odd sense of satisfaction; that, as much as anything, was why she had opened the inn in this spot, to see people find what he had found here.

And the pleasure she took in watching him had nothing to do with his looks, she told herself. Nothing to do with the striking combination of thick, nearly black hair and bright blue eyes, a walking explanation of the mixed heritage evident in his name. Nothing to do with his quiet smile and his way of moving with such easy grace. He wasn't overly big, a hair under six feet, she guessed, but he was solid, muscular and probably even stronger than he looked.

It was that unmistakable strength, so much greater than her own, that had made her wary. Not in the way any woman is by necessity wary of a more powerful male she didn't know could be trusted not to use that strength against her, but in the way of a woman who caught herself thinking of that power turned in other directions.

"He's a cop," she reminded herself fiercely.

Not that she needed reminding. She'd been so stunned when, just as he was leaving last year, he muttered something about putting the badge back on, that he stared at her in surprise. Her shock had turned to embarrassment and, flustered, she had waved him away hastily, wishing only that he would leave so that she could recover.

A cop. Her favorite guest, the man who so fascinated her, albeit against her will, was a cop. And she'd never known, never guessed. How could she? He was quiet, unobtrusive and seemingly bent on nothing more than utterly and completely relaxing while he was here. They'd never talked much about personal things, partly because she sensed he came here to escape them. And, having some secrets of her own, she wasn't one to pry. She had, despite her fascination, left him to his solitude, sensing how much he needed the peace he got from this place.

She'd never suspected why he needed it so badly. Never suspected that when he left, he went back to a job that had one of the highest death rates in existence, and divorce and alcoholism rates even higher than that. She'd sensed that there was something beneath his surface calm, that his quiet demeanor was deceptive, that there was hidden fire there, but never had she expected that.

Cruz Gregerson was a cop.

It still made her feel oddly off balance. She'd welcomed him here, to this haven she'd built. She'd looked forward to his visits. And he was a cop.

"And now you've made him suspicious," she muttered, getting up to pace her room. "At the worst possible time."

Just what she needed around here, a suspicious cop. That could endanger everything, could ruin all she was trying to do here.

She sat on the edge of her bed. It creaked, as usual, and she quickly stilled it, not wanting to awaken Melissa. The girl needed rest, badly.

She shouldn't have panicked, she thought miserably. All the times before, when Cruz was here, although perfectly friendly and congenial, he had never intruded on her any more than any other guest. He had never pried into her life or privacy, or asked her any questions she couldn't answer. She hadn't thought anything of it at the time, had just classified him as an innkeeper's dream guest: quiet, undemanding, pleasant.

She had even had an occasional meal with him, when he was the only guest and invited her to join him; the conversation had been light, interesting, amusing…and generally impersonal, without much effort on her part to keep it that way. Yet another reason why she had been so stunned to find out he was a cop. She'd imagined them as always asking questions, always skeptical, always suspecting.

She'd imagined them to be the way Cruz had been on the phone tonight.

"Thanks to you," she chastised herself aloud. She could probably have counted on his usual demeanor to keep him from finding out, she thought. He probably never would have even noticed anything. But now she'd gone and roused his suspicions. Cop suspicions.

She sighed. Oak Tree was the culmination of a lifelong dream, and now she'd endangered it with her own silly panic. Chances were Cruz's visit would have gone as all the rest had, quietly, uneventfully. Of course, during all his other visits, she'd had nothing to hide from him. But he probably never would have noticed anything different this time. She could have told him any number of things about Melissa. He would have had no reason to question them.

Except that he was a cop, and they had a tendency to question everything.

Without realizing it, she found herself back on her feet, pacing yet again.

"All right," she said to the empty room, "now what? You can't change what just happened, so deal with it. Just deal with it."

It always seemed to help, hearing it spoken aloud, even if it was in her own voice, instead of Cecelia's. It was from her that Kelsey had picked up the habit of bucking herself up aloud; it not only helped, but seemed to bring Cecelia closer. God, sometimes she missed her so much....

"You can't change that, either," she snapped, then shook her head wryly. Cecelia's soothing, logical advice had never been meant as self-castigation, only as a way of keeping going when it seemed things were impossible.

She couldn't change what she'd just done. She couldn't call back the panic that had made her do it, couldn't undo the call, couldn't undo the fact that Cruz was a cop and she'd roused his suspicions. So she had to decide what she *could* do.

And all that deciding would have to be based on the one thing she was reasonably certain of. It gave her a sinking feeling in her stomach, but she couldn't shake the feeling that it was true.

Despite her call, Cruz Gregerson would show up as planned.

Chapter 2

"It...turned out it wasn't as bad as I thought," Kelsey said.

Cruz simply looked at her, wondering if she knew how lame the excuse sounded; judging by her expression, she did. He'd seen too many people trying to hide things to mistake the signs, and even though her flustered air could have been put down to simple distraction, he knew it was more than that.

"You got it cleaned up in a hurry," he observed, glancing around.

"I did... It was in the kitchen, mostly. The tile floor helped."

It was good. It was logical. It was also a lie. He could have told by her tone, even if she wasn't avoiding meeting his eyes.

He wanted to say something, to ask her what was wrong, to try to help, but he couldn't seem to find the words. Perhaps because he'd worked so hard at keeping a safe distance from her. He'd been beyond wary of the first woman in a very long time who powerfully and irrevocably reminded him that he wasn't just a cop, that he wasn't just a father, the two roles he allowed himself, that he was a man. Red blood and all.

And Kelsey Hall set that blood pulsing as no woman had since his life began to fall apart six years ago. And made him start trying to remember just how long it had been since he held anyone in a real male-female way, how long it had been since he responded to the invitation in a woman's eyes.

And when he couldn't remember, when he realized he had no idea when the last time had been, he'd known he was in trouble.

But he kept coming back. He could resist the urge for a week, he told himself. He could resist anything for just a week. And Kelsey's own private nature helped; she never intruded on him, always left him to his own devices unless he made a point of seeking her out. He'd convinced himself she wanted it that way. He was hardly the type women fell for at first sight, anyway. That was reserved for smooth charmers like Quisto Romero, or dramatic, exotic guys like Ryan. Women tripped over themselves gaping at Ryan, who had eyes only for his wife. Even more now that they were remarried than before, although he'd been completely crazy about Lacey then.

There had been a happy ending for their tale, Cruz thought, although it had nearly killed them both to get there. There would be no such happy ending for him. Ellie was dead and buried now, and he'd lost her long before that.

And he didn't want to dwell on what it was about Kelsey that had him thinking about things like this at all.

"It looks...the same," he said, dragging his wandering mind back to the present.

He meant it; the main room looked as it always had, a charming haven of soft tans spiked by an occasional touch of rich, deep green or jewel red. Two comfortable sofas and a couple of temptingly cushioned chairs were arranged invitingly before a stone fireplace, and on the other side of the large main room sat an oak table and chairs, where breakfast was served. She always seemed to come up with unique dishes to add variety to the standard but tasty selection, un-

usual fruits, rich coffees, and the banana pancakes he found
himself thinking about like a kid thinking about his favorite
candy bar. She'd once laughingly told him breakfast was the
only meal she was capable of cooking, so she tried to make
it something special. He'd told her she more than succeeded,
then taken a quiet pleasure in her pleased smile.

"I'm happy with the look, so I don't tinker much," she
said now. "Besides, I think people like to have a permanent
feel to things when they're in a transient situation. It's like
coming to a home away from home."

Cruz blinked; he'd never thought of it that way, but she
had a point. He knew it worked for him, even though he'd
never been consciously aware of it; the sameness of the surroundings did make it easier for him to relax. And made the
process of unwinding quicker, so that he was at ease much
faster than he had been the first time.

Clever of her, he thought. But then, he'd always known
she was smart. And good at what she did. He wondered for
the first time if she'd gone to school for this. He'd never
asked, but he'd somehow gotten the idea that this was more
a calling than just a job for her. There had always seemed a
heart in what she did, despite the smoothness of her approach
to her guests.

But now, even her practiced innkeeper's smile was absent
as she led him upstairs to his usual room in the front corner
of the large remodeled old house. Not only was the smile
missing, but she'd taken on another habit, that of looking
around as if she expected something—or someone—to leap
out at her at any moment. But as they reached the top of the
stairs, she seemed to shake the mood off, and the smile was
there as she opened the door for him.

It was a comfortable, welcoming room, the warmth of oak
furniture and rich colors giving it a simplicity he felt instantly
at ease with. The windows gave an expansive view of the
rolling hills that spilled down to the Pacific, and if you looked
from just the right angle, the spreading branches of the oak
masked the sprawl of civilization and you could pretend it
wasn't there, that there was nothing but open land reaching

down to the sparkling water. It was hard to believe he was barely an hour from the city of Marina Heights, from the bustle and commotion of Trinity West.

She hadn't commented at all on the fact that he'd shown up even after her phone call; in fact, she hadn't even seemed surprised when he arrived despite her attempt to cancel. It was as if she'd expected him to come anyway, which made him wonder just what *he* had sounded like last night.

Nor had she told him again that the inn was closed; she'd simply said she was sorry for the confusion and welcomed him with her usual warmth.

But it was a warmth undeniably tinged with a wariness he hadn't seen in her before, and that alone kept Cruz's instincts at a high hum as he set his bag down on the padded bench at the foot of the four-poster bed.

"I'll let you get settled," Kelsey said. "Then come down for lunch if you want."

He gave her a sideways look. She caught it and laughed— a genuine laugh, for the moment free of whatever was bothering her. It lit her green eyes and sent an odd sensation racing down his spine.

"It's okay, Cruz, really. Dolores did the cooking, not me."

He grinned in spite of himself, and everything seemed suddenly as it had always been. Except that he was more aware than ever that this woman was a potent female package, dangerous to a man who'd been without for a very long time. With an effort, he hid his own reaction.

"Her youngest daughter is having a baby soon, so she won't be back until the day you check out, but she made a ton of that spicy chicken salad you like," she said.

"You remembered," Cruz said, his grin widening.

Kelsey nodded, the smooth, sleek fall of hair that reached just below her chin moving in a way that made him want to touch it. He'd always wondered if it felt as silky as it looked, wondered if it was somehow as warm as the fiery highlights that made it shine, but he'd been better at quashing his wayward thoughts before. He wondered if there was a connection somehow, if all the questions that were clamoring for answers had somehow made him unable to dodge the other thoughts as well as he once had, if in rousing the cop instinct she'd managed to rouse some others he'd thought long numbed beyond revival.

"Actually," she corrected, "Dolores did. She was flattered that you liked it so much."

"You mean amazed that I ate about a gallon of it?"

Kelsey grinned back at him, and for an instant he wondered that he had ever suspected this open, warm woman of anything at all. "Something like that," she agreed, with another genuine laugh. "Oh, and there are strawberries. Just picked this morning."

Cruz put a hand over his chest in a dramatic gesture. "Be still my heart. Heaven is truly here on earth."

Kelsey laughed again, and as she walked toward the door, Cruz unabashedly watched, liking the way she moved, liking even better the way she looked in neatly tailored black slacks that subtly cupped her eminently cuppable bottom and a pristine white blouse with long sleeves and French cuffs that made her wrists seem impossibly fragile. It was her uniform of sorts; she always wore it during the day at the inn, although he'd seen her wear faded jeans and an old sweatshirt to work in the garden that produced strawberries the size of eggs. Once he'd even seen her in an elegant green silk dress, when she was on her way to some function she called a political necessity, something to do with schmoozing the zoning commissioner who would decide if she could keep her permit to run the inn permanently without filling out several dozen more forms in triplicate.

As she pulled the door closed behind her now, he remembered how she'd looked that night, emerald-green silk subtly delineating feminine curves without a trace of obviousness, the dress satisfyingly but not blatantly short, just enough to show a pair of legs a man would have to be dead not to appreciate. And he'd thought then that any man, zoning commissioner or otherwise, would have a hard time saying no to her.

Just as he was having a hard time believing what his gut had been telling him since she called last night.

He'd encountered this before, he thought as he began to unpack, putting what clothes he'd brought in the drawers of the solid oak dresser, pausing only to toss his shaving kit into the compact but more than adequate bathroom that had been added when the house on the hill was remodeled.

He'd confronted such situations before, when his instincts were in conflict, when the cop in him warned him of trouble but his gut told him someone wasn't involved. There had been trouble in Kelsey's voice last night, and obvious wariness in her today, but he couldn't believe she was truly involved in anything serious.

Maybe she just didn't like cops, he thought glumly. There were certainly enough people in the world who needed no more reason than a badge to despise you. But he couldn't quite bring himself to believe that Kelsey Hall was the type to turn on him simply for that.

But he couldn't forget the look on her face when she'd found out he was a cop, either. Or her effort last night to keep him from coming at all, despite the relative normalcy of her greeting this morning.

Perhaps there was a simple reason for it, Cruz thought. Maybe she had some kind of personal problem, some family thing—although, he realized now with some surprise, he had no idea if she even had any family—or maybe she had some new fight going with the county zoning people that had her on edge. But that wouldn't explain the subterfuge of the water leak, a leak he'd seen no sign of. Why had she felt the need to lie to him? More importantly, why had she felt the need to keep him away?

"And why," he muttered to himself, "can't you just stop being a cop for a while?"

He meant it; this was the one time of the year when he truly, genuinely tried to put it all behind him for a week. He took a second vacation later in the year, but that was Sam's time, and while he loved it, it was hardly relaxing. It was the time he concentrated on making sure he and his daughter had some time alone, to make sure he still knew who she was; he didn't ever want to be one of those parents he saw too often, parents who had no idea who their children were, what their dreams were, what their problems were. The ones who said in stunned tones, "But I had no idea," when confronted with a child caught stealing, doing drugs, or sometimes even worse.

So he needed this time to recharge, to simply let go of it all, so that he would have the energy to go back and start again to deal with the danger of an often ugly job and the stress of being a single parent.

And he wasn't going to get the time if he didn't turn off his cop mentality. If he didn't quit looking for trouble around every corner, if he didn't quit trying to make something that was probably utterly innocent into something he should stick his nose into.

"You're out of your jurisdiction anyway, Gregerson," he said as he slapped a drawer shut, "so back off."

He only hoped he could follow his own advice.

It just wasn't fair, Kelsey thought as she set plates on the table and got out the tangy chicken salad Dolores had left in the refrigerator. He was so nice. She *liked* him. She had liked him ever since she found him sitting under her oak tree, three years ago.

She'd seen his big blue four-wheel-drive truck first; it had been easily visible from the front room where she'd just put the finishing touches of colored pillows. She hadn't put up any signs on the drive denying entrance to anyone—it had seemed contrary to the atmosphere she was trying to create here—but maybe she would have to, she'd thought. She'd been afraid she had some trespassing off-roaders to deal with and wondered if she dared approach them. But there had been no sound of revving engines, and the truck itself had never moved, so eventually she had steeled her nerve and walked toward the big tree.

She'd stopped some yards away, staring at the dark-haired man who sat so utterly still. His back had been propped against the tree's gnarled trunk, his head tilted back, his eyes closed. She'd studied his profile, the regular features, the thick darkness of his hair. Nice, she'd thought, but he'd looked strained, his jaw tight, his strong, muscular body tense and wire-drawn. As she watched, it had been an amazing thing to see the change that gradually crept over him, to see his expression relax, see the tension seep away as the moments passed. She'd wondered if it was a conscious thing, this letting go, wondered if he'd learned some technique somewhere to simply release all the pressure and let it flow out.

And she'd wondered wryly if he could teach it to her.

He'd heard her the minute she started moving again, and when he turned his head to look at her, she'd nearly gasped as warning bells clanged in her head. She hadn't been able to see him face-on before; if she had, she would no doubt have turned back. What had been simply nice, regular features in profile had now been turned into striking good looks by a pair of thick-lashed, vivid blue eyes, unlike any she'd ever seen before. They had seemed at odds with the slight bronze tint of his skin, a mixed heritage she'd understood as soon as he spoke.

"I'm Cruz Gregerson. I hope you don't mind. I was driving by and saw your tree. It was…irresistible."

"It is to me, too," she'd said impulsively, and been rewarded with a smile that made her breath catch.

They had talked for some time that day, long enough for her to find out that he'd set off simply to get away, looking for a likely place to spend a week's vacation. And she hadn't been able to resist offering him her just-finished main guest room, even though she wasn't due to officially open until the next weekend, when all four rooms would be done.

He'd hesitated—she wasn't sure why—but he had finally agreed. And he'd come back every year since, for a week each time, and each time she'd been glad to see him, even wished he would keep a little less to himself, although she knew it was just as well; she'd given up playing with dynamite long ago. And beneath the quite exterior, she sensed, Cruz Gregerson was just that—explosive.

She wasn't sure why she was so certain. There was no obvious reason. He was relatively quiet, never talking much about himself, unlike most men she knew. He always seemed more than willing to listen to her plans for the inn, and he encouraged her in her dreams for the future in a supportive way that surprised her. But she never quite lost the sense that there were depths to the man that were hidden, that he was walking, breathing proof of the old saying about still waters running deep.

They chatted amiably when they met, usually over breakfast in the main room of the house, sometimes with other guests, sometimes alone. Then he would be off on one of his long walks, or sitting alone under the oak, working in that spiral notebook he carried. She'd wondered if he was a writer, even asked him once, and he'd laughed and said no, he worked in Marina Heights, for the city, mostly pushing papers around on a desk.

Well, he hadn't lied, she thought ruefully.

But why did he have to be a cop? Why couldn't he have been a nice, boring accountant or something?

But if he'd been anything other than a cop, would he have needed the peace of this place so badly? It made so much sense now, that tension that she always saw in him when he first arrived and that she sensed gradually returning whenever he got ready to leave. And it explained the pager that was always attached to his belt, even when he was supposedly on vacation.

It wasn't that she disliked cops. Really, she didn't. She had once, but she didn't even blame them anymore. At least, not very much. She was sure that she'd outgrown that, that she'd finally come to see there hadn't been anything they could do to save the child she'd been, not under the circumstances. Not given the laws that they were bound to enforce.

But that didn't mean she trusted them. None of them had ever been willing to bend those laws, even a little, for the sake of a lost and bewildered child.

And they had that nasty tendency to ask questions, she thought as she rummaged in the drawer for knives, forks and spoons. She knew he hadn't believed her last night. She had heard it in his voice, even in the silences that had seemed to her so tense. He hadn't believed her, just as those long-ago cops hadn't believed her and had, instead of saving her, as she'd prayed they would, sent her back into hell.

With an effort, she wrenched her mind out of an old, worn track that was an exercise in futility. She really didn't think about those days much anymore, except to wonder and worry about Cecelia. There was nothing she could do to change them. She would be much better off concentrating on the problem at hand.

The problem named Cruz Gregerson.

Perhaps it would be all right. He'd seemed okay, once he got here. He hadn't even called her on the obvious lie about the water leak, although she'd seen in those incredible blue eyes that he knew perfectly well it had been a fib from beginning to end.

Maybe he would just let it go. Maybe—

"Kelsey?"

She dropped the silverware she'd been holding and spun around.

"I'm sorry, I didn't mean to startle you."

The girl who'd spoken hovered in the doorway to the kitchen, in the manner of someone unsure of her welcome and ready to run if necessary. Too-blonde hair, dark roots showing clearly, hung in lank strands over her face, the overgrown remnants of what had once been a trendy haircut. Her eyes were a medium brown, dulled now, dark-circled with exhaustion and scared-looking. She was an inch or so taller than Kelsey's own five-foot-four, but painfully thin. Even at nearly five months, her pregnancy barely showed.

She'd told Kelsey she was sixteen, but Kelsey suspected she was younger. She understood all too well that need for any kind of confidence, even the false confidence gained by pretending to be older than you were. Her heart went out to the girl, because she knew what it was like to feel so alone that you clung to even that small solace.

She also knew just how frightened the girl was.

"It's all right, Melissa," she said quickly.

"But…I saw that man come," the girl said hesitantly, looking more and more like a terrified fawn ready to bolt any second.

"It's all right," Kelsey repeated. One look at the girl's frightened face told her that she didn't dare explain the truth. "He's a regular guest. He's been coming for years."

The girl didn't look at all convinced. "Maybe I should just go—"

"It will be fine," Kelsey hastened to assure her. "He'll only be here a week. And I'll do my best to keep him…occupied." *Right,* she thought miserably. *Like you've ever had* any *luck keeping a man occupied.* "Just stay out of sight as much as you can," she added, telling herself it would do no good if she frightened the girl further. "With any luck, he won't even know you're here."

The girl hesitated, then nodded. "I—I'll eat in my room," she said hastily. "And stay there when he's in the house."

"That might be a good idea," Kelsey agreed, and helped the girl scoop food onto a plate. Melissa froze when they heard footsteps on the stairs. Then she grabbed the glass of milk Kelsey had poured and bolted out the back door of the kitchen.

Kelsey sighed and stepped into the main room to meet Cruz, wondering all the while if there was anything worse to have around than a suspicious cop, if you had a secret to keep.

Chapter 3

There was no doubt about it. He wasn't going to have to change his approach at all, because Kelsey had changed. Or her attitude had. And he wasn't sure what it meant, because she hadn't changed in the way he would have expected, had it been simply that she didn't like cops. She hadn't become more formal, more aloof; in fact, she'd done the opposite. Never before, in the three separate weeks he spent here, had he ever seen so much of her. In fact, he'd seen more of her in these past three days than he had all together before.

"Hi. Mind if I sit down?"

I rest my case, Cruz said to himself, but he closed the book he'd been reading without comment.

"I...don't mean to intrude," she said hesitantly.

"It's all right," he said, meaning it; whatever the reason, he'd found himself enjoying their conversations. "I'm not finding this particularly riveting."

She smiled as he gestured with the book. "I suppose not. Police books must seem old hat to you."

Well, Cruz thought, that was hardly the comment of someone who had it in for cops enough to not even want one around. "Mainly it's annoying," he said, again lifting the paperback. "They get away with things that'd get me suspended in a big hurry. But that's what I get for reading about what I'm here to get away from."

For a moment, she looked at the fire dancing on the hearth. It wasn't really cool enough tonight for it to be a necessity, but she said she liked the smell, look and sound of it, and he couldn't argue with that. He'd been nearly dozing off when she joined him.

"It must be...a very hard job, sometimes."

"Sometimes."

"Do you...have times when you wish you could do things differently?"

He studied her silently. Her words were casual enough, but that hesitation made him wonder if there wasn't some specific intent behind the question. Was she going to tell him what was going on?

"Often," he said after a moment, picking his words carefully. "Cops have a little leeway, but it's mostly in interpretation. You make a judgment call and hope it doesn't backfire on you. Sometimes you wish you could do more, but the laws won't let you. Sometimes you wish you didn't have to do something, but the laws won't let you not do it."

An oddly sad and wistful expression crossed her face. "I thought it must be like that."

There *was* more to this than casual curiosity, he thought. This was something personal, although somehow he sensed it wasn't immediate; that almost melancholy expression had been distant, as if it were about some long-ago memory, rather than whatever her current problem was.

"Kelsey—" he began, but before he could go on, she quickly and definitely changed the subject.

"Did you have a good walk today?" she asked brightly.

"Yes. Kelsey—"

"I saw you head up the hill. Did you go to the pond?"

He had, in fact, gone to the small pool of water that had once served as a reservoir for the house, before waterlines had been brought out this far. He'd sat on the small boulder that overlooked the pool of water and watched the reflections of the few puffy white clouds skid by across the glassy surface, trying to let all his tension go with them.

It had been a rough year, with the breakup of the Pack, the Marina Heights gang that had made the youth gangs look like a church choir, and with Ryan getting himself shot in the process. But it had been a good year, too. Ryan and Lacey were back together; Ryan had opened up enough to ask Cruz to be his best man at their remarriage, and now there was a baby on the way.

They'd also picked up a damn good cop in Quisto Romero, and Miguel de los Reyes was turning out to be exactly the kind of chief the department needed: trusted by his men because he'd come up the hard way, yet able to handle the politics and keep the confidence of the city leaders, who tended to make a cop's life more difficult than it already was with their unrealistic and sometimes ludicrous demands. Cruz did not envy de los Reyes the path he had to walk, but he admired the way he did it.

He'd reminded himself then that he was here to put all that out of his head, to spend as much as he could of this precious week not thinking about the job.

"I did go to the pond," he said now. "It's a good place to try not to think."

She looked startled for a moment; then a smile curved her lips in a way that had Cruz suddenly thinking how soft and warm her mouth looked.

"It's the perfect place for that," she said. "I like to watch the clouds reflected in the water, and if they're moving, I send my troubles along with them."

It was Cruz's turn to look startled. "Exactly," he said after a moment.

They both smiled then—the smiles of two people who have found common ground.

"You know," Kelsey said, the new easiness of her tone only now making Cruz aware that there had been a slight tension in her voice before, "this is the fourth time you've been here, and I just realized I've never really thanked you for always coming back."

"You don't have to thank me. This place is exactly what I need."

"A lot of people can't stand being away from things. No televisions or phones in the rooms makes them crazy."

Cruz grinned. "That's one of the things I like best."

Her smile widened. "I got that feeling. Most of my repeat guests are that way."

"Speaking of which, am I the only one here now?"

Something flashed across her face, a flicker of something that, if he was confronting a suspect, he would have called guilt. He hadn't meant to interrogate her, had even managed to pretty much put that mysterious late-night phone call out of his mind. But at the sight of that furtive look, the memory came charging back. Along with the odd sense he'd been having that there was someone else around; he'd thought it might be Dolores, but it was unlike the outgoing woman to come and go so unobtrusively, and Kelsey had said she wouldn't be back until her daughter had her baby.

"I… Yes," she said, recovering. "The rest of this month is light. You're the only guest registered."

Concern overcame his misgivings for the moment. "Are you…doing all right?"

"Yes. My bookings are heavier as summer really gets rolling."

"Heavy enough?"

He was genuinely concerned, and not simply because he would hate to try to find another place where he could be less than an hour away and yet feel as if he were in another world. He'd seen the enthusiasm and energy in Kelsey's voice when she spoke of this place and how she loved it, and he would hate to see her run into financial trouble.

Her expression softened at his unfeigned solicitousness. "Really, Cruz, I'm fine. The first couple of years were tough, but I…came into some money last year, so I have a nice cushion now. And more often than not nowadays, I break even."

"That's quite an accomplishment," he said, meaning it. "There aren't many people who can say they've even started, let alone made a success of, a business like this at your age."

"My age?" She started blushing the moment the words were out and she realized what they sounded like. "I didn't mean... I'm not..."

One corner of Cruz's mouth quirked upward. "Not fishing for a compliment?"

She put her hands up to hide her face as she shook her head in obvious embarrassment. "I'm probably older than you are," she said ruefully.

"Honey," he drawled teasingly, "it ain't the years, it's the mileage, and I've got more than you have on both counts, I'm afraid."

Her hands came down and she met his gaze, and for a moment Cruz saw something old and painfully wise in those green eyes. Perhaps she wasn't quite as young as she appeared on the surface. But sometimes it wasn't just the passing of time that put that kind of look in your eyes, he thought.

"I'm thirty," she said abruptly.

He lifted a brow in surprise.

"Thank you," she said, but her expression still held a trace of that cynicism that seemed so at odds with her appearance.

"You must know you don't look it. So," he said, purposely keeping his tone light, "we're even. We've both made it to the big three-oh."

For a silent moment, she just looked at him, and as if it were a drop of water vanishing before the sun's heat, he saw that weary look fade away, to be replaced by an oddly curious expression.

"Even though you've been here so often, I don't know much about you," she said.

"You know I like getting away from phones and TV. You know reading about fictional cops who get away with things I can't frustrates me. You know I like strawberries, your banana pancakes and Dolores's chicken salad. You know I like sitting on my butt staring at clouds for hours. You know I can laze the day away under your oak tree.'' He shrugged. ''You know a lot about me.''

''But I don't know...basic things. Like if you're married, or—''

Her hands flew back up to her face and again she looked horrified at what she'd said. Had she simply asked if he was married, he might have thought she was flirting, as uncharacteristic as it might seem. But her reaction to her own words either meant she was not very practiced at it or simply that she was afraid he would think she was flirting when she hadn't meant to at all.

Either way, he found her far too appealing for his own comfort.

''I'm not married,'' he said, as much to end his own speculations as to fill the uncomfortable silence.

''Oh.''

She seemed unable to meet his eyes, and by the color still staining her cheeks, he judged she was still embarrassed by what she'd blurted out.

''I thought you would have guessed that, since I've never brought a wife along.''

She looked at him then. The blush was gradually fading, and he saw a glint of that cynical look again. ''Some husbands prefer it that way. Or they bring their girlfriends.''

Cruz barely managed not to wince at the tightness in her voice. ''Ouch,'' he said. ''Did yours?''

''Mine?'' She blinked.

''Husband.''

''Oh. No. I've never been...''

Her voice trailed off and her eyes widened as she stared at him. He read her thoughts as clearly as if she'd spoken them; he'd easily gotten her to volunteer what she'd baldly asked.

''I've had a lot of practice, Kelsey.''

For a moment she looked as if she wanted to ask exactly what he'd had practice at, but if so, she held it back. She also looked as if she wanted to bolt but was afraid of being rude.

He wondered yet again if it was he himself who made her nervous or the fact that he was a cop. She'd never acted this way before she knew. And he couldn't picture her making that midnight phone call before, even if the water leak had been for real.

But whatever had provoked that midnight phone call, it certainly wasn't something obvious at first glance, now that he was here. And as far as he could tell, the only thing that had changed was that now she knew he was a cop. And apart from the sort of innate or learned dislike she didn't seem to feel, there was usually only one reason why people didn't want to have a cop around.

They had something to hide.

"Whatever it is, Kelsey," he said softly, "I wish you'd let me help."

She nearly jumped. She paled as she stared at him.

"Not me the cop," he added, trying to calm her. "Just *me*, Kelsey."

But she didn't answer. Finally she gave a rather wild shake of her head and got up, retreating hastily to the kitchen. Cruz watched her go, letting out a long breath as the door closed behind her.

Maybe he'd jumped the gun. Maybe he should have left well enough alone. Maybe she would have told him eventually if he hadn't pushed. But he hadn't quite been able to shake the thought that the real reason she was acting so out of character, the reason she was there every time he turned around, the reason she seemed to want to talk to him all the time, was not, however much he might like it to be, because she was irresistibly drawn to him, but because she wanted to keep him occupied.

And if she wanted his attention on her, it was because she didn't want it on something else.

And he would really like to know what that something else was.

She supposed she could be making a bigger hash out of this, but she wasn't sure how.

Kelsey let out a huge sigh as she heard Cruz make his way

upstairs for the night. She sank down into one of the kitchen chairs.

She should have known better than to even try; the few times in her life when she tried to gain a man's attention, she'd failed miserably. And she never would have tried it with a man like Cruz if she hadn't had to; men who looked like Cruz only paid attention to quiet, slightly too-round women like her out of politeness. And she felt awful about using that politeness, using his innate good manners, to intrude upon the stay he clearly treasured as a time of peace and quiet.

Although he'd never betrayed by action or word that he wished she would leave him alone. He'd never even hinted that she was being intrusive, or that he wished she would just go away. He'd never shown the slightest bit of irritation or impatience with her fumbling attempts to overcome her natural reserve and be sociable.

In fact, except for her unease, she'd quite enjoyed the time she spent simply talking to him. And although it was a bit wearing, always being on guard, she was finding it intriguing getting to know this man. Well, she had to admit she'd always found him intriguing, but she'd never dared indulge herself before. And finding out he was a cop had startled her so much that she hadn't been sure how she felt.

But now she had no choice; she had to keep him occupied. And as a result, she was finding he wasn't anything like she had imagined a cop would be.

Also as a result, she was finding herself more attracted to him than ever, so much so that if she hadn't *had* to do this, she would have run the other way; she couldn't have a cop around, no matter how appealing the idea of Cruz Gregerson around all the time might be. If word got out that she fraternized with the enemy...

She gave a low, rueful laugh at the thought of a man like Cruz, cop or not, even being interested in her. Not that she wanted him to be. It was pointless. If she'd learned nothing else in her limited experience with men, it was that. Richard, Alan, her father...

She scrambled to her feet. She *wasn't* going to go down

that old trail. She should be thankful it hadn't taken her long to learn that there wasn't a man on the planet she could trust enough to maintain any kind of relationship. And she wasn't the type who could have a string of casual affairs and never look back.

"So do without," she muttered as she looked for something to tidy or clean in the already spotless kitchen.

"Without what?"

Kelsey spun around, thinking that the pregnant girl should at least make some noise when she moved.

"Er...dessert," she said, only after she spoke seeing that what she'd said was truer than she realized; she had a good life, and she was safe and happy. She had the main course, she didn't need dessert. Not if she wanted to stay healthy. She didn't need a man who would no doubt mess up her world, didn't need to learn a painful lesson all over again.

"Oh."

Melissa looked rather wan tonight, and Kelsey wondered with a qualm if the girl had been working too hard. She'd insisted on helping, and indeed had been the one to scrub the kitchen when Cruz was out at the pond, but perhaps it had been too much for her.

"Are you feeling all right?"

"Fine."

"You look a little pale. Maybe you should sit down?"

"No."

The girl wasn't usually quite so laconic, and Kelsey's brow furrowed. "What is it, Melissa?"

"I... It moved."

Kelsey blinked. "What?" Then it struck her. "Oh. The baby?"

Melissa sat down after all, rather heavily, and Kelsey took back the chair she'd vacated. It was then, at eye level, that she saw the expression in the girl's eyes; she looked stunned. She didn't know what to say, so she reached out and took the girl's hand.

"It...didn't seem real, before. I mean, I knew, but..."

Kelsey understood then. Melissa had known she was pregnant, but until she felt the new life moving inside her, she hadn't really realized all it meant.

"How does that make you feel?" she asked quietly.

"I don't know!" Melissa wailed. "I should have done something, gotten rid of it—then I could just go home and everything would be like it was."

Kelsey sighed inwardly. The girl hadn't dealt with the reality of it still; nothing would ever be the way it had been again. She wasn't surprised by the denial; Melissa had told her she had ignored the possibility she might be pregnant until it became undeniable.

"I knew my parents would have a fit," she'd said. "And after they threw me out, and Doug got so mad at me, I decided to keep it. At least a baby would have to love me, wouldn't it?"

She'd sounded so forlorn that Kelsey didn't have the heart to disabuse her of that notion. The girl had refused to talk any more about either her parents or the baby's father. Kelsey had let her slide, with the warning that it would not be forever.

She saw the girl tremble and tried to ease her distress by changing the subject for a moment.

"Thank you for cleaning the kitchen so beautifully."

Melissa shrugged and pushed a lock of her dyed hair back behind her ear. "I wanted to help. You've been so nice." She gave Kelsey a sideways look. "He sure stays close by."

Kelsey nodded. "He comes here for peace and quiet, not to see the sights. He doesn't live very far away."

Melissa looked away. "He's…kind of cute. For an old guy."

Kelsey smothered a smile. "Yes, I suppose he is. For an old guy."

"You like him?"

"Yes," Kelsey said truthfully. "He's very nice."

"Is that why you've been hanging with him so much? Or is it me?"

Kelsey considered that for a moment, then settled on honesty as the best policy. She tried never to lie to kids; they sensed it, and when they found you out, they rarely forgave.

"Both," she admitted, but didn't add that she knew just how unwise thinking anything would come of it would be. She'd known that long before she ever knew he went home and put on a badge and a gun.

"I'm trying to stay out of sight."

"You're doing fine, Melissa," Kelsey assured her. "Don't worry about it. It probably wouldn't matter if he saw you. We could just tell him——"

The girl cut her off, shaking her head fervently. "No. I don't want anyone to know I'm here."

Not for the first time, Kelsey felt there was something the girl wasn't telling her. Her fear seemed beyond that of a young girl away from home, even one who was pregnant and scared about it. And if she was this afraid now, Kelsey could just imagine how she would feel if she knew who—or rather what—Cruz was.

"All right," Kelsey said soothingly. "We'll just keep things the way they are. It would be easier if I had other guests to add to the distraction, but we'll manage."

"If you had other guests, I'd have to dodge them, too," Melissa pointed out.

No, because they wouldn't be cops and already thinking something odd is going on because I'm the world's worst liar, Kelsey thought ruefully. So much for her vow, made years ago, that someday she would be where she never had to lie again, to anyone. All she'd done was manage to get so out of practice that she gave herself away even over the telephone.

"We'll do fine," was all she said. "Let's get you some dinner."

The girl had adapted so that she generally ate when Cruz was either outside or already upstairs in his room, but tonight he'd gone up rather late, so Kelsey imagined Melissa was hungry. She'd been good about clearing up after herself, too, so there were no telltale dishes left out, betraying her presence.

She thought Melissa would be fairly secure in the small room just off the kitchen; for a cop, Cruz showed little sign of being a snoop. For a cop, Cruz didn't ask nearly as many questions as she'd expected, knowing he knew she had lied about the water leak. For a cop, he was amazingly kind and thoughtful. She might even have said gentle.

But she'd always thought him a gentleman, from the first time he came here. It was only the knowledge of what he did for a living that had changed the way she looked at him.

And somehow that didn't seem quite fair, Kelsey thought. It wasn't as if he did something distasteful, not really. Just because she'd been let down long ago by the system he represented, that was no reason to condemn him. The fact that she was circumventing that system was reason to be wary, but was it fair to judge him just for being part of it? He was still the man whose visits she had looked forward to each year. He was still the man who took the same quiet pleasure in her home as she herself did. Did knowing he was a cop really change all that?

She wasn't sure, but she had the feeling now that not only was Cruz Gregerson not what she'd thought a cop would be, but, as a man, far more than she had ever expected.

Chapter 4

"So how did you end up with the name Cruz Gregerson?"

He blinked, a little startled at the personal question. Ever since that night in front of the fireplace, she'd kept the conversation fairly impersonal. They'd still spent more time together than during any of his other stays, but there had been no more betraying moments when her eyes were shadowed with remembered pain and unwelcome knowledge.

He'd been well aware that they spoke mostly of him, places he'd seen, things he'd done—although never of his work—and very little of her. He knew little more about her now than he had before. And he couldn't remember the last time he'd talked so much without mentioning his job; a cop's work usually permeated every aspect of his life, and even though he came here to get away from it, it was odd to be so carefully avoiding the subject.

But for some reason that he didn't stop to analyze, he didn't want to bring it up, didn't want it out in the open between them, didn't want to have to deal with whatever had made her react that way. He'd revised his estimation that she was in trouble; it seemed more likely that she was simply hiding

something she would prefer he not find out. Maybe she'd let
her car's license tags expire, he thought wryly; he'd seen
people panic over sillier things.

He might have been flattered that she seemed so intent
upon him had it not been for that nagging suspicion about
her motives. He was touched despite himself by the shy way
she went about it, and he had to admit that there seemed to
be a great deal of sincerity in her interest. In fact, if it hadn't
been for that suspicion, he would have thought her utterly
genuine.

And that bothered him as much as anything except his own
reaction to the idea of her genuine interest.

"Elena Cruz Santiago married Frank Gregerson," he finally answered.

Kelsey smiled as she moved her feet in the water of the
pond. She'd asked him if he would mind if she came with
him this morning and offered a picnic lunch as, she said, a
bribe to put up with her. He'd told her that she hardly needed
to do that, that he enjoyed her company. And he'd been a
little surprised to find that what could have been an automatic
polite response was more than a little true; his morning's jaunt
had suddenly become even more pleasantly anticipated at the
thought of her joining him.

And he managed to put out of his mind the growing certainty that, while she seemed to enjoy his company as well,
there was something else driving her to spend so much time
with him. If she was a little better at the small talk, if she
was more practiced, instead of acting as if she were very
unused to being alone with a man, he might have taken her
at face value. But between the change from her previous demeanor and the damning fact of that midnight phone call, he
couldn't quite quash his suspicions completely.

And he couldn't help wondering if there was a connection
to the still-niggling sensation he had of another presence,
evoked by the occasional unaccounted-for noise, or lights going on after he—and, he thought, Kelsey—had already retired
for the night.

No, he couldn't quite smother his suspicions. But he could

avoid thinking about them, he decided, at least for the moment. And that task was made easier by the fact that she had traded her black slacks for a pair of shorts for the walk, baring long, nicely curved legs, and had slipped off her shoes to dabble her feet in the water, baring equally nicely curved feet, small and high-arched, and making Cruz wonder when the hell he'd started finding feet attractive.

"I assume the blue eyes came from your father, then?"

"I hope so," he said, with mock fervency.

Kelsey gave him a startled look, then let out a hesitant laugh. He took pity on her and explained.

"It's an old family joke. I'm the only one with blue eyes in the whole family. Even my dad's are brown. If it wasn't for the fact that I'm a dead ringer for my grandfather, my mother would have had some explaining to do."

Her laugh was genuine then, and he had the idle thought that he would like to hear it more often. It was like the splash of the pond's sun-warmed water, light, cheerful, and somehow clean and pure in a way that was far too often absent from his life. And that thought should have had warning bells going off like mad in his head, but he was too lazily comfortable to worry about it.

"You grew up in a big family?"

"Not immediate. My folks just had me." He grinned. "Guess I was enough of a handful."

"You? Don't tell me you got into trouble."

"Constantly." His grin widened. "Nothing serious, though. I didn't dare. I have so many aunts and uncles and cousins scattered all around, somebody was sure to burn me."

She smiled, but her voice took on that wistful note again when she said, "Sounds nice."

"Sometimes. Sometimes, when a half dozen or so of them would come stay with us when I was a kid, or when one of them blabbed to my dad about something I'd done, it was anything but."

"What…did he do? If you did something…bad?"

He couldn't pin down the change in her voice; he only knew that it was there.

"Not much. He just stood there looking at me with that sad 'I'm disappointed in you, son' expression he had perfected, until I felt like—" he flicked at the water with a finger as he finished "—pond scum."

"That's all?"

"That's all it took, believe me," Cruz said with a grimace. "He had a way of making me want to do whatever it took to make sure he'd never look at me like that again."

"That," Kelsey said, "is a feeling I can relate to."

Her tone was far different from his, with an edge he couldn't define. Whatever her childhood had been—and he had no idea, since they had been so busy talking about his—it had clearly left behind some unhappy memories. And not for the first time Cruz blessed his parents for the solid, happy family they'd built with their love and sweat and tears, although he had to admit that sometimes—completely unintentionally—they made him feel like even more of a failure because he hadn't managed to do what they had and keep his own marriage together. Not that they'd ever criticized. In fact, they'd made it clear that they knew it was no one's fault, but their example was a tough one to live up to.

Maybe he would take Sam up for a visit this year, when the time for their joint vacation rolled around. Or maybe for the holidays. His mother had been hounding him for a couple of years, saying that she wanted her granddaughter home for Christmas.

"Do your parents live around here?"

He shook his head. "They still live up in Santa Rosa, where I grew up. They have a little restaurant. The Vineyard Inn." He glanced down the hill toward the inn. "In fact, they've been thinking about buying the big old house behind it and doing pretty much what you've done here."

Kelsey looked intrigued. "Really?"

He nodded again, then looked at her pointedly. "I should send them down here to take lessons from a pro."

She blushed prettily, and looked so pleased that he felt absurdly warmed by what his simple words had done. "I'll bet they'd do well there, in the wine country."

"Mom thinks so. Dad's not so sure."

"He doesn't think it would be successful?"

"It's not that. He worries about Mom, and the extra work it would be. She already runs the kitchen operation of the restaurant, and she's on the board of the Center for the Arts up there, and he's afraid of adding this to her load. Dad's got a good business head, but he doesn't know the first thing about what you do."

"Does your mother?"

"She's learning." He couldn't help smiling. "But then, she's always learning. She went back to school and got a degree in restaurant management before they opened the place. And she's back in school again for this."

"She sounds like…quite a woman."

"She is. She's a dynamo. I think this is going to happen whether Dad likes it or not."

Kelsey's brow furrowed. "Will that cause a problem?"

"Problem?"

"Between them. If she goes ahead and does something he doesn't want her to."

Cruz laughed. "If that were the case, they would have split long ago. She'll listen to advice and take it if it makes sense to her, but nobody tells my mother what to do."

Kelsey stared at him. "Even your father?"

"Especially him," Cruz said, curious about her expression. "He always says he married her for her spirit, so why would he want to crush it by trying to rein her in?"

"She—*they*—sound…remarkable." Kelsey's tone was hushed.

Cruz studied her for a moment, thinking that he'd been wrong when he thought he had learned very little about her in their talks this week. True, she hadn't told him her life story, not the way he seemed to be doing for her, but what few things he'd deduced were much more telling than all his light, amusing recollections. And he was sure he was learning more from her reactions to what he said than she knew she was revealing.

"They are, but they're not so unusual," he said, watching

her face. He saw what he'd expected, even though he wasn't sure why: a flash of reaction to his words, a look that bordered on, but didn't quite fall into, bitterness. She didn't speak, but she didn't have to for him to interpret that look.

"Your folks are different, huh?" he asked.

She went very still. "They're dead."

He winced at her bald tone. "I'm sorry."

"Don't be. It doesn't matter."

Yes, he was learning more than she realized, Cruz thought.

"So," Kelsey said, her voice now determinedly bright, "do you see your parents often?"

"Not often enough, if you ask them."

His mind wasn't really on his answer. He was thinking about how she diverted the conversation back to him whenever it strayed to her, or anything close to her. He wondered just how defensive she could be and set about finding out.

"So how did you get started in this business?" he asked, figuring that was innocuous enough to begin with. "And how did you find this place?"

"I got lucky. It was a rush sale, because of somebody's tax problems, at a time when I had some cash."

Cruz lifted a brow; even this far from the coast, property with a view, however slight, of the ocean didn't generally come cheap. "*Some* cash?"

She shrugged. "I'd been partners in a restaurant. It was fairly successful when we sold out. I needed to turn the profit over quickly, or I'd be the one with tax problems."

"Must have been quite a restaurant."

"It did well. It was in Marina del Mar, maybe you've heard of it? The Sunset Grill?"

Cruz blinked. "You owned the Sunset Grill?"

It was one of the trendier places in the wealthy resort town, with a menu that was never the same twice and a reputation for great ambience and better food. He'd been there a couple of times, with Kit Walker, and he'd liked the airy, open feel of it, with skylights to let in the sun and a unique design that made every table seem secluded and private.

"A quarter of it," she said. "And don't look so stunned.

It wasn't the Sunset Grill when I started working there. It was a little hole-in-the-wall kind of café that didn't have much going for it except a good location.''

"You started out working there and ended up an owner of the place?''

She smiled with a pride she had every right to, he thought, if it was true.

"I did. I worked there for six years. I got hired even though I had no experience, because I offered to work the first two weeks for nothing. I bussed tables, worked as a receptionist, then a waiter. I saved every penny I could, and when Mrs. Lerner—the owner—decided to renovate and start over, she let me buy in. On the condition I go to school nights and learn restaurant management. She wanted someone to help her run things.''

"And how soon were you running everything?''

Kelsey grinned. "After about a year. It's really amazing that she trusted me to manage the place, even though I was so young and had no real management experience. And she let me buy in more each year, until I owned a quarter of it.''

Cruz smiled back at her, imagining the stubborn determination she must have had even then. Six years, he thought. She'd been running this place for three years, and she'd told him she'd spent a year getting it ready. That was four, plus the six, and the year before she'd started managing the restaurant, plus however long she'd spent at that... No matter how you added it up, Kelsey Hall had been working hard for a long time.

She tilted her head to look at him when he didn't speak, and the sunlight turned her hair to warm fire. An answering warmth kicked through him, and his breath caught at the force of it. He wanted to bury his hands in that silken mass, wanted to plant a kiss on her upturned nose in the moment before he took her mouth with all the hunger that had suddenly awakened in him.

And if she could read his thoughts, she would probably dunk him in the pond, he told himself.

"But the place took off," he said hastily, trying to divert his wayward thoughts.

"It did. We hit the right combination of food and atmosphere. It was as much luck and the fact that the public taste ran in our direction at the right time as anything else. We sold it for twenty times what we'd put into it."

"If it was doing so well, why did you sell?"

A shadow crossed her face. "Mrs. Lerner got ill. Her heart. She had to retire."

She was staring at the glassy surface of the pond, her eyes distant, unfocused. And sad. Cruz floundered a little, not sure what to say; it was obvious the woman had been special to Kelsey.

"Is she...all right?" he asked finally, wondering if perhaps the woman had died and left her an inheritance, if that was the real source of the money she said she'd come into.

Kelsey brightened a little, and he knew that wasn't the case. "As well as can be expected for someone who never wanted to retire." She gestured toward the inn. "She's in Florida now, but she owns part of this place. She wanted to invest part of her share from the restaurant, and I couldn't talk her out of it." She smiled, a little sheepishly. "But then, I didn't try too hard. If it hadn't been for her, I wouldn't have been able to do it."

Cruz considered that for a moment before he said quietly, "All the more reason you had to make a go of it?"

She looked startled, then rueful. "Yes. I couldn't let her down. She was so good to me, all those years."

"She must be pleased with how you're doing."

Kelsey's mouth quirked. "Well, she hasn't lost any money, and she says that's enough. But I'm hoping for the day when I can actually pay her some dividends on her investment."

He looked at her steadily. "To go along with the dividends on her judgment?"

He knew she'd worked it out by the faint color that tinged her cheeks and the pleased smile. He wondered if compliments had been so few in her life that she still blushed at them.

"Thank you," she said softly. "I hope she feels that way."

"How could she not?"

"I'm not doing too badly for a kid with no degree and a mere three years of running a restaurant under her belt."

He couldn't help doing the math again; she'd run the Sunset Grill for three years before they sold it? That meant, he thought, backtracking quickly in his head, that she... Damn, it meant that she'd been sixteen when she started working there. Amazed, he stared at her.

"You've done well," he said at last.

He meant it. Not only had she started working younger than most kids, she'd also made a success of herself at a young age, in a very tough business, not to mention as a woman alone.

Or at least it appeared she was alone. He had an uneasy sense that Kelsey had spent too much of her life alone, one way or another. He was suddenly filled with a compulsive need that he couldn't explain, a need to know so much more about her, about who she'd been, about what kind of life had made her the capable yet vulnerable woman she was.

The compulsion made him uneasy, but he doubted it would matter in the long run; he was fairly certain she would dodge any attempt to make the conversation more personal. But he was going to try anyway.

"Have you always lived in California, then?"

He purposely made his tone casual, but his eyes never left her face. It was almost imperceptible, but because he'd been watching for it, he saw it, that faint tightening of her mouth, of the delicate skin around her eyes, as tension—or wariness—flooded back into her. He almost regretted doing it, but he couldn't seem to stop.

"I... Since I was sixteen."

And she'd gone to work right away, he thought. But he didn't pursue that, he kept the conversation on general things, feeling his way carefully, as if he were dealing with a frightened victim and everything he said, every move he made, were crucial.

"That's a tough age to move, having to leave all your friends behind in… Where'd you move from?"

"Back east," she said shortly, unspecifically. She pulled her feet out of the pond and drew her legs beneath her, as if she wanted to be able to spring up quickly. To run? Cruz wondered.

"You must have liked it here," he said, as if he hadn't seen her action or heard the edge that had come into her voice. "You stayed."

"There was nothing to go back to," she said, then looked as if she wished she hadn't said it.

She sat up on her heels, her hands moving restlessly over her knees. He noticed she had gotten her feet under her now and knew he'd been right when he thought she was acting as if she were preparing to run. Apparently it wasn't just his questions she would dodge, it was him, too. Her new interest in him did not, it seemed, mean it was a two-way street.

"I'd better get dinner started," she said, not looking at him.

"We just ate lunch."

She glanced at him, surprise mixed with that still-evident wariness in her expression. "That was nearly three hours ago."

He blinked. Had they really been here that long? He glanced at his wrist. It was bare. His watch was still sitting on the dresser in his room. For a man whose life was usually run by a clock, it was a big step to forget to put the thing on.

"Guess this means I'm really on vacation," he said, a little sheepishly.

Her wariness seemed to vanish, and she gave him a dazzling smile. "And it means Oak Tree is working its magic."

She did get to her feet then, but the feel of impending escape had vanished with the wariness. Now she looked like what she should be: an attractive woman well pleased with her world and what she'd accomplished in it.

"How does a pot roast sound?"

"Wonderful. But you don't have to feed me dinner. That isn't in the meal plan. I can go into town and get something."

"You're my only guest now. Until the first, in fact. I should take good care of you. Besides, it's no more hassle to feed one more. Especially when Dolores fixed it so all I have to do is put it in the oven."

His mouth twisted into a crooked grin. "Far be it for me to refuse a meal I didn't have to cook. But you have to promise me you'll let me take you out for dinner in return before I leave."

She drew back a little, as if startled, and she wasn't quite able to hide the look of surprised pleasure that glowed in her eyes. It warmed Cruz in a way he'd never known before; it had been a very long time since a woman lit up at the simple prospect of having dinner with him. But then, it had also been a long time since he asked a woman to dinner.

In fact, he admitted wryly as he walked with her back to the inn, trying not to notice the graceful, smooth way she moved, with that trace of a feminine sway to her hips, it had been too long, period. That must be what had him thinking this way, what had him fighting off heated, erotic thoughts even at the most ordinary times.

That, and the fact that Kelsey was more fascinating than he'd ever realized.

It's the cop in you, he told himself. *You just can't resist a puzzle. And she's one heck of a puzzle. Wrapped in one heck of a package.*

On a physical level, he supposed some men, those who preferred the kind of woman who graced most magazines these days, would find her just a bit too curved for their taste. Personally, he found her damn near perfect and enjoyed the fact that she didn't bemoan every mouthful she ate, worrying about her weight.

He also found himself spending far too much time gazing at those luscious curves, wondering if they felt as good as they looked, and knowing the answer deep in his gut, where an intense heat had been building for days now.

Maybe it was a good thing he was only here for two more days.

* * *

She couldn't remember an evening she'd enjoyed more,
Kelsey thought as they left the restaurant and walked back to
Cruz's big blue four-wheel-drive. The service had been amazingly quick, the meal delicious, topped off with a strawberry
pie that had her wishing she could get the recipe. The talk
had been friendly and painless, and looking across the table
at Cruz Gregerson had been anything but a hardship.

Except when she found her heart speeding up at silly
things, such as when he reached for his glass and she noticed
how beautiful his hands were, lean, strong and long-fingered.
Or when he was reading the menu and she noticed the long,
thick sweep of his lashes. And then when he looked up at the
waiter and she noticed the way the cords of his neck delin-
eated the hollow of his throat.

And such as the moment when, because she was stealing
glances at him, she nearly missed a step in front of the restaurant. She was struck by his solid strength as he caught
nearly her full weight, righted her, then steadied her, all with
one hand. She'd never felt so secure. So safe. Protected. Almost...cherished.

She was being silly, she told herself. Cruz was simply being...kind. He had exerted himself to be charming, had acted
as if he'd looked forward to this as much as if it were a date
with a woman he liked, rather than payment for a few extra
meals that wouldn't show on his bill when they got back
tonight and he checked out.

At least that was what she kept telling herself; she knew
that to think there was anything more to it would be beyond
foolish. And she tried to ignore the tiny voice inside her that
was saying she would truly miss him when he was gone.
Listening to it would be even more foolish.

So foolish that she had limited herself to a single glass of
wine with her meal, since she rarely drank. Cruz was driving,
but she was feeling far too attracted to him to risk exceeding
her tolerance for alcohol.

He opened the door for her and handed her up into the
passenger seat. As he walked around to the driver's side, she

remembered the warning he'd given her when they first got into the vehicle.

"You may regret this," he'd said.

"Why?"

He'd given her a wry look. "Dog. I try to keep him out of the front seat, but the hair seems to migrate."

"What kind of dog do you have?" she asked now, when he was in the driver's seat.

"Who knows?"

Kelsey smiled; she liked that kind of dog. "Who's taking care of him?"

"A friend who doesn't mind feeding the zoo."

"The zoo?"

He gave a long-suffering sigh that she was reasonably sure was feigned as he maneuvered out of the parking lot.

"At last count, besides the dog and I don't know how many fish, it includes a baby raccoon, a possum, two rabbits, a couple of birds and a squirrel. And," he added, a look of sheer abhorrence on his face, "Slither."

She stared at him. "Slither? Is that…what it sounds like? A snake?"

"It certainly is."

There was no mistaking his tone. "Er…why do you have a snake, if you dislike them so?"

"I *hate* them," he corrected as he made the turn onto the highway that would take them back to the road to the inn.

"Then why have one?"

"I don't. Sam does. She loves the damn thing."

"Sam?"

"Samantha." He gave her a sideways glance as he pulled the car to a stop in the left turn lane at the bottom of her hill. "My daughter. She has a habit of bringing home every wounded stray for miles around. Including, unfortunately, the legless ones."

Kelsey blinked. She'd forgotten. Cruz had mentioned, on perhaps his second stay, that he had a little girl. But she'd been trying so hard not to succumb to the interest he sparked in her that she hadn't wanted to hear any more, hadn't wanted—or hadn't dared—to indulge her curiosity about him.

"I'm sorry," she said hastily. "I'd forgotten her name."

"I'm not sure I ever told you," Cruz said. "And you never asked."

It wasn't said in an accusing tone, but Kelsey winced anyway. She was very aware that, for all her trying to keep him occupied, she had stayed away from really personal questions. She even knew why: asking him personal questions about his family and background would imply license for him to ask those questions of her, and she was in no way ready for that.

"Where is she now?"

"She's at camp, up near Lake Arrowhead. That's why I have to leave tonight. She's getting a ride home with one of the other parents, but I want to be there when she gets there." There was a break in the traffic, and he made the turn onto the hill road smoothly, evenly. "That's why I come here, close to home, rather than someplace a plane flight away. I want to be able to get to her if anything happens."

Kelsey felt a sudden tightness in her throat at his words and at the lack of any trace of resentment in his voice; it was clear that, in his eyes, this was nothing special. He said it as if such compromises in his more important adult life for the sake of his child's were...natural. Expected. And not at all cause for complaint.

"She's got my pager number if she needs me," he added, and Kelsey felt a pang of guilt at her assumption that he wore the pager because of his work, as if there could be no other reason, simply because he was a cop and therefore had no other life. "And from here I can get to her in a couple of hours."

If he only knew how special that seemed to her, she thought, blinking rapidly as they turned onto the drive to the inn.

"Does she look like you?" she asked, grabbing at the first thing that came into her mind to say before he noticed the moisture in her eyes.

"No, lucky for her. She's blond, and got the brown eyes.

She's only like me in temperament.'' He stopped the truck in one of the guest slots, turned it off and turned in his seat to look at her as he added with a grin, ''Stubborn.''

Kelsey smiled; she couldn't help it. ''How old is she?''

''Ten. Going on thirty.''

Her smile widened. She didn't know why she'd shied away from this; she loved learning more about him. ''Precocious?''

''I think she was just born with an old soul,'' Cruz said. ''But she's smart as a whip and has more energy than I can deal with sometimes.''

He leaned toward her, and for one heart-stopping moment Kelsey thought he was going to kiss her. She fought down an embarrassed flush when she realized he'd only been reaching for something on the back seat.

It was, she saw then, a spiral notebook like the one she'd seen him with in the great room last night, like the ones he always brought with him. Up close now, she saw that it was not a writing notebook, as she'd thought, but rather a sketchbook, and it seemed full of pencil drawings. This was what he'd been doing? He wasn't a writer, but an artist?

He flipped through a few pages, slid them to the back, then handed the sketchbook to her. And she had her answer; he was indeed an artist. A very, very good one.

Kelsey's breath caught. Her gaze shot to his face, then back to the pad she held. ''Oh, Cruz...''

She didn't know if it was a reaction to the quality of the drawing itself or the image portrayed there, but she felt stunned. The sketch was a marvelous piece of work, capturing not only the young, innocent beauty of the little girl, but the glint of mischief in her eyes, and the determined slant of jaw and chin that gave the truth to his words about her temperament. And while he might be right in saying she didn't look like him, there was nevertheless a sense of quiet strength, evident even in this child, that spoke clearly of her father.

''She's lovely,'' Kelsey said softly. Then, looking up at him, she added, ''And if I had to guess, I'd say she's a handful, too.''

Cruz grinned. ''That she is. But she's got such a good

heart, it's hard to stay mad at her for long. When she gets in trouble, it's usually because she's trying to help somebody else."

"Or something? Like a raccoon, rabbit, or the like?"

"Exactly," he said. "And they sense it, I swear. Every living creature she's around gravitates to her."

Kelsey stared at the drawing as Cruz got out of the truck. She hadn't assumed he would open the door for her, it was simply that she'd been so entranced that she forgot to open it herself. But he seemed to assume he would. He made no comment, merely nodded when she thanked him as she slid to the ground.

"She sounds…very special."

"She is. She's the best thing that ever happened to me."

Kelsey stared at him as he said it with no trace of hesitation or doubt, not a trace of false sincerity. He meant it, she thought. He absolutely meant it.

"She's going to do some good in this world," he said softly. "Maybe become a vet, if she doesn't outgrow the animal thing. It would suit her, I think. And she'd be a darn good one."

The intensity of the love and pride and protectiveness in his voice made Kelsey's eyes begin to brim anew. What must it be like, to have your father love you so very much? She stared down at the lively sketch. *Lucky, lucky little girl*, she thought. *I hope you know how lucky you are.*

She knew she was going to lose her composure, so she quickly flipped the page. And smiled at the vivid portrait of a shaggy dog, one ear pricked, the other flopping over, a tongue-lolling grin on his face.

"Frisbee," Cruz said in explanation.

She smiled at the engaging portrait as they walked up the steps onto the porch. "Frisbee? I gather he catches them?"

"Remarkably well. What he doesn't do so well is give them back."

Charmed, Kelsey laughed. Apparently he didn't mind her looking futher, since he took the keys from her to open the door and left her the book, so she turned another page.

"Oh, my," she said as she gaped at the drawing of the most dramatic-looking man she'd ever seen, his high cheekbones, strong jaw and long black hair, held back by a bandanna tied around his forehead, speaking of ancestors who had walked this country long before the white man had.

"Ryan Buckhart," Cruz said, his tone wry.

"He's…amazing."

"Yes." He pushed open the door and ushered her inside, then closed it behind them. "He's six-foot-two and looks like some kind of Native American god. Women tend to think he's amazing."

"I can see why."

"Lacey—his wife—is a tough lady, to put up with it. But she knows he's crazy about her, so I suppose that helps. As much as anything can help being married to a cop."

Her eyes shot to his face as they stepped into the great room from the hall. "He's…a cop, too?"

Cruz nodded. "He's my best friend on the force. I was best man at his and Lacey's remarriage a few months—"

A high, stifled cry came from across the room. They both spun around, Cruz going into a slight crouch that was so swift it had to be instinctive, while Kelsey simply yelped and nearly dropped the sketchbook. And then she groaned when she saw Melissa in the kitchen doorway, staring at them, wide-eyed and pale, wrapped in one of Kelsey's flannel robes; in her concentration on the drawings, she'd forgotten to give a warning knock before they came in.

"He's a cop?" the girl cried out in a tone of sheer horror usually reserved for ax murders, staring at Cruz.

Cruz's gaze shifted from the girl to Kelsey's face. His brows were lowered, his eyes probing, and she imagined that this was what he must have looked like when she called him that night.

And judging by his expression, he was even more suspicious now than he'd been then.

Chapter 5

"I can't believe this!" Melissa wailed. "I thought you were suppose to be straight with us—everybody said so!"

"Melissa—"

"I trusted you, because you didn't preach, or tell me what to do, you just said when I felt safe again I could decide what to do. But it was all a trick to stall me while you called the cops, wasn't it?" the girl cried accusingly, weeping now.

Kelsey felt Cruz's gaze on her. She glanced at him, then back at the girl, her heart turning over at the girl's obvious distress.

"Melissa, listen to me—"

"What a joke, you telling me to stay out of sight, when all along you had a damn cop here, spying!"

The girl whirled and ran back through the kitchen.

"You want to explain this?" Cruz said.

Gone was the charming dinner companion, gone was the clever artist she'd never expected to find, gone was the loving father who had unknowingly moved her to tears. She was looking at the cop now, and she knew it to the depths of her knotted stomach. If he'd been anybody else, she might have been able to bluff her way out of this, but the only thing in his unexpectedly blue eyes besides suspicion was a razor sharp intelligence that wouldn't be fooled. But she had to try.

"She's my...cousin," Kelsey began, then stopped when she saw the disbelief that was clear in his face. There was no point in going on. She shouldn't even have tried, that late-night phone call had taught her as much.

"I suggest you don't try that again, Kelsey," he said. "I've been lied to by the best, and believe me, you're not very good at it."

No, she wasn't, she admitted silently. Not anymore. There had been a time when she was very, very good at it. But it had been a long time since her very survival depended on her ability to lie convincingly.

But it had also been a very long time since she let herself be cowed just because someone was bigger and stronger than she was. She might have had to do as the cops said once, but she was an adult now, and he might be a cop, but this wasn't his...what did they call it? Jurisdiction?

She drew herself up straight and forced herself to meet his gaze head-on. "It's none of your concern," she said.

He drew back slightly, as if startled. Or hurt, she thought, then nearly laughed out loud at herself for the absurdity of that idea. And she knew how absurd it was when he spoke; his voice was cool, almost mild.

"She's been here all along, hasn't she? I had the feeling somebody else was here. The lights...and I didn't remember the place making that many noises at night. Why was she hiding? Why did you tell her to stay out of sight? Because of me? What's she done?"

Kelsey cringed inwardly at the barrage of questions, but she made herself hold his gaze. "I told you—"

"You also told me you had a water leak," he said, cutting her off, "to keep me from coming at all. She was the reason, wasn't she? I was right all along. You didn't want a cop here, did you?"

Anger sparked through Kelsey. She welcomed it, grasped at it, needing it. She'd spent too much of her life in fear, too

much of her life facing a man who fired question after un-
relenting question at her, to accept it easily now. She would
not let it happen again, would not live like that, afraid, intimidated. She'd fought hard to conquer her fears, and she wasn't
about to buckle to them again now. And anger was the only
thing that would help her.

"You're not on duty here, Cruz. And I'm not under any
constraint to answer your idle questions."

"Believe me, there's nothing idle about them."

His tone was ominous enough that her stomach took a little
leap. She ignored it; she would not revert to the frightened
child she'd once been. Not when Melissa was depending on
her. Not when the girl already felt betrayed by her.

"Then let's just say I don't feel compelled to satisfy your
cop curiosity. Why don't you just go home as planned and
forget it?"

He looked at her for a long moment, and she found it very
hard to meet those steady blue eyes without looking away.
But she did it, simply because she stubbornly refused to do
anything else.

"Maybe," he said softly, "because I'd like to help."

She wished she could believe him. But nothing she knew
of cops gave her reason to think that he would be any different than any other cop when it came to bending the rules,
no matter what the circumstances. It was a lesson she'd
learned early, and painfully well. And she couldn't put Melissa at risk on the hope that Cruz might be different, just
because he seemed that way. Or had. He certainly didn't seem
any different from any other cop she'd ever seen now. Not
when he was firing questions at her as if this were an inter-
rogation session.

"I'm not a suspect you've arrested, Cruz. Just go home,"
she said, stifling a sigh. "Please."

"Kelsey, whatever it is, whatever you've gotten yourself
into, maybe I can—"

"Go home, Cruz. Won't your daughter be waiting?"

He glanced at the watch he'd put on this evening in prep-
aration for going back to the world where time mattered. His

mouth tightened when he read the time. Then he looked back at her.

"Kelsey, whatever she's hiding, whatever you're hiding—"

"She's just a friend staying here for a while," Kelsey said firmly. "Don't assume there's anything…clandestine going on just because she didn't want to be sociable."

Cruz gave her a steady look. "Why not?" he said, his dry tone tinged with what sounded almost like disappointment. "You assume just because I'm a cop I… What? Just what is it *you're* assuming about *me?*"

Cruz's mouth thinned when she didn't answer, just looked at him miserably.

"It was all a scam, wasn't it? All the attention, the long talks, the—"

He broke off and looked away, and again Kelsey got that odd sense that he was, if not hurt, at least upset. The idea of such vulnerability in a cop startled her, and the thought that she had hurt him, however unlikely that seemed, stung.

"Cruz…" she began, but stopped when she realized there was nothing she could say that wouldn't make this worse.

"Some people don't like my looks," he said tightly, "or my heritage. I've been called everything from the worst Hispanic slur to half-breed."

Kelsey winced, but Cruz didn't stop.

"But the most consistent, unreasoning prejudice I've ever faced isn't because I'm half-Mexican and my skin color doesn't go with my eyes. It's because I have a badge. People who don't even know me assume they know who I am because of it. People who would never dream of calling me a wetback or a spic don't think anything of calling me 'cop' with the same kind of distaste in their voice."

He let out a compressed breath.

"I just never thought you'd be one of them."

He turned then, grabbed the bag that was packed and waiting by the door and was gone. Leaving Kelsey standing alone, thinking he'd learned well from his father, because the way he had sounded, the way he had looked at her, made her feel exactly like pond scum.

He'd been too damned hard on her, Cruz thought as he drove through the night. Whatever she was up to, whoever that girl was, they'd both been more scared than anything else.

Scared of him.

He supposed that was what grated. That, and that he'd been fool enough to convince himself that there was something more than just ulterior motives to all the attention she'd been paying him this week. He'd been hurt, something that hadn't happened in a long time, and he'd reacted nastily.

His mind veered away from that painful thought and settled on something else, something he could at least wrestle with without feeling like a fool. What on earth was Kelsey up to? Who was that girl, and why had she gone into such a panic when she heard he was a cop? Why had she been hiding in the first place, if she hadn't already known? What had she done that had made her want to hide from someone who was, for all she knew, just a guest at the inn? Had Kelsey told her some horror story about him, or was whatever the girl had done so awful that she didn't dare risk being found even by an average civilian?

He couldn't believe it. The girl was just scared, it had been written all over her young, weary face. Not the ugly expression of viciousness, just a scared kid. Besides, Kelsey wouldn't protect somebody vicious.

At least, he didn't think she would. But he hadn't thought she would turn on him because he was a cop, either.

Fine thing, he thought to himself wearily. *You become a cop to try to help people, and half the time they just run scared from you.*

Even Kelsey had been scared. He'd sensed it, beneath the determination, behind the grit, with which she faced him. She'd been scared, and he didn't like thinking that it had been because of him, for whatever reason.

He rubbed at his eyes, wondering if any of it had been real.

Had all of it—the companionable chats, the laughter, the moments when he'd caught her looking at him as if she were...interested—had it all been simply part of the plan to keep him from noticing the girl's presence? And what the hell had she expected him to do if he *did* notice?

I'm not a suspect you've arrested, Cruz.

Maybe he *had* come on a little strong, he thought as her words echoed in his mind. Sometimes that cop instinct just took over. When you were presented with someone clearly hiding something, it was a deeply ingrained habit to find out what and why. And he supposed Kelsey had no idea of his motivation for pushing for an explanation, other than what would be obvious to her, that he was a suspicious cop. How could she? Even he wasn't sure what his motivation was.

He was concerned about what she might have gotten herself into, nothing more, he told himself as he changed lanes, handling the big four-wheel-drive with automatic skill. He'd always liked her, and in this past week he had even grown fond of her, and that was all.

Except that this past week had all been a sham, an exercise in distracting the cop, keeping him busy so he wouldn't notice her phantom guest.

And there he was, back in that rut, forced to admit to what stung more than anything, and hating himself for letting it happen.

"You've been alone too damn long, Gregerson," he muttered as he took the freeway off-ramp that would get him home. "You let a pretty face, some soft curves and a pair of big green eyes lead you right where she wanted you to go."

But he knew it wasn't just that. He'd really *liked* the time he spent with her; he'd liked her quick intelligence and her quiet humor. And he'd more than once found himself wishing he could chase away whatever shadows haunted her, those memories that turned her eyes so sad and made her voice hollow.

He hadn't felt that way about a woman in a very long time. That her actions had apparently been all for show was a blow to more than just his pride. It crippled whatever fledgling feelings had been developing for this woman.

Just as well, he thought. He'd been a fool to let it happen, anyway. He and Sam were doing just fine; she was the only female he had time for or wanted in his life.

So why couldn't he put it out of his mind? Why did he still want to know what was going on, who Melissa was, what she had done, and why Kelsey was hiding her? There was only one explanation for that: he just couldn't stop being a cop.

Or else Kelsey had completely gotten to him, more than he even suspected, and that was why he couldn't let it alone.

He wasn't sure which explanation bothered him more.

Kelsey stifled a sigh and wondered if there was anything else that could possibly go wrong. She quickly retracted the thought, thinking better of tempting a fate that seemed determined to prove to her that there was *always* something else that could get messed up. She lifted her cup of coffee in mock salute, hoping the offering would stave off any further ideas that fate had about playing with her.

Cruz's last words still seemed to echo in the air, and Melissa hadn't set foot outside her room this morning, after refusing steadfastly last night to even listen to Kelsey.

Great, she muttered to herself. Now you've not only made him suspicious, you've made him mad.

She wondered if he would do anything. How deep did that cop mentality run? Would he pursue this, even though it clearly had nothing to do with him? Was he going to show up back here, demanding answers? Or since it wasn't his jurisdiction, would he call whoever's it was? Or would he just walk away?

And never come back?

Kelsey was startled by the strength of the pain that thought caused. She traced the wood-grain pattern of the kitchen table with a finger, pressing down hard, as if the pressure could relieve the ache. The idea that he might never come back— no, she corrected herself grimly, the likelihood—made her feel much more miserable than it should. He was only a guest, after all. True, he was a special guest, her very first paying guest, her first repeat guest, but that was all.

"God, you can't even lie to yourself," she said to the empty room, her words punctuated by a self-deprecating laugh.

It was true. Cruz had become much more than just a guest to her in the past week. How ironic, that the interest she'd always had in him had made it easier for her to concentrate on distracting him, yet had also resulted in her falling into the trap she'd set. She'd found him fascinating, charming, and far too attractive; it had been a long time since she met a man who made her wonder if another stab at love might be worth it. But she had found herself thinking that way about Cruz, wondering what it would be like...

She leaped to her feet, abandoned her coffee mug and fled from the kitchen into the great room, curling up on the sofa before the cold ashes of last night's fire. An appropriate setting for her mood, she thought glumly. The emptiness of the coming days was pressing down on her already. The Taylors would not arrive for another two weeks, and for once, instead of welcoming the break between guests, she dreaded it.

She knew she'd brought it all on herself. If only she'd thought it out when Melissa showed up on her doorstep, shaking, cold, hungry and scared. She'd listened to the girl pour out her story between gulping sobs, a confused tangle of cruel parents, an angry boyfriend and the police hunting her down. She had fed her, soothed her, assured her she was safe here...and then panicked when she remembered that Cruz Gregerson, due to arrive the next day for his annual visit, was a cop.

Now she let her head loll to one side, smothering a yawn; she hadn't slept much last night. Her weary eyes closed, then snapped open again as something she'd seen registered. She stared at the end table beside the sofa and the spiral-bound pad that lay there. The sketchbook Cruz had shown her last night. She vaguely remembered dropping it there after they'd

seen Melissa, and after their emotional confrontation before
he departed last night, Cruz must have forgotten it.

With a sad smile, she picked it up. She hesitated, then
decided she probably couldn't be any more miserable than
she already was and flipped it open.

A half-dozen sketches like the ones she'd already seen were
on the first few pages, different angles and moods of the little
girl who was clearly his favorite subject. And she saw again
that while it was true that the child didn't particularly look
like him, there was an undeniable resemblance in the set of
her chin and the steady determination in her eyes. It was, she
supposed, a tribute to his skill that even those intangibles
came across so clearly.

She turned to the drawing of that exotic, breathtaking man
he'd called Ryan Buckhart, seeing now the different approach
he'd taken here, the firm slash of lines, as opposed to the
gentle brushstroke type of technique he'd used for Samantha.

She fiddled idly with the book, wondering if he'd ever gone
to art school, or if the talent was so natural he'd never had
to learn. Yet another thing she never would have expected
from a cop, she thought, beginning to realize that she was
perhaps as guilty as he'd suggested of judging him simply by
the fact that he wore a badge. Maybe she should—

Her breath caught, sharply, audibly. She stared down at the
sketchbook she held, at the page it had fallen open to, the
back of the last page. It was as if he'd turned it over to start
fresh from the other side.

She stared at herself.

Shock enabled her to look at the portrait in a rather de-
tached way. He'd been kind, she thought numbly. Her eyes
were not that large or that pretty, her lashes not that long, her
mouth not that soft and warm-looking. Nor was her hair really
so smooth, sleek and beautiful-looking. And he'd taken her
stubborn chin and made it look somehow delicate. In fact,
he'd given the whole portrait a fragile air. But he'd caught
her nose as it was, turned up just a bit too much.

That he'd drawn her at all made her feel…she wasn't sure

what. Why? Why had he done it? Simply because she was the only subject handy?

She discarded that thought; he hadn't had his daughter handy, and it certainly hadn't stopped him from drawing her. Of course, he would know her features by heart. Perhaps he simply wanted a change from drawing from memory.

She would not read any more into it than that. She simply would not. She said it to herself fiercely, determinedly, as if that alone could make it so. As if—

"Why, that's lovely, dear. It looks just like you."

Kelsey gave a start as she jerked around to look at the woman behind her. Dolores Lamana gave a start in turn. Quickly Kelsey apologized.

"I'm sorry, I was...distracted." She frowned. "Do you really think it looks like me?"

"Exactly," the woman said, leaning over for a better look. She was wearing a pastel blue suit, and Kelsey guessed she had come from church; Dolores rarely missed a Sunday.

"I don't know, I think he was too...flattering."

"That," Dolores said briskly as she straightened up, "is because you have no idea how lovely you really are." Kelsey blushed. Dolores smiled widely. "And that, my dear, is part of your charm. Don't ever change. So, who did the drawing?"

Kelsey stood slowly, giving the woman a sideways look. In the past two years, Dolores had been her lifesaver in the cooking department around here; she brought extra meals in once a week when there were guests registered, carefully and deliciously prepared items chosen because they could be prepared ahead of time and frozen, and would keep until Kelsey needed them, adding great variety to her own breakfast menus. She provided the occasional dinner, as well, for Kelsey's own use, saying that if she didn't, she was afraid Kelsey would never see a hot meal.

She had also more than once pointedly told Kelsey that Cruz Gregerson was the most attractive man she'd seen in ages, and were she not twenty-five years too old and a grandmother three—now four—times over, she would set her cap for him.

"Cruz," she finally said.

Dolores's warm, dark eyes widened. "Really? I had no idea he was an artist."

And you still have no idea he's a cop, Kelsey thought, but she didn't say it. She doubted it would make any difference to Dolores, but the woman knew what Kelsey was doing here, and she didn't see any point in having somebody else worrying.

"Neither did I" was all she said.

Dolores started toward the kitchen to pick up her dishes from the meals she'd provided this week. Kelsey followed.

"I'm sorry I missed him this year, but that baby simply would not wait."

"You must be happy. I'm glad all went well."

"I'm delighted. Every one of my children has done their duty now and presented me with a grandchild to spoil." She looked back over her shoulder with a teasing smile. "Now I can concentrate on getting you settled with some babies of your own."

Kelsey laughed, as she always did when Dolores's thoughts inevitably turned in that direction, but this time it was a hollow-sounding laugh, even to her own ears. Once she'd believed the idea of a loving, happy marriage was a fantasy, far removed from the dreary and sometimes grim reality. She'd learned better since those early days, come to realize that there were good relationships, that it was just not in the cards for her. She hadn't really minded, hadn't felt she was missing much.

But Cruz had made her wonder. He had upset her hard-won equilibrium, and that it had happened because she had little choice but to make it happen was nobody's fault but her own.

It was all a scam, wasn't it?

His words, and the sound of his voice when he'd said them, rang in her ears.

No, she whispered silently to him, to herself, not sure who the pleading denial was really aimed at. *No, it wasn't all a scam. I had to do it, but it was still real. It was still real.*

"Kelsey? Are you all right?"

She hastily composed herself. "I... Yes. I'm fine. I'm just a little tired."

Dolores gave her a look of motherly concern. "You do too much, baby. Running this place would be enough, but the rest on top of it?" She shook her head. "I know you mean well, but you should think of yourself a little more."

"I'm fine," Kelsey insisted, although she made sure to smile; Dolores was her only confidante, the only one who knew, and Kelsey sometimes desperately needed that outlet.

"Well, at least Melissa came around."

"She hasn't yet. In fact, we're not communicating at all at the moment," Kelsey said dryly.

"Oh?" Dolores looked puzzled. "I assumed you'd gotten her taken care of, since her room is empty."

Kelsey went still. "What?"

"Her room—"

Kelsey didn't wait to hear the rest. She spun on her heel and ran for the small back room Melissa had been using. It was tidy, the bed neatly made...or never slept in. Kelsey walked quickly to the closet and pulled open the door. The girl hadn't had much, but even that was gone, empty hangers rocking from the air currents Kelsey had stirred with the door. The floor was bare, as well, although all that had ever been there was the one spare pair of tennis shoes Kelsey had bought for her.

There was nothing else, no sign anyone had been here, not even a goodbye note. But there was no denying the truth.

Melissa was gone.

Chapter 6

Cruz stared at the drink he'd poured, wondering why he'd bothered. It wasn't going to help him sleep. Nothing had helped much in the past two days. Here he was, on vacation, supposedly to relax and catch up on the sleep all cops found at a premium, and he was sitting in the dark, staring at a glass half-full of liquor from some bottle he hadn't opened since the day Sam broke her arm falling out of the tree beside the garage.

He would never forget that day, how his tough, gritty little girl had picked herself up and walked into the house to find him, cradling her left arm, her eyes wide and dark with pain, her cheeks streaked with tears and dirt as she faced him and said quietly, "Daddy, will you fix my arm? It really hurts." As if he were some kind of miracle worker. As if she had all the faith in the world that he could do it. And then she had truly blown him away by asking that he put the baby bird back in its nest first, before he tended to her.

He set the glass down untouched and got to his feet. Driven by an urge he knew from long experience was useless to fight, he walked across the living room, past the den that he'd long ago ceded to Sam's zoo, past his own bedroom, and quietly opened the door to his daughter's room.

As usual, she had kicked free of the covers and was curled up in a small ball at the top of the bed. She hated the confinement—that was something Cruz was sure was going to be a lifelong trait—even if she had to curl up for warmth. But he did as he always did, crept in quietly and pulled the blanket over her, not tucking it in, because he knew she hated it, and forgoing the extra weight of the quilt, judging it not quite that cold.

For a long moment he just stood there looking at her, this tiny miracle, this combination of gentleness and strength, this little being he'd helped create and who owned his heart in a way no one else ever would. Her long blond hair was a tangled mess he would have to deal with in the morning, and she'd missed a spot on her arm in her hasty washing before tumbling into bed.

She was beautiful.

He'd heard about nothing but the exciting week she'd had at camp since she got home on Saturday night. He'd listened carefully, grunting noncommittally at her assurances that Slither had been well behaved, made a mental note to keep track of the new interest she seemed to have developed in astronomy, and nearly cried when she stopped in the middle of her chatter to earnestly tell him that no matter how good camp was, she liked being home with him better.

Even now he found himself blinking rapidly at the memory, and his vision blurred a little as he watched her sleep. This was the only time he ever saw her completely still, the only time she didn't look as if she were about to burst into motion at any second.

You were a fool, Ellie, he thought. *This is what matters. This is where the real living happens. Not out there, wherever you went looking for it.*

He shook his head and backed quietly out of the room. Maybe he would have that drink after all; it had been a long time since he spent any time dwelling on his former wife. He'd long ago dealt with the facts and effects of what had happened and what she'd done, and thinking about it now would hardly change anything. He knew why she'd done what she did, he even understood it, and there was no point in dragging it out to look at again. It never changed. He just wished it would go away.

He went back to his chair, sat, picked up the glass, looked at it, then set it down again. And faced the fact that the last thing his stomach needed right now was the burning heat of alcohol.

The clock over the fireplace—Sam's whimsical choice, a bear on its back, balancing the dial precariously on its paws— ticked off the last few minutes before midnight. He let his head loll back, but a tug from the tense muscles of his neck stopped the motion. The chair wasn't as comfortable as the chairs at Oak Tree. Maybe he should find out where Kelsey had gotten them—

Stop it, he ordered himself, as he'd been doing for almost all of those two days now. The orders did little good, even though he knew this was damn near as pointless as thinking about Ellen, this constant wondering about Kelsey Hall and what kind of mess she'd gotten herself into. Just let it go, leave it behind. It's not your problem; *she's* not your problem. He chanted the phrases in his mind as if they were a mantra that would ward off thoughts of her, would enable him to put out of his mind what a fool he'd been to think there was something genuine in her sudden interest in him.

And what a fool he was because he couldn't seem to just drop it, couldn't forget the look on Kelsey's face when he saw Melissa, that look of distress and panic and fear. Having suspects afraid of him was one thing, having a woman like Kelsey afraid of him was something else. And no matter how much he told himself that she wouldn't be afraid of him un- less she had something to hide, and therefore it was her fault, not his, it didn't quite take.

And no matter what he did, he couldn't seem to put her out of his mind.

"You *have* been alone too long," he muttered.

But if that was all it was, then why the heck hadn't it

bothered him before? He'd been cruising along, doing fine, with few problems outside his caseload. And now that Lacey and Ryan had put their marriage solidly back together, relieving him of the awkward position of being caught between two people he cared a great deal about who were hurting each other and hurting *for* each other, his worries were minimal. Sam, of course, but she was amazingly—sometimes frighteningly—self-sufficient for a ten-year-old. Lieutenant Robards, who was going to drive him crazy with his cigar-chomping arrogance and old-school ways. And the constant worry that somehow that damn snake was going to get loose in the house.

But rarely had he thought about being without female companionship, except maybe early in the morning, when he rolled over and came stark awake from the shock of cold sheets. In fact, he'd thought himself cured of the need for it, when the few women he dated had failed to interest him beyond dinner and a movie, when he couldn't even stir up enough interest in his obviously open and amenable—not to mention attractive—next-door neighbor to stir himself to respond to her invitation to get to know her better. He had female friends, but not a one of them, not even Kit, great as she was, had made him consider it worth the possible loss of the friendship to make it into something else.

No, he hadn't thought a damn thing about it one way or the other until Kelsey Hall insinuated herself into his mind, until she resorted to throwing herself in his path to keep him too occupied to notice just what she'd been hiding.

And she'd succeeded nicely, he thought dryly. He'd been occupied, all right. He still was. So much so that he was even considering taking a drive back to the inn tomorrow. He could take Sam with him. She'd never seen where he stayed those weeks she was in camp, and he—

The scraping sound at the front door brought him up out of the chair in a rush. He confirmed the late hour with a glance at the bear clock and felt a rush of adrenaline as his cop's mind turned over the possibilities. They were few; most everyone he knew who would want to see him at this hour would have called first.

He thought briefly about getting his off-duty two-inch Colt, but it was locked safely in his desk drawer, for Sam's sake. He headed for the door instead. He peered through the peephole just in time to see a shadow turning away and heading for the porch steps.

His body tightened in the instant before he saw who it was, and he grimaced at the irony that his hormones had known it was Kelsey before his mind did. Belatedly his mind kicked in, and he yanked the door open and simultaneously reached for the switch beside the door. She spun around at the sound and the sudden flare of the porch light, her hand flying up to her throat as she let out a startled little yelp.

"Kelsey?"

He felt like an idiot the instant after he said it. Of course it was her, he knew it was. But he was so startled to see her standing right in front of him, as if he'd summoned her somehow by thinking about her so much, he didn't know what else to say.

"I... I'm sorry." She sounded as flustered as he felt; he could only imagine how he must have startled her. "I didn't knock because it's so late, and there was no light, so I didn't think anyone would be awake."

"I was..." His words trailed off into silence as he realized that the truth, that he'd been sitting in the dark thinking about her, was not something he wanted to admit. "I was awake," he amended awkwardly.

"I'm sorry," she repeated. "I didn't mean to bother you."

He glanced out toward the street and saw the green sedan with Oak Tree Inn painted on the door in white letters parked at the curb. He hadn't heard the car at all, which was highly unusual for him, and he supposed a statement on just how lost in those thoughts of her he'd been.

Then what she'd said registered. She hadn't meant to bother him? Then why was she here? Never mind that she'd been bothering him in one way or another for days...

His gaze slid back to her. She was edging toward the steps, away from him, and that stung in a way he'd never experienced before.

"I don't bite," he snapped. When she winced, he immediately regretted the sharpness of his tone and let out a short breath.

"Just don't look at me like you think I'm going to..."

He wasn't sure what she was thinking, only that he hated to see her acting like this. He forced a soothing tone into his voice. "What did you want, Kelsey?"

"I... Nothing."

He managed not to point out the obvious absurdity of her standing on his doorstep at midnight claiming there was no reason. But at least she had stopped edging away.

"You were just in the neighborhood?" he asked mildly.

She had the grace to look chagrined. "No, I...just wanted to drop that off. You forgot it."

She pointed down toward his feet. He followed the gesture, but because of his own shadow it took him a moment to see the dark blue cover of the sketchbook she'd left on the mat.

"Oh," he said, feeling a little silly himself that there truly was such a simple explanation.

He bent to pick it up, straightened, then went very still when he remembered that this was the book he'd just begun to use on this trip—and remembered what he'd put in it. His gaze shot to her face. Had she looked? It was in the back, maybe...

"I had your address on file," she said, as if he'd asked. "And I thought you might...need it."

Of course she'd looked. Why wouldn't she? She'd been effusive enough about his amateur attempts at portraits to be curious. Unless, of course, that had been an act, too.

"Thank you," he said abruptly, not wanting to dwell on that idea. And besides, it had just hit him that this explanation of her presence wasn't really simple after all, given the hour. "But you hardly had to drive out here at midnight to deliver it."

Her mouth quirked. "I was in the neighborhood."

He wasn't sure if she was teasing, using his own words back at him, but he smiled anyway.

"You really are very good," she said. "Have you studied?"

"No. My mother kept telling me I should go to art school, but..." He shrugged.

"But...you didn't want to?"

He shook his head. "I didn't want to be a doctor, either, like my dad wanted. All I ever wanted to do was be a cop."

She lowered her eyes. The light of the porch fixture threw stark shadows across her face, and he couldn't see her expression.

"He must have been...angry."

"Dad? No. Maybe a little disappointed. But he got over it. Then he tried to talk me into being a lawyer, if I was so set on something to do with the law."

"You didn't want that, either?"

"I told him I'd rather clean birdcages," Cruz said dryly.

He heard an odd sound, as if she'd caught her breath sharply. "You...said that to him? To your father? To his face?"

Cruz's brow lowered. He'd never met the man, and he supposed it wasn't kind to think ill of the dead, but right now he didn't care much for Kelsey's father.

"And lived to tell about it," he said quietly. "Dad's got a good sense of humor. And he finally got the point. Told me if that's what I really wanted, then he'd back me all the way. He cheered louder than anyone when I graduated from the academy."

She gave a tiny, almost forlorn shake of her head, and Cruz had to fight not to reach out and envelop her in a crushing hug.

He knew on some deep gut level that life hadn't been easy for Kelsey Hall; he'd seen the signs too often to mistake them.

"Why don't you come in for a minute?" he asked, knowing he was going to regret it, but unable to stop himself. He told himself it was just like Sam's animals; she'd never been able to resist a wounded stray, and apparently neither could he. There was nothing more to it than that. Kelsey was hurting, for whatever reason, and he couldn't turn his back on her. Not even for his own good.

"No, I have to go. But thank you."

She tilted her head back to look up at him then, and for the first time he saw her face in full light.

"God, Kelsey, what's wrong?"

He took a step forward onto the porch, reaching for her. He sensed she was about to draw back and quickened his movement until he had grasped her shoulders. He held her still, gently but firmly.

"You look exhausted," he said, staring down at the huge dark shadows that circled her eyes. "What the hell have you been doing?"

She looked away, and he felt the tension in her as she began to pull away.

"Never mind," he said shortly. "It's obvious that whatever you've been doing, it hasn't included sleep. Come inside."

She blinked. A tremor rippled through her, and he felt the weariness that caused it as if it had been his own. "Inside?"

"It's late, you're thrashed, come inside and rest. Whatever it is, it can wait."

She shook her head. "No. No, it can't."

He tightened his grip on her shoulders and urged her toward the open door. He got her to step inside, but there she stopped dead.

"It has to wait," he insisted. "You're dead on your feet."

"I have to keep going, I have to—"

He didn't know what was driving her. It didn't matter, not at the moment. "What good is it going to do if you collapse? Or maybe drive your car into a tree?"

"But—"

"Don't make me pull rank on you, Kelsey. I can't let you out on the street when you're too tired to even walk straight."

A shudder went through her this time. Her head slumped and her shoulders sagged. "Always the cop," she whispered.

"That has nothing to do with it."

Her head came up sharply, and her voice was suddenly angry. "It has everything to do with this."

"What it has to do with is you being too stubborn to listen to reason."

"What it has to do with is you making like a TV cop, snapping out questions, demanding answers, scaring people...." Her voice trailed away, and she lowered her head again.

"What," he said slowly, "does any of that have to do with

why you're standing here in the middle of the night, about to topple over?''

When she didn't answer, he lifted one hand and nudged her chin up, making her look at him.

"Kelsey?''

"This could ruin everything," she said, shaking her head slowly, as if she were in pain. She sounded as if weariness and fear had worn her down to a nub, and he guessed she was running on pure nerve and had been for a while now. He felt a surge of protectiveness he barely recognized, something he'd only felt toward Sam before. He wasn't sure he liked the revelation.

But he knew for sure he didn't like being accused of ruining everything, even if he had no idea what "everything" was.

"I'm the same guy I've been for the past three years," Cruz said, a bit weary of the whole thing himself, after spending all this time trying to figure it out. "What the hell have you done that you're so afraid now that you know I'm a cop?''

"Me?'' She wrenched free and glared at him. "You're the one who was firing off questions like a machine gun! You're the one who kept pushing. You're the one who scared her away!''

"What?''

"Melissa! She's out there now—'' she gestured wildly behind her, toward the city ''—all alone and scared and thinking she can't trust anybody because the one person she did trust called the cops on her!''

"Didn't you...explain?'' *What the hell had the kid done, to be so scared?*

"She didn't give me a chance, she took off. But what else was she supposed to think? She's just a kid, and she's scared, and then you show up right after she did... I have to find her.''

He blocked her as she started for the door. "That's what you've been doing? Looking for her?''

"Yes. Let me go.''

"When did she leave?''

"The same night you did," Kelsey snapped. "Now let me go. I have to find her, and soon."

"She's a runaway?" he guessed.

"Just let me go."

"But there's more to it, isn't there? She was more than just scared she'd get sent home. What else is going on?"

"What does it matter to you? She's just another kid in trouble, somebody to badger with questions and not listen to the answers."

Cruz frowned. There was an undertone of fierce emotion in her voice that triggered some deep, intuitive response in his gut. Kelsey wasn't simply worried about Melissa, there was something much deeper, much more personal, going on here. Every instinct he'd ever had, every knack he'd developed in nine years on the job, was telling him so. This normally quiet, almost reserved woman was beyond passionate in her empathy with the missing girl. And Cruz couldn't help wondering why.

"Kelsey—"

"Just let me go!" she cried out, twisting to try to get past him.

"Daddy?"

Cruz spun around as the tiny voice came from behind him. Samantha, clad in her beloved Tigger T-shirt, stood in the center of the living room, staring at the two of them, her eyes wide with worry and a touch of fear that made his stomach knot violently.

"Sam," Cruz breathed.

And cursed himself for being so distracted by Kelsey that he'd forgotten his daughter.

Chapter 7

"I heard yelling," Samantha said. And then, in a tone that was oddly, almost frighteningly adult, she looked at her father and asked, "Are you all right?"

Kelsey stared as Cruz crossed the room in two long strides, then bent to sweep the child up in his arms. In a movement that was clearly automatic, the girl's arms went around his neck and she hugged him fiercely.

"Everything's fine, squirt."

Wide brown eyes the color of cinnamon looked at him, then shifted to Kelsey, who was feeling nothing less than dismayed as Sam clung to him in a way that seemed both fearful and protective at the same time.

"Then why was she yelling?" the child asked. "And who is she?"

"She," Kelsey said, stepping forward and feeling utterly contrite at having frightened this lovely, innocent child, "is a silly woman who's very sorry she woke you up."

Samantha seemed to consider this for a moment, never relinquishing her hold on Cruz. He kept quiet, just looking at Kelsey, as if to point out that she had been doing the yelling, so she could deal with the result. But she noticed he never stopped rubbing the child's back, never eased up on his secure hold of her.

"I'm Kelsey," she said, taking another step forward when Sam didn't draw back. "And truly, I'm sorry if you were frightened. I didn't mean to yell."

"I was worried," Sam said after a moment, still eyeing Kelsey warily. "My dad puts bad people in jail, and sometimes they get mad."

"I...imagine they do," Kelsey said. Her gaze flicked to Cruz. He looked back at her levelly, as if he knew perfectly well she'd never thought of that aspect of his work, that by its very nature he lived under the constant threat of revenge.

This time Sam's expression and voice were doubtful. "But you don't look bad."

Cruz didn't make a sound, but Kelsey saw him bite his lip, as if to keep from smiling. Kelsey grimaced. She knew all too well what she looked like. And didn't look like.

"No, I don't," she said. "I look...nice."

She's such a nice girl, that Kelsey.

Kelsey, you shouldn't try to wear that dress, it just doesn't suit you, it's too...sexy.

You shouldn't use all that makeup, Kelsey. You have that fresh-scrubbed look, and it just looks wrong on you.

She'd heard it all her adult life, the well-meant reminders that she wasn't the kind of woman who stopped traffic. At least not the male kind. Not with her plain, no-more-than-pleasant appearance. She'd told herself for years that she was grateful for that fact; she didn't want a man in her life, because she was certain it was all highly overrated. But underneath it all had been the niggling thought that it would be nice to have the choice.

"No," she added, unable to help sounding a bit sour, "I'm just the girl next door."

"No, you're not," Sam said, clearly taking it with a ten-year-old's tendency toward literalness. "Tammy is the girl next door. Her dad died. Now her mom likes my dad."

Of course, Kelsey thought. What woman wouldn't?

"Of course she does," Cruz said quickly, but in an entirely different tone, as if he were uncomfortable with how his daughter's words had sounded. "Because I help her out now and then, that's all. And now you—" he reached out and tapped Samantha's tiny, upturned nose "—need to get back to bed. It's late."

"The zoo. I have to check—"

"I know. Come on, we'll make sure everybody's okay." He looked back over his shoulder at Kelsey. "Don't take off, all right?"

"She can come see the animals," Sam suggested, apparently having decided Kelsey wasn't any danger. And Kelsey had no doubt it was the danger to her father that concerned the child more than anything else.

"If she wants," Cruz agreed as he flipped on a light in the hallway.

Kelsey didn't want. She didn't want any of this. She didn't want to watch anymore while Cruz comforted the girl who had moments ago been so frightened for him. She didn't want to see how exquisitely gentle he was with her, how tenderly he soothed her fears and brought her world back to safety. She didn't want to see the zoo, including the detested snake he put up with for the simple reason that he loved his little girl so much he would do anything to make her happy.

What she wanted was to run. To get away from him and the incredible pull he seemed to exert on her. In all the time she spent searching for Melissa in the past two days, he had never been far from her thoughts. And coupled with the memories of how much she'd enjoyed the time she spent with him last week was the nagging awareness that she hadn't been quite fair to him. If she stayed now, all she would end up doing would be piling up more memories that would haunt her, more images that would taunt her with her own longings and loneliness.

She *should* run. Far and fast. If she had any sense at all, she would.

But what she did was follow meekly, her eyes fastened on the little sprite who still clung to Cruz's neck, not quite over the last vestiges of her scare. Her blond head was a startling contrast to his dark one, but they were the same in one very important way: the sheer love that radiated from them.

It was a tangible thing, a cocoon spun around them. Kelsey didn't think she'd ever felt so shut out. Not just shut out from the connection between these two, but from ever having known that kind of feeling, that kind of ultimate love between parent and child. It was not a new sensation, but she hadn't experienced it in a long time. She'd thought herself over this.

But then, she'd thought herself immune to such foolish feelings as Cruz Gregerson evoked in her, too.

She watched as Cruz flipped on a light and then gently set the little girl down in the doorway of what looked, from the wood paneling and shelves, as if it had once been a den or library of sorts. But now the shelves—the lower ones, at least—were full of a variety of cages and aquariums. Some of them were empty and set to one side. Some were obviously in use, and she heard a rustling as some tiny creature moved in response to their presence.

She guessed that a glass aquarium, topped with a piece of screen fastened with a very secure-looking latch, held the snake loved by the daughter and detested by the father, although she couldn't see from where she was. Two more aquariums, these serving their original intended purpose of holding brightly colored fish, sat against the far wall, bubbling cheerfully.

Kelsey wondered where Frisbee the dog was, and why he hadn't set up a fuss when she came to the door, or when she was being such an idiot inside, yelling at Cruz and waking up this little sweetheart.

"Where's the dog?" she asked. "I half expected to hear him waking up the whole neighborhood when I came to the door."

"Frisbee? He doesn't bark much," Samantha said, adding matter-of-factly, "That's 'cause he's deaf. He can't hear anything to bark at."

So even the dog was a recipient of Sam's generous compassion. And Cruz's seemingly endless patience. With his daughter, at least, Kelsey amended; he didn't seem to have that much with her.

Samantha moved from cage to cage with the sureness of long experience. Cruz watched with the same air, and Kelsey realized this was a long-established routine. Sam peered into each cage, chattering soothingly to the occupants one by one in a tone that, Kelsey realized with a sense of poignant wonder, she had clearly learned from her father.

"It's okay, Bandit," she murmured, Kelsey supposed to the baby raccoon Cruz had mentioned. "You just go on playing."

Samantha glanced at Kelsey. "He's a raccoon. They're nocturnal," she explained, not stumbling at all over a word Kelsey doubted many ten-year-olds would know. "That means they're awake at night."

"I see," Kelsey said with a nod, not having to fake being impressed.

"So is Nosy. He's a possum. It's really *opossum*, but that sounds funny."

Kelsey smiled; she couldn't help it. The girl was enchanting, with her tousled blond locks and those big brown eyes, and her solemn air as she introduced the visitor to her obviously precious zoo.

"Yes, it does," Kelsey agreed.

"Bandit got hit by a car, and Nosy got in a fight with a cat, like the rabbits. But they're both almost well now," Samantha said. "And the rabbits will be soon, too."

"Then what happens?" Kelsey asked.

Sadness shadowed the little girl's eyes, but she spoke with utter conviction. "I have to let them go. I don't want to, but Dad says it's not fair to keep them caged after they're well."

Kelsey looked up at Cruz, moved by his daughter's utter, total belief in him.

"I'm sure he's right," she said softly, still looking at the father instead of the child. After a moment Cruz shifted, as if uncomfortable with her steady regard.

"Okay, squirt, that's it. Everybody's fine. Back to bed with you."

The child ran to him, holding her arms up. Cruz picked her up in a smooth, practiced motion, and they planted noisy kisses on each other's faces. Again Kelsey knew she was seeing a long-standing routine. And again she stifled the tiny ache inside her, knowing it was the child she'd once been who was hurting.

Cruz set Sam back on her feet and watched as the child scampered down to her room and went inside.

"She's a wonderful, smart and obviously happy child, Cruz," Kelsey said, meaning every word. "You should be proud."

"I am," he said softly, still looking down the hallway after his daughter. "Very proud."

"What about her mother?" The words came out before Kelsey could stop them, although she instantly wished she could call them back.

He turned sharply. "What about her?"

"I... I'm sorry. I just wondered. It's obvious you have custody...."

"She's dead."

More than ever, Kelsey wished she hadn't asked, and she floundered for something else to say, to get that awkward moment behind her. "This is wonderful," she said hastily, gesturing at the room and its occupants. "What she's doing here."

He looked at her for a moment, then apparently decided to let it pass, to Kelsey's relief.

"The vet bills when she finds one she can't handle are a little steep," he said with a shrug. "And it's tough on her when she finds one beyond saving. But she deals with it, and I can't seem to say no to her."

"I can see why." Not that that made the fact—and the admission—any less touching, Kelsey thought.

"She has a way with them. Even when they're hurt, they seem to know she's going to help them."

"It must be hard for her," Kelsey said, remembering the child's expression, "when she has to let them go."

"She hates it. She'd like to keep them, even when they've healed. But Ryan's been helping with that."

"Ryan? You mean...the man in the drawing?"

Cruz nodded. "He's a great wood-carver."

He pointed to a collection of whimsical carvings that graced one of the shelves above the cages. Each one was small, yet all were so beautifully done that they fairly radiated personality. A tiny squirrel, its tail fluffed out over its head...and missing part of one forepaw. A bird—a pigeon, she thought—softly plump-looking...and with a very crooked wing. Another squirrel, this one with a decided kink in a tail that had obviously been broken.

"He's been carving each member of the zoo for her, so she'll always have a piece of each one to keep before she has to let them go."

Kelsey knew she was gaping, but she couldn't help it; the idea of that man in the picture, that dramatically handsome and more-than-a-little-intimidating man, doing such a thing, boggled her mind.

"And he's...a cop?" she said in amazement, even though Cruz had already told her it was true.

"Yes," Cruz answered dryly. "And in his spare time he spits and roasts small children."

Kelsey felt herself flush. "I didn't mean—"

"I know what you meant. Or rather, what you assumed. It doesn't matter to you that he got shot trying to shut down the worst street gang we've ever seen in Marina Heights. Or that he got a medal of valor for pulling three kids out of a burning house and nearly died of smoke inhalation doing it."

"I didn't know—"

"You didn't know that behind the badge is just a man, a man who felt unbelievable pain when he and Lacey lost their first baby, a man whose divorce devastated him because he never stopped loving his wife, so much so that he changed himself, his entire approach to life, to get her back. You don't know any of that. You just know he's a cop, and that's all that matters to you."

Kelsey absorbed the emphatic words, knowing she deserved the sting of them. She *had* never thought of cops as people, not really; they were just the ones who hadn't saved her, the ones who had thrown her back into hell. She'd thought she didn't blame them anymore, but perhaps she'd been kidding herself.

"There's one thing I do know," she said as Cruz, apparently embarrassed by his own outburst, pushed himself away from the wall and turned to leave the room.

He looked back at her, waiting, silent, and she smothered a qualm at the weary look in his eyes. She wondered how often he had to fight this battle. And that he'd had to fight it with her upset her in a way she didn't care to look at just yet.

"Ryan is lucky to have you as a friend," she said quietly. He let out a long breath but still didn't speak. "I'd better go," she said.

He shook his head. "Let's go sit for a minute."

She hesitated, but when he gestured her into the hallway and turned out the den light, she went. And when they got to the living room and he indicated a chair, she sat, not quite sure why she wasn't heading for the door.

Cruz flipped a switch, and a pair of small track lights up above came on. She saw then that the room was furnished with matching oak tables that suited Cruz and designer-type chairs that didn't, and guessed that the choices were a legacy from his marriage. She suppressed a shiver at her stupid blurting out of that question about his wife. But she'd expected they would be divorced, not that she'd died. Poor Sam, to have lost her mother so young. She had lost her own even earlier, had barely had any memories of her, so she knew how hard it could be. If it hadn't been for Cecelia...

"I'm really sorry I disturbed Samantha," she said hastily, diverting herself from the old memories. "But I'm glad I got to meet her. She's an adorable child."

"Yes, she is." He grimaced. "I try not to think of what it's going to be like when she's a teenager."

Encouraged by his gracious acceptance, albeit tacit, of her apology, Kelsey went on. "Teenage girls," she said, nodding.

"They can be…difficult. It's a tough time. They can so easily get in trouble. Like Melissa. I would never have gotten so upset if I wasn't so worried about her."

Cruz ran a hand over his hair, shoving it back from his forehead, where it had fallen in a thick fringe she'd been itching to push back herself, just to see if it was as thick and silky as it looked. His mouth twisted, and he let out a compressed sigh.

"I'm sorry if me being there scared her into running away again," he said.

Kelsey was surprised by his words and more surprised by her own sudden turnaround as she spoke impulsively. "You couldn't have known. And it was my fault. I usually made sure she had warning enough to get out of sight."

He gave her a level look. "And if we hadn't been talking about Ryan being a cop, which set her off, you would have…what? Stuck to that lie about her being your cousin?"

Kelsey stiffened automatically, but there was nothing of accusation in his tone, only what sounded like mild curiosity.

"I don't know," she said, sagging wearily back in a chair that had obviously been chosen for looks rather than comfort.

"You know, if you'd just said she was your cousin in the first place, and not tried to hide her at all, I probably wouldn't have thought a thing about it."

"I realized that later. After I…panicked."

"You mean you just thought 'cop' and panicked?" She gave him a sideways look, but didn't answer. He shrugged. "I guess it's sort of a moot point now, isn't it?"

"Until I find her," Kelsey said determinedly.

Cruz sighed again, and Kelsey felt a start of guilt at having disrupted his night.

"Do you have any idea where she might have gone?" he asked.

"I had a couple," she answered wearily, "but I ran through them on Sunday. Today I started looking in town, and I have a couple more places I haven't—"

She broke off and went suddenly still, realizing for the first time just how much she'd admitted to him. To a cop. God, she must be tired; she had actually stopped thinking of him that way for a moment. It must have been the sight of him with Sam, she thought. He'd seemed so...human, then, just a father with his daughter.

Just?

The irony of her own thought swept over her; a father as loving as Cruz obviously was, was something far outside her own experience. And she'd let the seductiveness of the picture they presented lull her into betraying far too much. If word got out that she was even talking to a cop, it could destroy everything she'd tried to do, to build.

"Whatever happened to you to make you distrust the police so much?" Cruz asked abruptly.

She wasn't about to get into that, no matter how much his perceptiveness startled her. "It's not that I distrust cops," she began, then faltered, knowing that to a certain extent it was a lie. And realizing she really didn't like lying to this man.

"Then it's me specifically you don't trust?"

"No! I was just afraid you'd expect me to turn her in."

"I didn't say I wouldn't. It seems obvious that there's more to this than a simple case of a runaway kid. There has to be, because there's so little we can do with juveniles anymore."

It was obvious who the "we" he was referring to were. "Just throw them in jail?" she suggested.

To her surprise, he didn't react to her edgy words. "Not for long," he said. "We can only hold them for a few hours. If their parents can get there, fine. If not...they walk."

"And when the parents are the problem?"

"Look, every family has problems, but that's not for the police to get—"

"God, do they teach cops that line in the police academy? 'We can't get involved in family problems'?"

"We can't," Cruz said.

"You mean until it's too late and somebody's been beaten up, molested or killed? Then you can get involved, but it's too damned late for the innocent victim, isn't it?"

It was an old refrain for her, and she was too tired to put

much heat into it. Cruz seemed to sense that, because he answered in the same weary tone.

"You may not believe this, but it's as frustrating for us as anyone," he said. "But this isn't the time to discuss the limitations and dire straits of modern law enforcement. It's after midnight. Let's discuss it all in the morning."

Kelsey blinked.

"The sofa in the den folds out into a decent bed, if you can stand the company of all the critters."

The thought of just curling up and going to sleep right now was so alluring that Kelsey couldn't stop the look of longing that crossed her face. But still she eyed Cruz warily, uncertain whether she should accept his invitation. Uncertain whether she wanted to subject herself to trying to sleep under the same roof with him, in his home, which somehow seemed incredibly more intimate than when he'd been a paying guest under her roof. And she already had enough trouble fighting off constant thoughts of him.

As if he'd read her doubts, he grinned suddenly, stopping her breath short in her throat.

"You'll be more than safe, Ms. Hall, if you sleep in the den." He grimaced eloquently. "That snake will keep me from coming anywhere near you, trust me."

Kelsey couldn't help smiling at his fierce distaste; snakes had never really bothered her, and the idea of the big, brave cop being intimidated struck her as amusing. She liked even more the fact that he wasn't too macho to admit to his aversion.

And she hushed the small part of her that wished she was the kind of woman a man would brave even his worst nightmare for. She knew she wasn't, especially for a man like Cruz, who could no doubt pick and choose, from his widowed neighbor to just about anybody else who might interest him.

So there was no need to worry about it, and staying would be better than driving back to the inn, or trying to find a place in town to stay this late, she supposed. And if she did stay, she could get an early start looking for Melissa in the morning. She intended to start checking the popular local beaches next; it was warm at night there, easy to stay lost amid the crowds during the day, crowds that always left behind uneaten food. And the teenager had more than once mentioned that someday she meant to live at the beach.

It made sense. And maybe, she thought with wry self-knowledge, a night of telling herself what a fool she was for letting her thoughts dwell on a man who was impossible for so many reasons might drive the lesson home.

"Thank you," she said, before she could change her mind. "I could use the rest."

"I'll get you a blanket" was all he said, as if he invited women to stay all the time. As, she thought dryly, perhaps he did.

But somehow she doubted they slept in the den. And the thought of those women, whoever they might be, sleeping curled up in the safety of Cruz's arms gave her a pang she couldn't quite smother.

Chapter 8

He'd done stupider things in his life, Cruz supposed, but right now he couldn't quite remember when. He'd spent the night alternately dozing and jerking awake, most of the time not sure which was worse, lying awake trying not to think of the woman down the hall, or sleeping and having the thoughts run loose in ways that had him groaning aloud.

No, I'm just the girl next door.

Kelsey's words, tinged with that undeniably sour note, came back to him now, in the gray light of dawn.

Girl next door? Not in his life. He'd grown up next to Coreen Carter, a viper-tongued brunette who had never missed a chance to remind him, as if he could or wanted to forget, that he was half-Mexican. When he had, on a whim, gone home to Santa Rosa for his ten-year high school reunion, he'd been stunned to realize that the predatory bottle blonde who had her hands all over him was the infamous Coreen, who had apparently gotten over her distaste for his heritage.

He'd looked her up and down, gauging the figure that he remembered as being much rounder on the bottom and not nearly so round on the top, muttered something about preferring the original equipment, and walked away. It hadn't been kind, he knew, but he hadn't been feeling benevolent enough to pass up the jab. Her quick return to the vituperative Coreen he remembered had only made him glad he hadn't.

No, Kelsey was not the girl next door he'd known. Not in any way. Whatever else she was, Cruz could not doubt that she was real to the core. And he had to admit her soft curves and vivid, clearly natural coloring were far more appealing to him than Coreen Carter had ever been, brunette or blonde, original or replacement parts.

And he didn't know what to do about it. Didn't know if he wanted to do anything about it.

Worse yet, he didn't know if he could stop himself from doing something about it. Nor did he know why. He'd been aware of her before, maybe even interested, but all of a sudden he was so hot for her that he couldn't stop thinking about her. What had changed? Was he simply ready now, when he hadn't been before? Or was it that he hadn't really known her before?

With a sigh, he rolled over and made another futile attempt to pound his pillow into submission. When he dozed off again, it was to drift into a dream of the pond at Oak Tree, only this time Kelsey had more bare than just her long, curved legs. And this time the jolt when he came sharply awake was more than just groan-inducing, it was downright painful. The only bright side he could see was that it was genuinely morning now, and he could give up this farce and get up. A shower would wake him up completely, he thought, rubbing at gritty eyes.

And he told himself that waking up was the only reason he made it colder than usual. Much colder.

He felt almost in control by the time he tugged on a pair of faded blue jeans and a black Willie Nelson T-shirt Sam had picked out for him because it had a horse on it. In fact, he felt almost good as he walked out of his room. Sam's door was open, and the sound of voices from the den told him where—inevitably—she was.

Soft voices, he thought as he walked down the hall. Feminine voices. He stopped for a moment, listening. Not to eavesdrop—he wasn't close enough to hear what they were saying—but simply to listen to the unaccustomed sound. He smiled when Sam giggled; it was one of his favorite sounds. Then he heard an echoing laugh, one that had an entirely different effect on him.

So much for a cold shower's lasting effects, he thought wryly.

He walked on then, trusting Sam's presence to keep his suddenly awakened libido in line. He reached the doorway to the den and looked in, smiling when he saw both of them sitting cross-legged on the floor, heads bent over something Kelsey was holding.

The smile froze on his face, his libidinous thoughts vanished and his pulse kicked into instinctive overdrive when he saw just what it was they were so intent on. When he saw the long black-and-white-striped shape curled with apparent contentment around a very unperturbed Kelsey's arm.

All the old horror kicked through him in a rush, and it took every bit of his restraint to keep from shouting furiously at Sam for this violation of the single prime rule that allowed her to keep Slither in the house.

"Sam."

Despite his efforts, it came out biting. He saw her go still, then turn a guilty face to him.

"Uh-oh," the child said. "Busted."

Kelsey looked over her shoulder at him, her expression amused rather than fearful. Until she saw his face. He knew what he must look like, from the way the amusement drained away. Kelsey looked quickly at Sam, who sighed and reached for the snake.

"It's the big rule," she explained. "Slither can only stay in the house as long as he's never out of his cage."

The reptile moved, sliding from Kelsey's arm to Sam's with apparent willingness, its tongue flicking in and out rapidly. Cruz fought down his revulsion at the sight of the snake and his little girl, knowing that if he had his way the damn thing would be dead within the minute—harmless, even helpful king snake or not.

"Back in the cage," he snapped, the instant she had it. "Now!"

Samantha jumped to her feet. To his surprise, so did Kelsey. What she did next surprised him even more; she took a quick step that put her between him and Sam, her chin up and a light in her green eyes that he recognized as a combination of fear and determination.

"It was my fault," Kelsey said. "She took Slither out to show me. Don't blame her. I shouldn't have asked her to."

It hit him then, where he'd seen that look before: in the eyes of women protecting their children. It took him a moment to realize why he was seeing it now, that Kelsey had stepped between them because she thought she needed to protect Sam from his obvious anger. She was trying to deflect it, to take the blame on herself, because...

Because what? What the hell did she think he was going to do?

"It's okay, Kelsey," Sam said calmly. "I knew better."

She turned and efficiently put the snake back in the aquarium and fastened the lid. Then she looked up at her father.

"I'm sorry. I shouldn't have broken the rule." She picked up the aquarium carefully. "I'll take him out to the garage now."

She started toward him, and Cruz stiffened. Rigidly he backed up a step as she went past him. He fought it, but at the closest point, he lost the battle and closed his eyes so that he didn't have to look at the cage and its occupant.

When he opened his eyes again, he found Kelsey staring at him. He shrugged sheepishly.

"My mother told me I was bitten by a rattler when I was two. It was sunning on a rock after a storm, and I nearly stepped on it. Only the fact that I had rain boots on because it was still muddy out saved me. I don't remember it, but the lesson took." He tried a smile, but wasn't sure how steady it was. "And to think I hated those damn boots."

Kelsey kept staring at him. "But you let her keep it?"

"I try not to infect her with my fears. She'll have enough of her own to deal with."

She shook her head slowly, her eyes wide, astonished. He remembered then the moment when she'd leaped between them, ready to fight, as if Sam were her own. It was an image he would not soon forget. And he didn't know which hit him harder, that she'd done it, or that she'd thought it necessary.

"I love my little girl, Kelsey," he said softly. "And I would never, ever do anything to hurt her."

And why, he added silently to himself, *would you think that I would?*

But he was afraid he already knew the answer to that.

"Hurry, Dad, it's almost seven-thirty. I don't want to be late. It's kata today, and I want to practice my form before class."

Kelsey looked from Cruz to Samantha, then back again.

"Karate class at eight," Cruz explained as he finished the simple breakfast they'd put together of toast and fruit and cereal.

"Tae kwon do," Sam said. "My *sensei*—that's the teacher—says I'll have a green belt soon."

"Oh," Kelsey said, wondering why she was surprised; it was obvious that Cruz supported his daughter's interests, even if he didn't share them. Like Slither.

And there was no sign of lingering tension; a rule had been broken, and the expected punishment meted out, and they had gone on. Sam's demeanor was slightly chastened, but there was no trace of fear or anxiety in her, nor was there any sign from Cruz that the punishment had only begun, that it would go on for days, until he was satisfied she'd learned her lesson.

Kelsey watched as they went through what was clearly a routine of clearing the dishes into the dishwasher. Cruz and Samantha Gregerson obviously had this down to a science, she thought, and fought down another tug of that wistful feeling she'd been battling ever since she saw them together the first time.

It was a wistfulness that grew with the realization that, as angry as he'd been, Cruz would never have taken it out on Sam. It was a revelation to her; in her experience, anger had always meant a loss of control, and no one could make a father angrier than a wayward, rule-breaking daughter. The years since had taught her that such was not always the case, but while she'd learned intellectually, she was discovering it was a far different thing to see it in action.

Abruptly it was all too much, and she got hastily to her feet. Both Gregersons turned to look at her.

"I... Thank you. For the sleep, and breakfast."

"Is this goodbye?" Cruz said it lightly, but Kelsey sensed the deeper query, whether she was going to leave without telling him any more than she already had.

"I... Yes. I have to go. I have to—" she broke off with a quick glance at Sam, then ended awkwardly with "—finish what I was doing."

Cruz took the last bowl Sam held out to him, then sent her off to get her things for her karate class. When she was gone, he turned back to Kelsey, folding his arms across his chest. Arms that were strong enough to hold and comfort, a chest that was broad enough for a woman to shelter against. And for the first time in her life, Kelsey longed for that kind of shelter, the kind that didn't take away anything, only gave, the kind that didn't mean you weren't capable, but just meant that you didn't have to carry every burden all by yourself. The shelter of a quiet, strong man. A man to trust.

And that longing scared her. Terrified her, she who had been determined to always make it on her own, who had constantly reminded herself that there was only one person she could always count on, and that was herself.

"I have to go," she repeated, not looking at him, when his silence became too much.

"'And don't ask where, Cruz, because you're a cop and I don't want or need your help,' is that it?"

She looked up at him then. For an instant she wanted to trust him, to have faith that he indeed did genuinely care, that he would truly try to help and not simply toss Melissa into a system that would grind her up and spit her out as it had so many others. If it had been only her, she might have done it. But it was Melissa's welfare that was at stake, and she had no right to gamble with that.

"She would only run if she saw you," she said, knowing it was the truth, but not the whole truth. And Cruz just looked at her, as if he knew it as well as she did.

"And you're afraid if I found her, I'd drag her off, handcuffed, kicking and screaming, right?"

"No," she said, "not like that. Not you. But you'd have to do something. Call her parents, something."

"So she does have them?"

Kelsey blinked.

"Parents," Cruz prompted.

Kelsey drew back, sucking in a breath. She had to get away from him. She just couldn't think straight around him, and she always seemed to be giving away more than she meant to, telling him things she'd never meant to let out. And she didn't know why. All she knew was that if everybody reacted to him this way, he must be a damn good cop.

"I have to go," she said for a third time, aware that she sounded almost desperate. And before he could say anything else, she turned and literally ran.

And tried to convince herself that she was running *to* something, instead of away.

He wouldn't have done it, Cruz told himself, if the karate studio where Sam took her lessons wasn't just a few blocks from Trinity West. It wasn't as if he were going out of his way or anything, it was just handy, so he stopped in. Sam would be so intent on her lesson—as she was on everything that interested her—that she wouldn't care if he was there or not, so he had an hour to kill. And he was curious, that was all. So he'd gone to the station to poke around a little.

"Hey, Gregerson, I thought you were on vacation!"

"Damn, you wouldn't catch me here if I didn't have to be!"

"Never figured you for a workaholic."

The salutes rained down on him as he went down the hall,

and he grinned and waved them all off without speaking. This place was his second home, and the very walls welcomed him. Not that it was a particularly homey place; Trinity West was a square, uninteresting-looking two-story building, with tall, rectangular windows all around that mostly overlooked other buildings and a weed-filled empty lot. They still laughed about those windows, the dark laughter of cop humor; the regular glass that had been installed when the station was originally built had been belatedly replaced with bullet-proof material when a sniper explicitly demonstrated what marvelous targets the windows were at night, when lit from inside.

Cruz saw Lieutenant Robards headed down the hall toward the men's room—that gait that was a cross between a swagger and a waddle was unmistakable—and dodged into the detective-division office before he was spotted; he was in no mood to deal with the dinosaur. Fortunately, a visit to the men's room was usually good for at least a half hour—there had been a time when the Robards bathroom pool had been a going concern—if not longer.

Bypassing his own small office, Cruz headed across the large room filled with desks in various stages of disarray, set up in pairs, back to back, in clusters of varying sizes, separated by waist-high portable dividers. At this time of the morning, most were occupied by investigators doing what it sometimes seemed they did most: making phone calls and shuffling papers. Phones rang regularly, adding to the backdrop of blended voices; it was a familiar mixture of sounds to Cruz.

He turned left at the far wall, where a long, low case held the books that were also familiar to any detective division; penal codes, the *Physician's Desk Reference,* and the ubiquitous tools of any investigator, telephone books from all over. Above the bookcase was a bulletin board with the requiite wanted posters, crime warnings and advisories from other departments on missing persons, property and unidentified bodies. Cruz supposed it was like any other police agency in the country; he'd visited enough others to know that they were all alike enough to give a sense of comfortable familiarity to almost any cop.

He stopped beside one of the neater set of desks, behind a low divider labeled with a sign that said Juvenile and Sex Crimes. The name plaque declaring the closest desk the domain of Detective Gage Butler was half hidden by a pile of file folders—the paperless office had yet to arrive, and probably never would at Trinity West, Cruz thought; their budget didn't run to fancy computer systems—and the chair was empty.

He grimaced; he'd been hoping Gage would be here. But then he noticed the battered leather jacket hanging up beside the suit coat most detectives kept handy in case they had to make an unscheduled court appearance, and he knew Gage had to be around somewhere. He wore that jacket as if it were a talisman, had worn it ever since Cruz had known him.

Cruz heard a peal of laughter from the reception area, where Pam, the steel-gray-haired woman who ran the office with an iron hand, had her desk.

Barely a second later, a tall, rangy man with a shock of thick pale blond hair that fell forward over his left brow stepped into the office through the reception area. Tan and fit, he looked as if he should be lolling on the beach ten miles due west, at Marina del Mar. He also looked barely old enough to have graduated from any police academy, let alone be a cop with seven years under his belt.

His youthful looks were something the department had put to great use when he first came on board, sticking him undercover in the local high school before he ever did a day on the street. When he came out, after racking up a string of impressive arrests and cutting off a drug supply line that had kept a large number of Marina Heights kids strung out most of their waking hours, he'd had quite a reputation. There had been some grumbling when he was handed this detective position shortly after, but it hadn't lasted. Not when they'd seen the job he was doing.

Cruz had quickly learned that Gage Butler was possessed of a quick mind and a prodigious memory, and was a man utterly driven; he himself had spearheaded the drive to shut up the grumblers by making it well-known that Butler was doing the ugly job better than anyone ever had. So well that when the time came that Gage would normally have been rotated out of the assignment, no one had really wanted to take his place, knowing they would have an incredible record to try to match. So Gage had stayed, continuing to do the job no one else wanted.

And Cruz kept to himself the thought that it was costing Gage more than anyone else. It showed in his eyes, which held an expression Cruz had never quite been able to define, but that unsettled him nevertheless.

The green-eyed blonde with the baby face spotted him then, and smiled widely as he approached.

"Hey, Sarge, what are you doing here?"

"You flirting with Pam again?" he countered, grinning.

Gage laughed. "Sure. Keeps her from trying to set me up with her granddaughter."

Cruz laughed; Pam's granddaughter was eighteen and, as one of the less gracious members of the department had once said, tended to wake up in a brand-new world every three minutes or so.

"So what brings you into this place on your vacation? You looking for Kit?" he asked, referring to Kit Walker, his boss, the sergeant in charge of the Juvenile/Sex Crimes unit. "She's out on an interview."

Cruz shook his head; the last person he wanted to see right now was Kit, with her too perceptive mind and wry humor.

"Actually, I wanted to see you."

Gage looked surprised. And the tiniest bit wary, a common enough occurrence in a cop confronted with a sergeant, even if it wasn't his immediate supervisor.

"Officially?" he asked.

"Relax," Cruz teased. "You're safe. Robards didn't send me."

Gage grimaced. "That man..."

"I know. But he's our cross to bear. Besides, he likes you."

"That's not saying much, and if it's supposed to make me feel better, it doesn't. Worse, in fact."

Cruz knew that Gage was tremendously uncomfortable with the fact that the arrogant, vindictive lieutenant was pleasant only toward him, as opposed to the man's vicious, diligent attempts to make everyone else's life a living hell. And Cruz had discovered when he and Gage went on an extradition flight to Denver a couple of years ago that Gage knew perfectly well that it was his all-American-boy image that kept Robards off his back. And kept the heavy-jowled lieutenant on the backs of cops like Ryan Buckhart and Cruz Gregerson.

Only Gage's complete dedication and determined refusal to curry any favor with the detested Robards kept the rest of the section from ragging him about literally being Robards's fair-haired boy. In fact, Cruz suspected Gage occasionally went out of his way to tick Robards off, just to keep the playing field more level.

"I'll bet it kills him to take orders from Chief de los Reyes," Gage said with a grimace. "And he's ten times the cop—and the man—Robards is."

"Yes, he is." And there wasn't a man in this department, save Robards, who would dispute that; Miguel de los Reyes had the utter and total respect of his line officers.

"Sorry," Gage said. "Didn't mean to go off on you. And he's been...almost subdued lately. Ever since Ryan took down the Pack, he hasn't had much to say."

Cruz grinned. "What could he say? Ryan pulled off a miracle."

Gage grinned back. "Yeah. And he had to admit 'that Indian' was a hell of a cop. Must have hurt."

"Badly," Cruz agreed.

"Does the heart good, doesn't it?" Gage quipped. Then, joking aside, asked, "What was it you wanted?"

"I'm just looking for information. On a runaway."

"Well, I've certainly got that," Gage said, gesturing toward the stack of papers on his desk. "From every state in the union, every size, shape and condition, I got 'em. More in the computer, if it's working. What are you looking for?"

"I don't have much," Cruz warned. "Don't even know if she was reported."

Gage grinned. "Ah, a challenge. Hit me."

"Female, about fourteen to sixteen, I'd guess, first name Melissa. About five-five, kind of thin, brown hair dyed blond, but a while ago, it's kind of two-tone now. Brown eyes, I think." Gage scribbled as Cruz ran through his sketchy description. "I'd say she's either been on the run for a while or she's ill. She looked pretty hollow-eyed."

"Long-distance, you think?"

Cruz considered that, then, slowly, shook his head. "I don't think so. I'm not sure why, but I get the feel it's more local. She looked...California."

He didn't mention Kelsey at all; it was hardly something that would help Gage. If, indeed, he could do anything at all with the little bit of information he'd been able to give him.

"Anything else?"

"Afraid not. I only got a glimpse of her."

"What made you think she was a runaway?"

"Just...a feeling."

Gage nodded, not questioning, accepting that sometimes that was all a cop had to go on. Just a feeling.

"I know it's not much," Cruz said.

Gage shrugged. "I've started with less. She at risk?"

The phrase used by the Department of Justice to designate missing persons whose welfare was considered in danger because of the circumstances of their disappearance had been in Cruz's mind all morning.

"I don't know," he finally said. "I know she was scared, but that might just have been of me."

"Of you? Hard to believe," Gage said with a grin.

"Thanks," Cruz said wryly.

"Hey, we all have our crosses to bear. I've got my face, you've got whatever it is that makes people open up to you like oysters."

"Interesting analogy." Cruz's tone was dry. And he couldn't help thinking that there was at least one person who didn't open up to him like an oyster or anything else, who, in fact, was more of a clam, sealed up tight, beyond his reach. "Just do what you can," he said. "And let me know."

"Okay. I'll get right on it."

Cruz hesitated, considering telling the detective there was no rush, especially given the caseload he knew Gage carried. But when he opened his mouth, that wasn't what he said.

"And this is…unofficial, okay?"

"I haven't seen you and you didn't ask," Gage said easily.

"Thanks, buddy."

A good man, Cruz thought, not for the first time, as he headed back out to his truck. And he wondered yet again what it was that drove Gage Butler. All the officers who worked with him came away shaking their heads in wonder. "The man never stops," they always said. "I don't know what he runs on."

Neither did Cruz, but he thought Trinity West should be damn grateful they had him.

He glanced at his watch as he settled into the driver's seat; he still had better than half an hour before it was time to pick up Sam. Maybe he would swing by and pick up some lunch, maybe her favorite junk food, with a ton of fries. Sort of make up for this morning. Not that she hadn't broken a cardinal rule, but he knew that simply having one of her beloved creatures exiled to the garage was punishment enough for the tenderhearted Sam. And she'd taken it well, not arguing, not letting Kelsey take the heat for her. Yep, he was pretty proud of that little scamp.

"Cruz! Wait up!"

He glanced up and saw Gage sprinting across the parking lot toward him. He held a piece of paper, and when he skidded to a stop beside the truck, Cruz saw that it was one of the familiar interagency flyers.

"What you said about her hair being dyed blond a while ago made me think. This came through a few days ago."

He handed the paper through the window. Cruz stared at the photo. It wasn't the best of reproductions, and she looked older, wearing makeup and with her hair pulled back, and she was much thinner now, but there was no mistake.

It was the girl he'd seen at Kelsey's.

And she was in more trouble than he'd thought.

Chapter 9

"Is that her?"

Cruz nodded. "It's her."

"I was afraid of that. But you were right. Ventura's pretty local."

Cruz's mind was racing. He knew he could simply call the reporting agency, the sheriff's office, and find out the status of the girl and the circumstances around her disappearance. It would be the logical next step, but he found himself retreating from the idea. And he grimaced inwardly, because he knew exactly why he was doing so: Kelsey. Until he knew exactly what was going on, he didn't want to make this any more official than he had to.

He looked from the flyer to Gage. "You know anybody up there?"

Gage looked thoughtful, then shook his head regretfully. "Sorry. Only guy I knew up there left a couple of years ago." He gave Cruz a considering look. "I gather you want this off the record?"

"For the moment," Cruz answered.

"Okay. Why don't I call them and make a routine request

for a copy of the report? I can just say I'm working a case that probably isn't related, but I'm trying to cover all the bases."

Cruz considered that. He knew it was a common enough practice, and that it would rouse little curiosity on the other end, without any follow-up. It happened all too often when agencies had a dead body they couldn't identify; you called for any missing-person report that even came close.

And more importantly at the moment, he knew he could trust Gage to keep his mouth shut if asked.

"I could have them fax it, if you've got time to wait," Gage added.

Cruz nodded. He got out of the truck, and they walked back toward the Trinity West building.

After Gage had made the call, Cruz, with one eye on the clock, calculating how long he could wait and still make it to pick up Sam, waited by the fax machine. It was in the records section of the department, and he'd already taken more ribbing from the clerks there about being unable to stay away from the place even on vacation. He would have waited at his own desk, maybe even looked through what had been piling up since he left, but Robards was back in his office, and Cruz had no desire to ruin his day by seeing the man.

Idly he wondered when the chief was going to run out of patience with Robards and reel him in. The man was an anachronism, an old-school cop who had stubbornly and arrogantly refused to adapt as times—and law enforcement—changed all around him. For a long time, the running joke had been that irony meant Robards being torn between hating technology and computers, yet wanting to use them to spy on his subordinates.

He was also a bigot, a sexist and a few other things that were even more pernicious. And it was this that kept him from being simply a joke. He'd been in tight with Chief Lipton and he'd exploded in wrathful incredulity when Miguel de los Reyes was chosen by the city council as interim chief after Lipton had been gunned down. He would be damned, he'd shouted, if he would take orders from a greaser.

Nobody knew what had been said in the closed-door session that followed in de los Reyes's office, but Robards had not been heard saying another word against the man—at least, not within the walls of Trinity West. Yet another thing to admire the chief for: whatever he'd done, it had shut Robards up. And there hadn't even been any blood spilled that he knew of, Cruz thought.

But the man's tyrannical reign over the detective division continued. Not that there was much de los Reyes could do, not to a cop with thirty years on, not unless he screwed up really badly.

We can but hope, Cruz thought, then turned as the fax machine beeped and came on, dragging him out of his reflections. Fifteen minutes to spare, he thought, grabbing the pages as they were spit out. Long, he noted. Simple runaway reports were usually two to three pages. But then, he'd suspected there wasn't anything simple about this one all along.

Going the long way around to avoid Robards, he went back to Gage's desk, scanning the pages as he walked corridors that were as familiar to him as those of his house.

"Got it?" Gage asked, putting down the case he'd been reading.

Cruz nodded. "Thanks for pushing them."

"No problem. Anything more there?"

Cruz's mouth twisted. "Yeah. And I'm afraid it's even worse than we thought."

"Worse?"

"She's pregnant. Report says when the parents found out, there was a big fight."

"That's when she took off?"

"That night. Parents didn't find out until the next morning she was gone. When they realized she'd packed a bag this time, they called the sheriff."

Gage sighed, the sigh of a cop who's seen this so often it only makes him wearier.

"And that isn't all of it." Cruz gestured with the last page. "According to the supplemental report, she ripped her folks off when she left. Took some of her mother's jewelry and a camera. She must have sold the stuff for traveling money.''

And that, no doubt, explained her reaction to him, Cruz thought; she knew she'd done something criminal, something that could get her in real trouble.

"So she's really on the run."

"Yeah. And her boyfriend, the baby's father, is a real prize. Has a long record, theft, drugs, including violent offenses. Usually carries a knife, and it says he threatened to kill her because he doesn't believe the kid's his."

Gage winced. "Guess that answers the at-risk question."

"Yeah," Cruz said glumly. Then, with a sideways look at Gage, he added, "It also makes this…trickier."

He knew Gage knew what he meant; with an at-risk missing juvenile, it wasn't easy to keep things off the record. There had been too much public outcry over too many dead kids, resulting in the creation of the at-risk category, which required more stringent action. It also meant that as soon as the detective on Melissa's case found out that a copy of the report had been requested, Gage would be getting a call.

"I'll stall as long as I can," Gage said. "Tell 'em it's just a possible sighting and I'm having witness trouble or something."

"Thanks," Cruz said. "Do what you can without getting yourself in a jam."

"Been there before and survived," Gage said.

"Haven't we all?" Cruz muttered in assent.

"Leave me a copy of the report, why don't you? Maybe I can turn something. At least I can check the pawnshops, in case she tried to dump the camera and jewelry there."

Cruz eyed the stacks on the man's desk. "You've got enough to do. And this is…"

"Personal? I figured that. Leave it anyway. I'll find some time. And you never know."

Cruz studied Gage for a moment. In the begininng, he'd been thrown off by the pretty face, and perhaps, Cruz admitted ruefully, the blond California look. But now, looking at those tired eyes, he thought of the sense he'd always had that

Gage was driven beyond a mere dedication to the job, beyond even a sincere dedication to what justice could be found in a system that sometimes seemed painfully distant from that goal. And what the people who'd worked with him said came back to him again.

The man never stops. I don't know what he runs on.

"Don't run the well dry, my friend," he said softly.

Gage gave him a level look, and Cruz knew he wasn't the first to have said something like that to him.

"When it starts out dry, you don't know the difference," Gage said, and his voice was so bleak it made a shiver creep up Cruz's spine.

He was still thinking about it as he went back out to his truck. He didn't know much about Gage personally, just that he was one of so many other cops who had lost a marriage to the job, and that he didn't spend much time hanging out with the guys. Mainly because he was always working, in one way or another. Cruz had seen more than one cop on the edge in the past nine years; he hoped Gage wasn't another one.

But he had no doubt Gage would do just what he'd said. If there was anything more to be found, he would find it. And he would do his best to stall any curious questioning from Ventura, at least for a while. The keep-it-vague ploy would work at first, but not for long, Cruz knew. He was going to have to move fast.

The inquiry he'd made out of simple curiosity was going to have an effect he hadn't counted on, and he doubted Kelsey was going to like it much. Nor did he like the idea of Kelsey being somehow dragged into an active investigation because of something he'd done. Something she'd asked him not to do.

He started the truck and pulled out of the lot, lifting a hand automatically to acknowledge the marked unit that was coming in as he was leaving. When he saw that the driver was Quisto Romero, the gesture became a genuine wave; he'd come to like the former member of the Marina del Mar elite. Not only had he taken his return to street cop status with good grace, despite his years of detective experience, he'd worked hard since his transfer from the upscale department to rougher, tougher Trinity West, hard enough to impress everyone with his sincerity and how quickly he was picking up the nuances of his new territory. Including Chief de los Reyes, who would no doubt be keeping Romero's record in mind when the next detective slot opened up. And everybody already knew and respected his wife, Caitlin, who ran the Neutral Zone club for street kids. Quisto was well on his way to full acceptance.

The thought of the gutsy redhead who had taken one of the smoothest ladies' men in the state out of circulation brought his thoughts full circle, back to another woman with a touch of fire in her hair. A woman who was not going to be happy with him for setting wheels in motion that, judging from what she'd said, she was certain would grind a scared girl to bits without thought or compunction. That it had been inadvertent would not, Cruz guessed, cut much ice with Kelsey.

Nothing would, except finding Melissa. Fast. And to do that, he was going to have to pry everything he could out of the reluctant Kelsey. Which meant he had to find her first.

Tossing aside one of Frisbee's ubiquitous chew bones, he picked up the cell phone he'd bought mainly so that Sam could always reach him. He couldn't remember the number for the inn, so he threw fiscal caution to the wind and had information put him through.

He hadn't expected her to be there; he remembered what she'd said, that he was her only guest until the first, a good week and a half away. The answering machine that picked up confirmed his expectation, and he hung up without leaving a message, mainly because he had no idea what to say.

As he drove back to the large converted machine shop that had become the karate school, he wondered why the heck he was feeling so guilty. He was a cop, Melissa was a runaway—and, as he now knew, in more trouble than just that. He'd only done some checking; it wasn't his fault Kelsey had been hiding more than he realized.

If she even knew, he thought as he pulled into the small parking area.

Did she know the girl had stolen from her parents? He couldn't guess. But she had to know the girl was pregnant; it would explain why she was so desperate to find her that she'd run herself to near exhaustion searching. But what was her connection to the girl? He didn't believe that cousin ruse for an instant; even Kelsey had given it up before really trying to convince him.

And then Sam was there, chattering happily about her lesson, and he turned his attention to her as she clambered into the car, tossing her small gym bag in the back seat. And as always when he heard of a story like Melissa's, he made a quiet vow to himself that his little girl would never feel as if she had to run away rather than face him, no matter what happened.

"Who'd you call?" the observant child asked when she noticed the phone was turned on.

"I...er, I was trying to call the Oak Tree Inn."

"That place you go? Isn't that where Kelsey lives?"

So, they'd gotten that far in their chatting this morning, Cruz thought as he pulled out into traffic. "Yes."

"But she isn't there."

"I know."

"Then why did you call?"

Sometimes, Cruz thought, her logic was inescapable. "Just in case she went home."

"But she went to the beach."

He blinked, and as they came to a stop at a light, he turned to look at his daughter. "She what?"

"She went to the beach," Sam repeated in the tolerant tone she used to explain something her slower companions didn't quite understand. All too often, Cruz felt he was permanently relegated to that category; her quick, agile mind was unmistakable.

"She told you that?"

Sam nodded. "She said she had to go look for a friend of hers, and she thought she was at the beach."

Bless his brilliant child. "Thanks, Sam."

"The light's green, Dad," she pointed out patiently.

With a rueful smile, he turned his eyes back to the road and his driving.

It made sense, he thought. The local beaches, with their warm temperatures and big crowds, were a haven for runaways. The officers who patrolled them joked about how you could live just on the food beachgoers left behind. With public rest rooms and showers, you could get by nicely, if you were careful not to get caught out at night.

The question was, would Kelsey—or rather, would Kelsey guess that Melissa would—head for the Marina del Mar hot spots frequented by lots of kids, or to the state beach farther south, which was more of a family gathering place?

If he was a runaway, dodging the police, he would head for the family beach, simply because there were fewer problems and therefore less police presence. But he didn't know if Melissa was thinking that clearly. She might gravitate toward the place with kids like her. But if she did, she might later realize she would be better off somewhere else. So he would just have to look everywhere.

He glanced at the little girl beside him. "How about a hot dog at the beach for lunch, squirt?"

Sam looked at him consideringly, that too-wise, too-adult expression in her eyes. It worried him, that look, because he didn't know if it was just that she was so very bright, or what had happened in their lives, that had put it there.

"So you can look for Kelsey?" she asked.

Cruz swallowed, feeling oddly nervous. "What makes you ask that?"

"Something's wrong. You want to help, and she doesn't want you to."

She'd summed it up so succinctly that he couldn't help gaping at her. "How'd you figure that out?"

"Kelsey said this morning that she was worried about her friend. I told her you could help, but she said that wouldn't work. That's what you were arguing about last night, wasn't it?"

She should have my job, Cruz thought. He reached out and tweaked her nose. "Are you sure you're only ten?"

"Oh, Dad," she groaned at the oft-heard jest. "I liked Kelsey. She didn't call me 'honey' or something else stupid like some grown-ups do when they don't even know me. She didn't talk to me like I was a little kid."

"You had...quite a talk, then?"

"She was neat. She even liked Slither."

And that put her a few points up on me, Cruz thought glumly.

"How about that hot dog?" he asked at last.

"Can I have a corn dog instead?"

"If that's what you want."

"And a milk shake, too? Chocolate?"

"If you can stand it," Cruz said, the sound of the combination making him feel a bit less hungry himself.

"Okay," Sam said agreeably.

A half hour later, when he was helping Sam wipe up the stream of ketchup she'd dripped on her shirt, he found himself smiling in near relief at the mess. She really was just a kid, it just seemed sometimes that she was old beyond her years. They'd told him since she started school that she was very bright, warned him that she would probably have to go into accelerated classes or she would be so bored she would get into trouble, but so far her animals, and learning all she could about them, had kept her occupied. He was glad. Cops' kids had it rough enough, he didn't want her singled out for other reasons any sooner than she had to be.

He soon discovered, when he checked with the lifeguards on duty at the crowded family beach, that Kelsey had already been here.

"Green-eyed redhead? Oh, yeah, I remember her," one of them said with a smile of pure male interest. "I hadn't seen the kid she was looking for, though." The tanned face behind the mirrored sunglasses shifted into a frown. "She didn't mention the police were looking for her, though."

"I...don't think she knows." *Yet,* he added silently, ruefully.

"She checked the beach out pretty good, was here for a couple hours, at least. She talked to a lot of people."

And you watched her every step of the way, didn't you?
Cruz thought, then gave a wry inward smile at his own unexpectedly possessive reaction.

"I suggested she should check out the Strand, because
that's where most of the kids hang out," the young man said.

Cruz nodded and thanked him, barely managing to keep
himself from asking what else the man had suggested.

It only took them ten minutes to make the drive, but another fifteen to find a place to park amid the summer crowds.
They made their way to the wide sidewalk that wound its
way along the beach. On this sunny summer day, it was full
of pedestrians and, in the marked lane, bike riders, enjoying
one of the great perks of living in California.

"Y'know," Sam went on, her voice as sunny as the day,
"I could probably help you look better if I was up higher."

Cruz gave her a look of mock suspicion. "Is that a tricky
way to get out of walking?"

"You said they teach you to always take the higher ground
if you can."

"Oh, great," Cruz teased. "My kid quoting tactics at me."

But he grabbed her arms and swung her up, and with a
delighted giggle Sam settled on his shoulders in her accus-
tomed place. Although she was small for her age, she was
still getting so big that soon he wouldn't able to do this. And
soon, he thought sadly, she wouldn't want him to. She would
be caught up in that teenage-girl thing, and he would have to
work twice as hard to keep some kind of solid place in her
life. But he would do it. He would do whatever it took. Sam
had been deprived of too much in her life. She'd done without
a mother all these years, so her father was going to do his
damnedest to make up for that.

He only prayed it would be enough.

He listened to her chatter away as he walked toward the
pier where most of the kids who frequented the area hung
out, coughing slightly as a busload of tourists passed, envel-
oping them in diesel fumes. If this didn't work, he thought,
he would put in a call to Quisto and ask him if there was

anyplace else in this five-star town where runaways congregated.

Sam was in the midst of recounting a boating escapade from camp, something about canoes and balancing, when she interrupted herself with an excited shout.

"There she is!"

Cruz looked in the direction the girl was pointing, but he couldn't see past the group of tourists who were pouring out of the bus that had just parked in the lot at the base of the pier.

"Are you sure?" he asked.

"Of course, Dad." He was back in that slightly slow category, Cruz thought, smothering a grin. "I can see her hair," Sam explained kindly.

I'll just bet you can, Cruz thought, remembering how Kelsey's hair lit up in the sunlight, turning from a rich auburn to pure fire.

"Okay, okay. Just tell me which way to go."

"Go straight. She's by the ice cream stand."

He threaded his way through the mass of people, who all seemed to have cameras and be from someplace where they only sold black socks. And then a tall, wide man in a garish flowered shirt stepped aside, and he saw her. As with Sam, the burnished sweep of hair caught his eye first, then the way she held her head, as if intently interested in whatever the teenage boy she was speaking to was saying.

He didn't find it odd that it was such a thing that made him certain it was her; he'd been thinking enough about her of late to have just about every move she made committed to memory. He didn't find it particularly comforting, either, that even her tiniest habits were so engraved in his mind.

She was wearing the same faded jeans she'd had on last night, but somewhere along the way she'd changed from the sweater she'd had on to a more-appropriate-for-the-weather sleeveless blouse, crisp white and knotted at her waist. No, there was no way anyone would ever mistake her for a boy, even at a distance, Cruz thought. No skeletal thinness for her, only a collection of curves that would make any man look twice. This was the kind of woman you wanted to come home to, the kind you wanted to snuggle up to on a cold night....

And you'd better get your mind back to business, he told himself in the instant before Sam called out to Kelsey.

He hadn't really planned what he would do when he found her. It was only when she looked up and saw him, when she gave a sudden start and he saw the swift calculations flitting through her mind as if they were written across her expressive face, that he realized there was every chance she would take off to avoid him.

Then Sam called her name again. He saw Kelsey look at the little girl, saw her draw a deep breath and let it out slowly. And he saw her change her mind and decide not to dodge him after all.

He tried to pretend it didn't sting that she'd only decided to stay because of Sam.

Chapter 10

"**Y**ou did what?"

Kelsey stared as he told her again what he'd done.

"I knew you'd do something like that," Kelsey said bitterly. "I just knew it."

"Kelsey, listen—"

"To what? You've stirred up a hornet's nest, and Melissa's caught in the middle."

She saw his jaw tighten, and then he reached up and lifted Samantha from his shoulders and put her down. He dug a couple of wadded-up bills out of his pocket and handed them to her. "Why don't you go get us some ice cream, squirt?"

Sam wasn't fooled. She looked from him to Kelsey and back. "So you guys can fight again?"

"No," Cruz said.

"Yes," Kelsey said.

The girl eyed them both, then shook her head at the vagaries of adults, grabbed the money and darted over to the ice cream stand and got in line.

Kelsey eyed Cruz warily, very much aware that he had intentionally removed the buffer his daughter provided. When he moved toward her, Kelsey backed up instinctively. He moved again, and she tensed, wondering what he was going to do out here in public.

"Hold still, will you?" he finally said, sounding exasperated. "I'm just trying to get to where I can watch out for Sam."

"Oh." Feeling more than a little deflated, Kelsey stood still.

"Look, there's nothing official, at least not yet."

"Yet," Kelsey repeated ominously. "Why did you have to butt in at all?"

He sighed. "I never expected what it would turn into. I thought she was just a runaway." He gave her a pointed glance. "If you'd told me what was going on, I—"

"You would have what? Kept your nose out of it?"

Cruz checked on Sam, then folded his arms across his chest and looked at Kelsey. "So far you've got my nose and my butt involved," he said wryly. "Any other parts you're particularly interested in?"

Caught off guard by the quip—and the now too-familiar and too-frequent thoughts his words brought rushing to mind—Kelsey drew back slightly. She stood there for a moment, just looking at him, at his lean, straight body, the thick dark hair and bright blue eyes set off by the golden tint of his skin. Oh, yes, there were other parts she was interested in, she thought. More interested than she dared be. More interested than she had any right to be.

"I just wish you hadn't gotten involved, that's all," she said, a little breathless as she struggled to find the anger she seemed to have lost.

"All I did was have our juvie detective make a routine request for the report. Normally that wouldn't even raise an eyebrow."

"But it did."

"Because of the circumstances of the case, it probably will, yes." He glanced at Sam again, although Kelsey doubted she was ever really out of his field of vision. But then, for a moment, he focused on her intently. "I presume you know she's pregnant?"

She let out a compressed breath. "Yes. Why do you think I'm so worried about her? She's scared, Cruz. She doesn't know what to do."

"Why did she come to you? Do you know her, or her family?"

"That doesn't matter," she said, trying to divert him from questions she couldn't answer.

"Don't want to talk about that? Okay, so we let that slide for the moment. Did she tell you she ripped off her folks when she left?"

Kelsey lowered her eyes; God, he knew it all. Everything. No wonder he'd come looking for her; he was probably hoping she would lead him to Melissa, so that the girl could be arrested for stealing or something. Explanations leaped to her lips, all the reasons why a kid could be so desperate to get away, but she bit them back. He was a cop, what would he care? Even though he seemed so nice, even though he was so wonderful with his daughter, hadn't he just proved he was pure cop by insisting on stirring up trouble for Melissa, even if it had been unintentional?

She looked up at him again. His eyes were flicking from Sam, still waiting in the long line, to her and back again, quickly. Somehow the thought that even in the midst of a rather heated discussion he never lost track of his little girl both comforted her and brought on that wistful feeling again. She fought both sensations off.

"I just have to find her," she said stubbornly. "That's all that matters."

"I don't think so," Cruz said, and there was an edge in his voice now that she'd never heard from him before. It startled her, how different he sounded. "How about her boyfriend, Sutter? Did she happen to mention him?"

"Doug? Only briefly. He...doesn't want the baby, she said. Or her, now that she's pregnant."

Cruz let out a short, harsh laugh. "She didn't tell you what a charmer he is?"

Her chin came up. "I know he...hit her, if that's what you mean." Her mouth twisted. "She bought the classic old line, that it was because he loved her, that if he didn't care he wouldn't bother to hit her. I tried to explain how wrong it was, but I don't know if she believed me. It's so hard to convince—"

"I mean," Cruz said sharply, interrupting her, "that he has a record back to age ten, including two arrests for assault with a deadly weapon. Did she forget to include that?"

Her gaze snapped back to his face in shock. "I... Yes. She never told me that," she said, a little weakly.

"He'd be in the custody of the youth authority right now, on the last ADW, except that the only witness mysteriously recanted his statement. Sutter carries a knife big enough to carve a turkey, and he's carved up a few people with it. And he's threatened to make Melissa next."

Kelsey blanched. "Melissa? Why?"

"Apparently he doesn't believe the baby is his. He's threatened to kill her for cheating on him."

"Oh, God," she whispered. "Why didn't she tell me?"

"Yes, why didn't she tell you?" Cruz said, his tone sharp. "Maybe because she figured any sane person would call the police if she did?"

She knew he was aiming that at her. But she didn't care, not now, not when she was struggling to absorb this revelation.

"I can't believe she didn't tell me her life was in danger. No wonder she was so terrified. I thought it was just because she'd taken those things from her parents, and I kept telling her that could be worked out, but she was just so scared. No wonder she ran when she saw you. You'd make her go back, and then he'd find her."

"I don't believe you!" Cruz snapped incredulously. "This kid doesn't bother to tell you that she's got a half crazy, knife-wielding boyfriend after her, and all you can think about is that she was scared? What about you, Kelsey? Did you ever stop to think that she put you in danger, too?"

"Me?"

"What if he found her? And you with her?"

She hadn't thought of that; it hadn't even occurred to her. "Why would he hurt me?"

"Damn it, use your head!"

The minute the curse slipped out, he glanced toward the ice cream stand, where Sam was at last at the window, as if afraid she might have heard him. Despite being upset, Kelsey was touched by this further bit of parental concern. But when he turned back to her, the spurt of warmth faded, despite the unexpected heat in his blue eyes.

"I suppose you'd just stand by and let him take her away?" He ground out the words.

"Of course not," Kelsey protested.

"Exactly. You'd try to interfere. And just what do you think would happen to anybody who tried to stop him?"

She hadn't thought of it that way, either. And she didn't know quite what to think of him being so certain of what she'd do.

"Kelsey, listen to me. However you got into this, or why, it's too much. You're in over your head. Let the police handle it."

Everything he'd told her was spinning in her head. And it all somehow got mixed with her own memories of being scared and on the run. Her memories were different, but no less ugly, just in a different way, a way that made a threat with a knife somehow almost clean, or at least honest. She bit her lip, trying to think, to sort it all out.

Sam was headed back now, three ice cream bars of some kind in her hands. In the part of her mind that wasn't reeling, Kelsey was touched by being included, even by a child. As she watched the bright-haired girl approach, her perception shifted oddly, as if she were seeing Samantha years from now, as she would no doubt be, thanks to her father: smart, self-confident, strong, never having been scared in the way Melissa was. In the way Kelsey herself once had been. The image shifted again, and she saw herself years ago. At Sam's age, she'd already lost most of her childhood innocence.

The images whirled, blurred, spun. She was vaguely aware

of taking the ice cream bar Sam offered her, but her thoughts kept spinning. Gradually, one thing overpowered them all: the knowledge of just how scared Melissa must be. She'd been that scared in her life before, Kelsey thought. So scared she hadn't known who to trust. And when she'd finally had no choice but to trust someone, when she'd had to make that choice, she knew what it would have done to her if that one person had let her down.

As terrified as Melissa was, she had come to Kelsey for help. She had come to her because she had no one else to turn to, nowhere else to go.

But she had lied. Or, at least, left out a crucial, dangerous piece of information when she poured out her sad story. There was that to consider, too.

Did you ever stop to think that she put you in danger, too?

Cruz's words echoed in her mind. He was right, she supposed. She was certain it hadn't been Melissa's intent, but it was the result, nevertheless.

Just as it hadn't been Cruz's intent to start rolling wheels that couldn't be stopped. The thought came to her suddenly, and she wondered if he hadn't just been being a cop, if maybe, just maybe, he really had only meant to help.

And maybe, just maybe, she needed that kind of help. A scared, pregnant girl was one thing. A half-crazed, vindictive, knife-carrying boyfriend was something else.

She couldn't give up on Melissa. She just couldn't.

But what should she do?

"Your ice cream's gonna melt," Samantha pointed out kindly, jarring Kelsey out of her confused thoughts.

"You're right," she said, peeling back the wrapper. "I guess I should…rejoin reality, huh?"

She said the last with a sideways glance at Cruz, seeing by his face that he got the underlying meaning.

"We've got another couple of miles of beach here," he said quietly. "Let's keep looking. You can eat while we go. And think."

Kelsey felt a tightness in her throat at his understanding. At every turn, this man was showing her he wasn't the kind of cop she thought most of them were. Maybe things truly had changed since she needed their help and they failed her. It had been more than fifteen years, after all. Maybe cops were different now.

Or maybe it was just that Cruz Gregerson was a different kind of cop.

Had it been just her, she would have risked it. But then, if it had been just her, there would be nothing to risk. She was safe now, and had been for a long time. No thanks to anyone who wore a badge, but only to the one person in the world she'd been able to trust, the one person who hadn't let her down.

Melissa had thought Kelsey was that person for her.

But the teenager had also broken one of the few cardinal rules.

Kelsey sighed as they started walking. Her eyes searched the crowds on the sidewalk and out on the sand, looking for Melissa, or any likely-looking group of kids. She was worried that none of them would talk to her with Cruz along, until common sense reasserted itself; he wasn't in uniform, and it wasn't like he wore a sign saying "Off-duty Cop." And he didn't work down here in plush Marina del Mar, so chances were nobody would recognize him.

She glanced at him, at the darkly handsome man with the unexpected blue eyes, his hand protectively on the shoulder of the live-wire child with the sunny blond hair, and thought that "cop" was the last thing anyone would think when they saw them.

Or maybe it was just her point of view that was skewed. Maybe she still held more hurt and blame inside than she realized. Maybe other people saw cops as just…people, people who weren't paid nearly enough to do what others didn't want to, risking their lives so that others didn't have to, trying to keep the peace so that others could go about their lives without thinking about such things as crime and death and ugliness.

Why on earth anyone would want to do it was beyond her.

Why Cruz would want to do it fascinated her.

Why it fascinated her made her very nervous.

It was well into the afternoon when Kelsey finally had to admit they weren't going to find the girl here. And since she'd already exhausted her other ideas in the two previous days of searching, she was at a loss. She came to a halt and sat wearily on the seawall at the edge of the sidewalk.

"Dad?"

"Yes, squirt?"

"Are we done yet?"

Kelsey felt a pang of guilt; the child hadn't complained at all, despite all the walking and the heat. Although Cruz had picked her up and deposited her back on his shoulders a couple of hours ago. Which meant he had to be tired, too, but he'd never said a word about stopping.

"I'm sorry, Sam," she said. "I know this must be awfully boring for you."

"Sometimes important things are boring," the little girl said wisely from her perch. "Dad says so, huh?"

"I suppose he does," Cruz said, swinging her down to a seat beside Kelsey, then sitting down himself.

"Even important police stuff is boring sometimes," Sam informed Kelsey solemnly.

"Is it?" She looked at Cruz. "I never asked…exactly what you do."

"No, you didn't."

Kelsey felt her stomach knot at his flat statement. He didn't say another word, but she knew what he was thinking. She hadn't bothered to differentiate but had lumped all cops together, then lumped him in with them.

"He's a detective sergeant," Sam said. "He's the boss of the F unit."

Kelsey blinked. "The what?"

"Felony unit," Cruz explained. "An impressive name for me and two overworked detectives."

"But they're the best, huh, Dad?" Sam added.

He reached out and tugged at the girl's breeze-tangled hair. "That they are, squirt. Best in the county, officially. Best unit in the state, if you ask me."

"They work on the really hard stuff. Right, Dad?"

"That's why they call it the felony unit," Cruz said with a shrug.

The girl turned back to Kelsey and said proudly, "And he's got all kinds of awards and stuff, and they even gave him a medal—"

"That's enough of that." He cut off the bragging and looked at Kelsey. "What now, Kelsey? Will you let me help?"

She hesitated, torn between the need to keep Melissa safe and the growing feeling that, as he'd said, she was in over her head. What good would it do if she found Melissa and then Doug found them?

He has a record back to age ten, including two arrests for assault with a deadly weapon.

If that was true, and she supposed Cruz had no reason to lie, then she couldn't stop him. He clearly wasn't about to listen to her if she tried to talk to him, and while she might be the fool Cruz probably thought her, she wasn't fool enough to believe she could do much against a knife.

"So my choices are to keep trying to find her myself, and if I do, pray Doug doesn't find us, or turn things over to the police and then do nothing while Melissa gets sent back to the parents who kicked her out?"

Cruz sighed. "Look, her parents reported her, obviously they're worried about her."

"According to Melissa, they're more worried about what their friends and family will think than they are about her."

"Why did her parents kick her out?" Sam asked with great interest. "I didn't know parents could do that."

Cruz looked at his daughter. "We'll talk about it later."

Sam let out an exaggerated sigh. "It's one of those things that I'll understand when I'm older, right?"

"Yes. Kelsey?"

"I just realized," she said morosely. "I really don't have a choice, do I? It's already in the hands of the police. You."

He gave her a look that made her wonder if he was going

to ask her again what had made her distrust the police. But he said nothing for a moment. Then, finally, he spoke.

"I can try to keep this quiet a little longer. We can stall off Ventura for a while, but not long. If you'll give us whatever else you have, when Melissa showed up at Oak Tree, anything she said, I can ask Gage to do some checking off the record."

"Gage?"

"Gage Butler. He's in the juvenile and sex crimes unit. He's the best there is. He's got incredible sources we don't even question anymore, and a dedication to the job that's borderline obsessive. If anyone can get results in a hurry, he can. It's not Trinity West's jurisdiction, but he'll do it if I ask him to."

"He's nice, too," Sam offered. "Even if he is sad most of the time."

Cruz blinked and stared at his daughter. "Sad?"

Sam nodded. "He looks like my animals do when they're hurt. They can't say it, so it shows in their eyes."

Cruz drew back slightly. "Out of the mouths of babes," he murmured. "So that's what it is."

"What what is?" Kelsey asked, watching the exchange curiously, wondering yet again at the wisdom that came wrapped in this unlikely ten-year-old package.

Cruz looked at her. "I've always wondered what it was about Gage that…made it hard to look him in the eye sometimes. Not like he was hiding anything, but…"

"Because he wasn't?" Kelsey asked.

"Yes."

Kelsey stared down at her shoes, then past them to the sand scattered across the concrete sidewalk, tracked into swirling patterns by countless feet. The thought of a sad cop rattled her perceptions nearly as much as Cruz had. And she began to wonder if maybe they weren't perceptions at all, but preconceptions she'd never bothered to question. She had done, it seem, an awful lot of assuming in her life.

"He really is the best, Kelsey. Let him do what he can."

"Why?" she finally asked. "Why do you want to get involved in this?"

"I didn't want to," Cruz said dryly. "I wanted a nice, quiet vacation."

"Then take it. Just let it go." She wondered even as she said it what on earth she would do if he turned and walked away. She'd run out of ideas, run out of possibilities, and had no idea what to do next.

"I can't do that, Kelsey," he said, and then, with an odd sort of emphasis, added, "Not now."

"Why?" she repeated. Some tiny part of her mind admitted that she knew perfectly well what she wanted to hear, just as she knew both that she wouldn't hear it and that she wouldn't know what to do if she did.

"It's Melissa's best hope, and it'll keep you safe."

"It's Melissa I'm worried about."

"I know that. So since you won't, somebody else has to worry about you."

The implication that that somebody else was him threatened to make her blush furiously; it was too close to what she'd wanted to hear, that he wouldn't let it go because of her. She turned away, just in case her cheeks were coloring anyway; she couldn't really tell, after being out in the sun so long.

"I know you won't drop this," he said, "and that means you could easily be in danger."

"How do you know I won't drop it?" she asked, feeling a little reckless after his implication about worrying about her; perhaps, as she'd been thinking about him, he'd been thinking about her, just a little?

"I can feel it, just like I can sense when a suspect's going to give up. You won't."

Well, that was romantic as can be, wasn't it? Kelsey asked herself ruefully. *What else did you expect?*

"You tried, Kelsey," Cruz said. "And if it was just Melissa, things might be different. But this is too much for a civilian to handle. There's a wild card involved, and you're risking too much. Let me help."

"My dad's really good at helping people," Sam offered.

It wasn't so much the words the little girl said as the simple, pure faith with which she said them that made up Kelsey's mind.

"All right," she said, knowing she really had little other choice. But inwardly she swore that if he let her down, if Melissa got hurt because she'd trusted him, she would never forgive him.

And, worse, she would never forgive herself.

Chapter 11

It had been nearly fifteen years, yet it seemed like just yesterday that she had been in a building like this one. She had to suppress a shiver and remind herself that she was no longer a scared, helpless kid, that this time she could get up and walk out if she wanted, that there was no man with a smiling face and a black heart on his way for her.

She felt a gentle touch, stopping the ugly memory before it could form. Cruz, his hand on her shoulder, comforting, as if he'd guessed something was wrong, as if he'd sensed the horror that tormented her. She glanced swiftly at him and saw the accuracy of her guess reflected in the warmth of his eyes.

She looked away before foolishness made her do or say something she shouldn't. She made herself study her surroundings instead. She supposed there were certain things common to all police stations; the constant ringing of phones, the cubbyhole offices, the piles of papers, notices on the walls, wanted posters. The computers hadn't been in evidence when she last set foot in one, but apart from that, this one didn't look very different.

Except that the officers all looked younger, she thought with a wry smile at herself.

Sam wandered ahead of them down the hall. The girl was clearly quite at home here, and Kelsey couldn't help contrasting the child's ease with her own discomfiture. The irony of it made her smile—outwardly, this time. And she noticed, as well, that Cruz, who had never let the child out of his sight or reach all day, seemed unworried about her here.

"Kit!"

She looked up as Sam cried out the name in the tone of one greeting a dear friend. Coming toward them was a tall, slender, attractive woman with a short, tousled mop of light blond hair, dressed in a pair of yellow slacks and a yellow-and-white-striped blouse that emphasized a trim figure. The woman's face lit up at the sight of the little girl.

"Hi, Sam!" she exclaimed, and when the child was close enough, the woman bent to hug her rather fiercely. "How was camp?"

Sam chattered away happily for a moment, until Kelsey and Cruz came up even with them. The greeting between Cruz and the woman was that of old friends, Kelsey thought, full of warmth, but devoid of heat.

Or at least that's what you want to think, Kelsey told herself ruefully as the woman looked at her. Kelsey was aware of the intensity of the other woman's scrutiny, but not of what it meant. Before she could dwell on it, Cruz was performing introductions.

"Kit, Kelsey Hall. Kelsey, this is Kit Walker, detective sergeant and stand-in animal feeder extraordinaire."

"She takes karate classes where Lacey and I do, huh, Kit?"

"That I do," the woman said with a smile at the child.

Cruz eyed Sam then. "Did you thank her for feeding your critters?"

"Of course," Sam said. "Didn't I, Kit?"

"Yes, you did," Kit said, tugging on the girl's hair, which was almost as sunnily blond as her own. "And very nicely, too."

Then she held her hand out to Kelsey. "Nice to meet you."

Kelsey took the offered hand, but forgot to shake it when Kit added, rather archly, "Dare I hope this is a social visit?"

Kelsey blinked, at a loss.

"Sorry, I suppose I should ask Cruz." She turned to him. "So, have we finally rejoined the dating world?"

Kelsey blushed then, realizing what the woman had meant. Kelsey was puzzled by the tone of open hopefulness in the woman's teasing question, but Cruz's quick denial diverted her.

He didn't have to be *that* quick, she told herself. As if it were not only not true, but absurd to boot. Not that it wasn't, of course....

"My social life isn't your problem," Cruz added, sounding a bit testy.

"Your social life isn't *any*one's problem," Kit countered, "because you don't *have* one."

Cruz glared at the woman, but Kit appeared unruffled, though Kelsey was wishing she could retreat, anywhere. Sam seemed unmoved by the discussion, and Kelsey could only guess it was because it had taken place before, or something like it.

"Why don't you go on down to the lunchroom, Sam?" Kit said. "I'll be down in a minute, and we'll see if there's anything evil to eat in the vending machines."

Sam gave Kit a knowing look that was universal to kids who knew perfectly well they were being sent out of the way so adults could talk, but she went without complaint, disappearing through a door labeled Stairway with no hesitation. Kelsey wished she could follow, but she had no good excuse.

After the girl had gone, Kit glanced at Kelsey, then back at Cruz, and her expression seemed to change, to soften. "Sooner or later, Cruz, you're going to have to deal with it. It may be in the past, but you haven't let go of it yet."

"And you haven't learned to keep out of it," Cruz said, his voice tight.

"You're my friend," Kit said to him, putting an odd emphasis on the last word while looking at Kelsey.

"Then go make sure Sam doesn't con the jailer out of an ice cream bar. She's had enough junk today."

"Okay," Kit said easily. "I'll buy her a nice, healthy candy bar instead."

"Fine. I'll send her to you when the sugar crash hits."

"You do that," Kit said, glancing at Kelsey. "Nice to meet you," she said, then went through the stairway door Sam had used.

Kelsey searched for something neutral to say but decided to say nothing at all when she sensed Cruz's sudden tension. And when he ushered her farther down the hall, she went without comment.

They'd barely gone two yards when Cruz stopped dead, stopping her, as well, by grabbing her elbow.

"Damn," he muttered under his breath.

Kelsey looked at him and saw that he was staring down toward the end of the hall, where a heavyset man in polyester pants and a garish plaid jacket, with brush-cut white-blond hair and a cigar clenched between his teeth, stood next to a young-looking man in uniform who clearly would rather have been somewhere else. Anywhere else. If the cigar smelled anywhere near as badly as it looked from here, Kelsey could understand why, even if not for the fact that the older man was obviously chewing as hard on the officer as he was on the butt of the cigar.

"Sorry," Cruz whispered into her ear, and propelled her physically through a door to their left and closed it behind them.

It was a very small room. The door had had a number on it, she thought vaguely. Number three, maybe. Inside were a single straight chair and a metal table with a fake wood-grain top. And in an instant Kelsey was twelve again, sitting in a room very like this one, waiting, knowing she was about to be sent back to what passed for her home. She fought off the sensation, lectured herself that she was not a child anymore, that if she wanted to, she could get up, open that door and leave, and neither Cruz nor anyone else had the right to stop her, had the right to make her do anything she didn't want to do. They couldn't make her go back....

She sucked in a deep breath and ordered her stomach to unknot, her muscles to ease up and her heart to slow down.

"Kelsey?"

Cruz was looking at her with concern, and she could only imagine what she must look like. He glanced around the room, which couldn't have been more than six feet square.

"Claustrophobic?" he asked gently.

"Only in police stations," she said, trying to sound glib but only managing to sound slightly panicked. She tried again and was pleased to hear that she sounded steadier this time. "I'm fine. But what was that all about?"

He looked at her for a moment, as if wondering what past experience in police stations she might have had, but, thankfully, he let it go. "Not what. Who."

"The man at the end of the hall?"

He nodded. "Lieutenant Ken Robards. The bane of our existence."

"He looked a little...nasty," Kelsey said tentatively, a bit bemused by his tone and words; she'd thought all cops stuck together, no matter what.

"He looks a lot nicer than he is," Cruz said. "And I refuse to ruin my vacation by dealing with him if I don't have to."

For the first time, it really struck her that he'd been doing all this on his own time, and vacation time at that.

"I...didn't mean to ruin your vacation," she said contritely.

He looked startled, then smiled gently. "You didn't. As I recall, it was me who butted in where I wasn't wanted."

"It wasn't that, it's just that..."

"You don't trust cops," he finished when she didn't. "And someday," he added, in the tone of a promise, "you're going to tell me why."

Just the suggestion of that much of a future between them rattled her, and she looked down at the table that took up at least half of the tiny room. The imitation-wood surface was scratched and gouged, apparently randomly, except for the occasional set of initials dug into it. She understood the need so well, whether it was in a desk or a tree or on a wall, that need to leave something permanent, some sign that you'd been there, some sign that you'd lived, even though it didn't seem to matter to anyone else.

"He should be gone now. We can get out of here."

She looked up at him just as he reached for the door. "How can you be sure?"

"He had his jacket on. He only puts it on when he's on his way out."

"What if he was on his way in?"

Cruz shook his head. "The cigar. The chief won't let him smoke them anywhere other than in his own office, and that one hadn't been lit yet."

She gave him a lopsided smile. "Guess that's why you're the detective, huh?"

He let out a low chuckle as he pulled open the door and looked down the hall. Then he stepped back to let her go first. She had to brush against him to get by, but he never moved to take advantage of the mere two inches' clearance. She could feel his heat and caught his scent, something undefinably male, underscored by a mix of salt air and some sort of spice-tinged aftershave.

And ice cream, she thought with a smile. The thought helped her steady her pulse, which had started to race crazily all over again. She was beginning to wonder what was wrong with her, but she managed to ignore the idea that formed in the back of her mind that her nervousness was as much due to the close proximity of Cruz as to being in a police station. But she had to admit, Trinity West didn't seem like a particularly threatening place; in fact, everyone she'd seen was smiling and friendly, if a bit…edgy.

No, that wasn't right. Not edgy. They seemed…alive. Very, very alive, with the kind of vitality common to people who were doing, not just existing. As she walked with Cruz down the hall, she tried to remember what she'd read about this place. The murder of their chief in a drive-by shooting nearly two years ago had been front-page news throughout

the state, and probably, she guessed, because of the shocking
nature of the crime, across the country. And, perhaps, because
of the position of the victim. She somehow doubted a rank-
and-file street cop would have gotten that kind of press.

Trinity West had been a department under siege when their
chief was murdered, she remembered reading. But Miguel de
los Reyes, the captain who had replaced him, a man who had
also been wounded in that drive-by shooting, had taken hold
and begun running things with almost a siege mentality,
adapting techniques that were sometimes called by detrac-
tors—most of whom didn't have to live in Marina Heights,
the writer of the article had pointed out—nothing less than
guerrilla warfare, and would no doubt have been frowned
upon if they didn't produce such spectacular results. The law-
abiding residents of the town had spoken of nominating Chief
de los Reyes for sainthood, and his interim appointment had
been made permanent with little protest.

Perhaps that was why she'd been so stunned, she thought
now. She'd always heard they were a different breed, a little
rough around the edges and a little cold in the eyes, and that
their reputation for now being the toughest, most effective
small police force in the county was well deserved. None of
which had disposed her to trust one of their number.

And finding out that Cruz was one of them had been more
than the shock of discovering he was a cop, it had been the
shock of learning he was a Trinity West cop. One of the tough
guys, the ones who lived on the edge.

She supposed they had to; Marina Heights had every ex-
treme, from the near wealthy residents of the western section
to the comfortable middle class of the east, but it was the
grim, gritty world of downtown, with its street gangs and
graffiti-festooned walls, with barred windows and doorways
blocked by the homeless, that got most of the attention, at
least in the news. She wouldn't expect the people who policed
those mean streets to be the same as those who worked in,
say, affluent and sheltered Marina del Mar, just a couple of
miles west.

But she hadn't expected it to be so obvious, even inside

the bastion of the Trinity West station. But it was, and she felt as if she'd wandered onto an action-movie set, where everything was a bit tense, a little larger than life.

And reconciling this setting with the quiet man who visited Oak Tree was becoming more difficult every moment.

When he turned and gestured her into a large room filled with ringing phones and talking people, she recoiled a little at the barrage of noise. Desks, at least a dozen of them, were set up back-to-back, separated by waist-high partitions. Along the far outside wall was a large office that she guessed belonged to the apparently despised Robards. Along the opposite, nearer wall were three much smaller offices, and she barely had time to register the names—Gregerson, Everett, Walker—before Cruz turned and headed down the aisle formed by the partitions.

Kelsey saw the gleam of pale blond hair as they neared one of the occupied desks. It had that healthy, childlike shine and that way of falling that always reminded her of mischievous little boys about to get into trouble.

When the man lifted his head as they approached, she blinked; she hadn't been far off, she thought. She knew he had to be in his twenties, at least, but with that baby face he looked more like that boy than—

She stopped her own thoughts the instant she saw his eyes. Never had she seen eyes so shadowed, so old, and they gave the lie to the youthful arrangement of his features. This was a man who had seen some ugliness in his life, she thought, and moreover, he had never, ever forgotten it.

He stood up as they came to a halt beside his desk. "Cruz," he said with a nod; his voice was also a contrast, low and rumbling and very male.

"Kelsey, Gage Butler. He's the best in the county at what he does. Gage, Kelsey Hall. She's…interested in that MP case I had you pull."

Gage looked at her for a moment. Intently. So intently that she had the feeling of being studied, assessed and classified, all in the space of a few seconds. Then those world-weary green eyes flicked to Cruz for an instant before turning back to her, and Kelsey had the oddest feeling that he wanted to ask what Kit Walker had asked. The feeling was so strong, she spoke hastily to avert the possibility; she wasn't up to another of Cruz's swift denials that there was anything at all between them. No matter that it was true.

"Glad to meet you," she said politely. "I've heard a lot about you."

"Oh?" Gage said as he shook her hand with a grip that was firm and warm, yet not crushing. "You've known Cruz awhile, then?"

Now there was an interesting question, she thought. Three years…and just over a month. Both were true answers. "Yes and no," she said finally.

"Kelsey runs the place I go to every year, up the coast an hour," Cruz explained.

"Ah," Gage said with a nod that said he understood her confused answer. "So what's your connection to the missing girl?"

Kelsey flushed, sending a sideways glance at Cruz. Telling her part in this hadn't been part of the deal when she agreed to come here.

"Melissa just showed up there. It…doesn't directly affect the case," Cruz said, meeting her glance with one of his own that clearly told her he was going to be greatly unhappy if he was proved wrong. "But Kelsey can give you some exact dates that might help, and tell you what the girl said while she was there."

Gage looked at them both then, as if he suspected there was more to it than Cruz was saying. But he didn't ask. Instead he reached down and fished something out of the stack of papers on his desk. When he held it out to Cruz, Kelsey saw enough to tell that it was a mug shot. Cruz looked at it, then, silently, handed it to her.

The young man in the stark photo, holding a numbered plaque up in front of him, looked more than a little wild, with a sparse reddish mustache and chin beard, and a closely shaved head. Most of all, he looked angry, and there was something in his eyes that made her skin crawl.

She swallowed, then looked at Gage. "This is...Doug Sutter, I presume?"

"You've never seen him?"

Why did cops always answer questions with questions? she wondered. "No. Melissa described him to me, but obviously she doesn't...see him this way."

"Even when he's thumping on her?" Gage asked pointedly. "The supplemental report says they're sure he's sent her to the hospital a couple of times, but she would never cooperate, denied everything, and there were no witnesses who would talk."

Kelsey grimaced.

"You knew she was pregnant?" Gage asked. Kelsey nodded. "Did he rape her?"

She stiffened. "Does it matter? Would that make Melissa's case more important to you?"

"It just means," Cruz put in gently, "that if Melissa has that trauma to deal with, on top of being pregnant, she might react...differently."

Kelsey felt her instinctive anger drain away. "Oh," she said, wondering how long she'd been so ready to jump to unwarranted conclusions. And how many times she'd done it without realizing it. Odd, since she instinctively trusted Gage to do what he promised. And that realization didn't help, either; why did she trust Gage, but not Cruz?

There was only one obvious answer, and she didn't like it much; the difference between them was that with Gage, her heart wasn't involved.

"No, I don't think so," she answered at last. "She thinks she's in love with him," she said sadly. "And she thinks he loves her. Or did."

"That doesn't give him the right to—"

Gage cut himself off abruptly. Kelsey looked at him, struck by the fierce intensity in his face, in those eyes. And she suddenly knew what Cruz had meant when he said the man's dedication to the job bordered on obsession.

"Tell me what you know," the blond man asked her peremptorily. "I swear I'll do everything I can to help her."

She believed him. She had no other choice in the face of that earnest intensity. Whatever was driving Gage Butler, she had no doubt that his goal was not arrests or glory. She wondered if he even knew himself what drove him.

"I don't know much. She arrived late at night, a week ago Friday." She didn't dare look at Cruz, didn't want to be reminded of that foolish call she'd made in her panic when the girl showed up. "She didn't talk much at all, but she mentioned coming to the beach, that she'd heard it was easy to get by there."

She really didn't know much more, just a couple of names Melissa had mentioned of kids who hung out at the beach, but since she had no last names to go with them, she doubted they would be much help. But she told Gage anyway, and he wrote down everything she said. He asked a few more questions, none of which she could answer, then put down the pad he'd been writing on.

"Okay, I'll get on it."

"Thank you," she said, meaning it. "I know you have other things to do, and this isn't really your—"

She stopped when he held up a hand. "It'll be payback time for him later," he said, nodding toward Cruz with a grin. Kelsey lowered her gaze, feeling more awkward than she had in a long time.

"Any chance she'd head back home?" the detective asked.

Kelsey shook her head, looking up at him once more. "She said she couldn't ever go home, her folks had thrown her out when they'd found out she was pregnant. She was almost as afraid of them as she was of Doug. They'd always been very harsh, she said, and now they really hate her."

"Which is why they bothered to report her missing," Cruz, who had been oddly silent, observed mildly.

"I know that," she retorted, looking at him at last. "I know I only get one side of the story, and there's always another, but I also don't think this is something you take chances with without knowing all the facts for sure. If she's telling the truth, then sending her back would be…more criminal than anything she's done."

"She's already lied to you," he pointed out.

"People lie when they're scared sometimes," she snapped. "Of course, you wouldn't know about that, would you? You've probably never been really scared in your life!"

She felt like an idiot the moment she'd said it. His eyes narrowed, and he just looked at her. The man was a police officer, for God's sake, of course he must have been scared at one time or another. But before she could say anything— and probably make it worse, she thought in chagrin—he spoke.

"Wait here. I'll go get Sam, and then we'll leave."

He was gone so quickly that she felt a little breathless. And more than a little foolish.

"He's been scared before," Gage said, his voice so neutral she knew it was intentional. "He was pinned down by a barricaded suspect once, caught in the field of fire. And he disarmed a bomb in a crowded high-rise a few years back, when the bomb squad couldn't get here before it was set to go off. They gave him a medal of valor for that one. And I've never seen him more scared than when his little girl was hurt last year, even though it was only a broken arm."

He was saying it casually, almost chattily, but every word made Kelsey feel worse. She didn't feel any better when he added, "It's easy to be what people call brave if you've got nothing to lose. Cruz has Sam, and he loves her more than life, but he goes out and does the job anyway. And does it damn well."

Kelsey grimaced. "I think I'll go outside and sit with my own stupidity," she muttered. "If you'll point me in the right direction?"

He gestured toward the door they'd come in. "Out and to the right, then down the outside stairs."

But he stopped her before she could move, with a gentle hand on her shoulder.

"He's a good man, Kelsey. The best. I don't know what's going on between you, but I can tell you that anybody on the force here would trust him with their life. Or the lives of the ones they love. And a lot of them have. He's never let them down.''

Nothing was going on, Kelsey thought glumly as she followed Gage's directions out to the parking lot. Not a thing was going on between them. And it was just as well. He was a cop. She couldn't have a cop in her life.

And she didn't know if what she was feeling was relief or disappointment.

Chapter 12

"My mom ran away, just like your friend did," Sam said blithely.

Cruz winced; he had known Sam would likely pick up on what was going on, she was too bright not to, but he'd never expected her to come out with an observation like that. He didn't know which bothered him more, that she'd done it at all, or her matter-of-fact tone. He'd never used the phrase *running away* when he talked to her about her mother; apparently she'd come up with it on her own.

He felt Kelsey's puzzled gaze and remembered that he'd told her Ellie was dead. It hadn't been a lie, he told himself. True, over the years it had become a defense, a quick way of stopping a line of conversation he didn't wish to continue. But it was the truth. As far as it went.

He waited, not knowing what to say now, and dreading Kelsey's inevitable question.

It didn't come. Instead, Kelsey turned her attention back to Sam, who was, at Cruz's insistence, seat-belted securely in the back seat of the four-wheel-drive.

"I suppose everybody feels like running away sometimes," she said to the girl with gentle compassion.

He let out a compressed breath, silently thanking Kelsey for not opening a can of worms he didn't want to deal with right now.

"My mom never came back," Sam said. "Do you think your friend will?"

"I...hope so."

"You'll be okay, even if she doesn't," Sam said soothingly. "Dad and I are, huh, dad?"

"Yeah, we're just fine, squirt."

"I don't remember her much."

He did, Cruz thought. He remembered more than he wanted to. He remembered things that he'd just as soon forget. Things he'd kept nicely buried, and he would just as soon they stayed that way. Even if he did have the grim feeling on occasion that he'd buried them alive.

He was thankful when the quicksilver Sam spotted a fast-food restaurant and wheedlingly suggested a stop for some dinner before they took Kelsey back to where her car was parked at the beach.

"I don't think so," Cruz said. "You've had nothing but junk all day, anyway."

"Da-ad," Sam said in an exaggeratedly drawn-out tone.

"Well, I haven't," Kelsey said brightly. "And I'm overdue for some good, greasy junk food."

"See?" Sam crowed in delight. "Let's go!"

Cruz grumbled about being outvoted, but his heart wasn't in it. A short while later, Sam abandoned the last remnants of her hamburger and fries for the kids' playground outside. Cruz watched her go, made sure he could see her from where they sat, then turned to Kelsey.

"Thank you for...handling what she said about her mother without..."

He trailed off awkwardly, not knowing exactly what to say.

Kelsey's mouth turned up at one corner in a half smile that was full of understanding. "Is she really...dead?"

He nodded. "Five years ago. But she left us...long before that."

"Ran away, like Sam said?"

"Sort of."

Kelsey looked at him speculatively. "You must have married very young."

He nodded. "I was nineteen. Ellen was barely eighteen." His mouth twisted. "Everybody said we were too young, tried to talk us out of it. But we were so sure we were right, that our love was different, that we'd prove them all wrong...."

"You think things like that, at that age," Kelsey said gently. "So...you both changed?"

He saw where she was heading and shook his head. "Not like that. I mean we didn't just grow apart or something. It didn't just happen."

He stopped and ran a hand over his hair, shoving it back from his forehead. He hadn't talked about this in so long that he was finding it very difficult. In fact, he hadn't really talked about it much at all, and he was a little surprised at finding himself trying to do so now. But Kelsey was looking at him with that expression of warm concern and understanding, and the words began, as if a dam had been breached.

"It wasn't like that. And it wasn't Ellie's fault. She was in an accident on Sam's third birthday. A bad one. She nearly died. When she finally got better, she...said she'd had a lot of time to think. And that almost dying made her realize she'd never really lived. She'd been sent a warning, she said. She had to have some time to herself, to figure out what she wanted."

He didn't tell her what a shock it had been, didn't tell her how panicked he'd been, wondering how he was going to deal with taking care of Sam alone, didn't tell her how he'd felt when Ellie looked at him, tears streaming down her face, and told him everyone had been right, they'd been too young, they hadn't had a real life. And that she was going to grab hers now, now that she'd learned how uncertain life really was. He didn't tell her any of that, but she was looking at him as if he had, as if she knew.

"Did she figure it out?" Kelsey prompted softly.

"Oh, yeah," he said, unable to stop himself from sounding sour. "Six months later, divorce papers arrived. She didn't even ask for visitation. She wanted out, and neither Sam nor I were part of whatever life she planned to grab before it was too late."

"I'm sorry, Cruz."

He sighed. "No. It turned out she was right." He jammed his fingers through his hair again, reining in the simmering anger he'd thought he'd conquered long ago. "She died a year after that. A stroke. From a blood clot. Probably the end result of that accident."

Kelsey made a small sound, he wasn't sure if it was sympathy or commiseration, but he didn't want either.

"It was nobody's fault. Not Ellie's, not mine, not Sam's. It happened. It was just…chance. There's nobody to blame."

It came out more sharply, more vehemently, than he'd intended, and Kelsey looked at him first with surprise, then thoughtfully.

"This is what Kit was talking about, when she said sooner or later you're going to have to deal with it, isn't it?"

Cruz tensed. "Kit talks too much. She's always…looking for deep, dark reasons for everything."

"Even in her friends?"

His jaw tightened. "We…dated for a while. Before we realized we were wrecking a great friendship trying to make it something it wasn't. But that makes her feel free to…butt in."

He hoped that would divert her; women tended to fasten on things like that, he thought. But, not for the first time, he found he'd underestimated Kelsey Hall.

"But she's right, isn't she? You haven't let go of it."

"There's nothing to let go of. I told you, it wasn't anyone's fault."

Damn, he sounded as wound up as he ever had; where was all his hard-won equanimity? He'd struggled for so long to not be angry, and yet here it was again, as hot and fierce as it had ever been.

"That's my point," Kelsey said simply. "Maybe you haven't dealt with it exactly *because* there's no one to blame."

"What's that bit of psychobabble supposed to mean?"

"I just mean that the natural way to deal with abandonment is to blame the one who left you. But in your case, you don't feel you can, because she died."

Cruz turned his attention to a solitary leftover french fry, bending it between his fingers, as intent upon it as if the fate of the world depended upon discovering how many bends the thing could take before it broke.

"Dying doesn't make someone right, Cruz," Kelsey said. "We tend to sanctify people for the simple act of dying, because we're taught not to speak ill of them. But the fact that she died doesn't make your wife a saint."

"It wasn't her fault," he insisted, chanting what had been his watchword for so long, whenever the anger and frustration would boil up inside him too hotly to be ignored.

"Maybe that's true. Maybe she did what she had to do, but you and Sam paid the price for it. And the circumstances made it worse, because there was no outlet for the feelings you had."

The fry tore in half. He looked up at her. "What do you know about what I felt?"

"I know, Cruz. I know about…abandonment. I know those feelings of anger are only natural. But you didn't have anyone to blame. At least I had my father to hate—"

She stopped suddenly, and Cruz knew he wasn't mistaken when he thought she'd gone slightly pale, even though she quickly turned her head away. She stared out the window into the playground, where Sam was scrambling through a network of plastic pipes that looked like child-size hamster-habitat tunnels.

"Kelsey?"

"Sam looks like she's having fun," she said, her light tone clearly forced.

He wanted to ask, wanted to know exactly what had happened between her and her father. And at the same time, he didn't want to know, because he was afraid the truth might be too close to the many ugly stories he'd seen in nine years of police work; there had been clues enough to make him think so.

And he also knew what it was like to be pushed into talking about something as painful as this apparently was for her. Although, he thought wryly, it hadn't seemed to take much pushing for her to get him to spill the miserable story of his marriage and its aftermath.

He watched her as she stared out the window. Was she right? he wondered. Was that the reason it had never really gone away for him, why he still felt so angry when he thought about Ellie? Was it that simple, that he just hadn't had anyone to blame? Because there had been no one to vent his anger on, had he carried it around bottled up inside until those times when it boiled over?

Gradually he sensed the tension quivering just beneath the surface in Kelsey. Did just the thought of her father do this to her? Or was she afraid that because he'd spilled his guts to her, he would expect her to do the same?

He was curious. He wanted to know. But he also sensed how skittish she was and knew that if he did push her, she would simply close up on him. Kelsey Hall might be the confident, competent woman who ran Oak Tree with practiced efficiency, but she was also a woman with secrets. And a woman who would not be pushed.

So instead, still not sure why he didn't just walk away, he chose another tack.

"So where do we look for Melissa next?"

Kelsey's head snapped back around, and the look of relief that flashed across her face told him that she had been afraid he was going to press her with questions she didn't want to answer.

"You've done enough already," she said.

He couldn't tell from her tone if she was being sarcastic. "Still mad at me?"

She looked surprised. "No," she said, then understanding

flashed in the green eyes. "I meant that, really. You're on vacation—"

"I told you, I'm the one who made that choice. It's not your problem."

"But it's not fair to Sam, to drag her along like today."

Cruz couldn't argue with that. "You're right. But there are other options."

He crumpled up the napkin he'd wiped his fingers with after the destruction of the french fry and tossed it on the tray. A shrill electronic beep sounded as his pager went off. He checked it, saw Gage's number and glanced at Kelsey.

"Will you watch out for Sam for me while I make a call?"

The smile she gave him was astonishingly bright. "Of course I will."

It wasn't until he was halfway to the telephone in the back of the restaurant that it hit him; she was flattered that he trusted her to look out for Sam.

He was a little surprised himself. Yet somehow he knew that, whatever else she was or might be up to, Kelsey would die before she let Sam be hurt. He wasn't sure how he knew, only that it came from the same source as that gut instinct he'd learned to trust as a cop. He just knew.

Gage answered on the first ring.

"Are you 10-35?" he asked, using the code asking if Cruz was clear for confidential information. Used like this, Cruz knew it could mean only one thing: Gage wanted to know if Kelsey was within earshot. He felt his fingers tighten around the receiver and forced himself to relax them.

"Yeah. Go ahead."

"Nothing on the Bargman girl," Gage said, "but I thought I recognized your Ms. Hall's name. So I did some checking. Called a couple of kids I know."

Cruz knew that Gage had reliable sources; he'd helped enough kids to have built a reputation among them as tough but fair, and he kept in touch with those he'd helped get their lives straightened out. It usually paid off for him later, sometimes in unexpected ways.

"And?" Cruz prompted.

"They know about your lady."

Cruz opened his mouth to protest the appellation but found himself asking only "What do you mean? Know what?"

"The word's been out for a couple of years now that Kelsey's place is a haven. That if you're a runaway and want to get off the street, she'll help you. Hide you out until things cool down, give you a roof and food and time to get your act together, think things through."

Cruz went still. "Go on," he said, his voice a little tight.

"She's not running a crash pad or anything like that. Apparently she has some pretty tough rules, and she sticks to them, and that doesn't appeal to a lot of these kids."

"Rules?"

"Yeah. I found a kid who'd gone to her. Remember the Acklin kid, last year? The one who got caught up in that convenience-store holdup?"

"I remember," Cruz said.

He'd caught the case, one underage teen caught in a mess with three nineteen-year-old punks who had robbed the store and pistol-whipped the manager. The boy had insisted that he hadn't known they were planning anything like that, that he'd thought they were only going to steal some beer. Eventually Cruz had come to believe the kid, in part because the only things on his record were several runaway reports. Gage had gotten him started in the emancipated-minor procedure, and once out of an abusive home, the kid had turned it around.

"What about him?"

"He went to her once. But she kicked him out when he broke one of her four cardinal rules."

"Cardinal rules?"

"That's what she calls them, apparently. No drugs, no booze, you agree to get some kind of help to resolve the problem you're running from, and you tell her the truth. That's why the hard-core runaways don't bother, it's too much like being at home. But the ones who are just confused, who maybe want to go home but don't know how...those are the ones she helps."

"And she uses Oak Tree as a cover?" Cruz asked, shaking his head slightly.

"I don't know about that. But it would be an easy way to account for having kids coming and going. Her customers are only there a short time, so who would notice?"

"No wonder she didn't want me around," Cruz muttered.

"Is that what all that was about this afternoon?"

"Sort of."

"Why? I mean, unless she's doing something that could get her on a contributing rap—"

"Kelsey? Hardly."

"I didn't think so. But even then, at the most it'd be a misdemeanor. What does she think you're going to do?"

"She has some…definite ideas about cops," Cruz said. "If nothing else, I think she assumes I'd nail her for harboring a criminal."

"Harboring a—oh. The stuff the kid stole."

"Yeah. From what Melissa told her about her parents, I'd guess Kelsey believes they'd try to have Melissa held for that."

"Some parents would," Gage said.

"I know. Thanks for the info, Gage. Keep me posted."

"Right."

For a moment after he hung up, Cruz stood there with his hand on the receiver, considering. Then he dialed again, punching out his credit-card number swiftly from memory. After a quick conversation, he was on his way back to the table.

He paused a few feet away. Kelsey was, true to her word, keeping a close eye on Sam. The late-afternoon sun was streaming through the window, lighting her hair to crimson fire and silhouetting her profile; her upturned nose was at odds with the sensual fullness of her mouth, and he thought it was indicative of her whole personality; an unexpected innocence at war with an undiscovered sensuality.

And if he didn't stop thinking things like that, things that made the heat kick through him in sudden spurts, he was going to be in big trouble.

He started moving again and sat down opposite her.

"What next?" he asked.

She looked at him, and he saw the weariness in her expression. "Maybe I should ask you," she said, her voice mirroring her expression. "You're the cop."

"Then I'd say we go back to the house, and you get some rest. We'll start again in the morning."

"But I should go home."

"Do you have guests?"

"Well, no, not until next week, and Dolores is checking on things for me, but—"

"You're too tired to drive for over an hour."

"That's what you said last night."

"It was true then. It's true now. So we get some rest, then tomorrow we'll try again. Maybe we can find those kids Melissa mentioned. At least that gives us three to look for instead of just one."

"But we only have first names."

"I know. But you said she said they hung out at the beach, right?" At her nod, he went on. "That implies they don't live there. Which means they'll be out, and visible, not in a house. Makes it a little easier."

He didn't point out that *easier,* in this case, was a relative term; there was nothing easy about finding one kid amid the summer beach crowds that numbered well into the tens of thousands. But he also knew that a good part of police work consisted of ignoring the fact that the odds of you finding what you were looking for were stacked so high against you and going ahead anyway.

"Unless, of course," he went on before she could protest again, "the lodgings weren't to your liking. I can understand that. Not everybody likes to share a room with a menagerie."

"I didn't mind at all," she said quickly. "The bubbling of the aquariums was kind of soothing. And they were all very considerate. Slither, in particular."

This last seemed rather pointed, and he eyed her warily. "That snake," he muttered.

"He's really very well mannered," she said.

"Did Sam put you up to this?"

"Up to what?"

"Trying to sweet-talk me into letting that thing back into the house."

"Oh. No. But I do feel badly. It was mostly my fault. She was so excited to have somebody to show him to who didn't…"

Her voice trailed off awkwardly, and Cruz finished for her, rather grimly, "Hate the sight of him?"

"Something like that."

He gave her a steady look. "She still knows the rule. She broke it, and the snake's in the garage."

She looked down at the paper place mat, staring at the child's game printed on it as if it were the text of the Magna Carta and she had to memorize it.

"It's…good for kids to have some rules," she said after a long silent moment. "But there can be too many rules, too."

"I know. That's why I don't give her many. But those I give her are inviolable. I think you know you have to have at least a few…cardinal rules."

Her head came up sharply, and she stared at him, her tired green eyes searching his face. He waited for her to speak, to say something that told him she was ready to talk, to trust him enough to tell him the truth.

She looked down again without saying a word.

And Cruz was surprised at how much that hurt.

Chapter 13

Kelsey didn't know quite how she felt about this. At first she'd felt bad for Sam, but the little girl had been so excited that feeling sorry for her was impossible. Then she'd felt a recurrence of her pangs of guilt for taking up Cruz's vacation time, but he'd again made the point that it was his decision, not hers. And then she'd felt wary, not sure she liked how much the idea of his help—and his presence—appealed to her.

And above all, she was totally bewildered about why he was doing it at all. Asking Gage Butler to make a few phone calls was one thing; physically going out with her and spending hours on what would probably just be more fruitless searching was something else again.

And she didn't dare think about last night. Didn't dare think about how many times she'd awakened in the night and how hard she'd tried to blame it on some tiny movement from one of the little creatures she was sharing space with, when she knew perfectly well it was simply the presence of this man, down the hall from her.

She'd never had dreams like this, never had to quash urges

like this. She didn't even know what these urges were, other than a need to see and touch far more of him than she had.

Thank heavens for ten-year-old chaperones, she thought.

"Dad used to get mad at me for this," Sam said cheerfully as she plopped her feet up on the back of Kelsey's seat. "But then he stopped."

"Oh?" Kelsey said, looking at the girl curiously.

"He said he could always get another truck, but not another me," Sam explained, and Kelsey wondered again if the child had any idea how lucky she was. She stole a sideways glance at Cruz, who seemed more engrossed in making a left turn than was strictly necessary.

At last he pulled the truck to a stop in front of a small split-level house that had the look of an invitingly secluded cabin, thanks to the wealth of greenery and flowers that surrounded it.

Sam, who hadn't stopped chattering all morning, scrambled out of the truck, clutching her small suitcase.

"Come on," Cruz said, leaning in to look at Kelsey when she didn't exit the truck. "Ryan's still here. You can meet the real thing."

She thought of the drawing and wasn't at all sure she wanted to meet him, but at Sam's excited urging, she slid out of the truck and followed them. The front door of the house swung open before they reached the porch, and Kelsey heard an exaggerated female squeal of delight.

"Sammy!"

"Hi, Lacey!" Sam returned, sounding as delighted as the woman had. "I get to stay for three whole days!"

"I know, sweetie. I'm so excited. Come on in."

The child disappeared inside the house. Cruz paused at the top of the three steps, looking back at Kelsey. Slowly she came up even with him, looking at the woman who stood holding the door open.

"Kelsey Hall, Lacey Buckhart," Cruz said. He'd been doing a lot of introductions lately, Kelsey thought.

"Hello, Kelsey," the woman said.

Kelsey hesitated, although she wasn't sure why. There was

nothing intimidating about the woman in the doorway, Kelsey thought, and her voice had been warm, as if the simple fact that she was with Cruz was enough to warrant welcome.

Like Kelsey herself, she wasn't model-thin or overwhelmingly gorgeous, there was no reason why she shouldn't feel comfortable with her. She had light brown hair cut in a smooth sweep almost like her own, and fair skin that was a bit unusual in this land of sun-worshippers.

And if Kelsey had ever doubted the validity of the phrase *glowingly pregnant*, Lacey Buckhart would have convinced her. She remembered that Cruz had said they'd lost one baby; perhaps that had something to do with the happiness that seemed to shimmer around Lacey Buckhart now.

"Come on in. Ryan's getting ready for work."

They stepped inside. Kelsey felt an immediate sense of liking. The soft, muted peach of the living room walls perfectly set off the rich jewel tones of the chairs, sofa and pillows. The room was as warm and welcoming as the woman herself.

"Would you like some coffee?" Lacey asked. "That is," she added with a laugh, "if you can stand what Ryan calls coffee. I've sworn off."

"Lacey's gonna have a baby," Sam explained to Kelsey.

Lacey laughed and patted the gentle protrusion beneath her sweater. "I think she can probably tell that."

"Congratulations. When?" Kelsey asked; Lacey appeared further along than Melissa, but perhaps it was just the difference of being happy and well cared-for.

"Thank you. We're very happy about it. And four months," Lacey added with a smile, then turned at a sound from across the room. The look that crossed her face then gave Kelsey that oddly wistful feeling again; never in her life had she even seen anyone literally light up at the sight of someone else, let alone felt that way herself. But there was no other way to describe it. Slowly she turned to look at the man who stood in the hallway, talking to Cruz.

Ryan Buckhart was everything Cruz's dramatic drawing had promised. And more. Tall, broad-shouldered, solidly strong, with his long dark hair, bronze skin and high cheek-bones, he was exotically striking. He stood there in a pair of dark pants and an unbuttoned white shirt, baring a wide strip of ridged belly and broad chest. Powerfully, uncompromisingly male.

Kelsey knew she was gaping, but she couldn't help it. Her gaze flicked to Lacey as she wondered what kind of woman it would take to keep up with this man. Lacey was watching her with an expression that said she'd seen this reaction countless times before.

"Better you than me," Kelsey whispered, just loud enough for Lacey to hear.

Lacey looked startled, then smiled, her expression this time one of friendly appreciation. "He is...amazing, isn't he?"

There was such pure love in her tone that Kelsey couldn't help smiling.

"Uncle Ryan!"

Sam's delighted cry made both Kelsey and Lacey smile, and as the girl ran to him and he bent and picked her up easily, swinging her in the air as she laughed, Kelsey knew that there were tender depths to this man that weren't immediately apparent.

"That's Ryan," Lacey said. "Charms women of all ages."

Kelsey looked at her, but there was no sign of resentfulness in Lacey's voice or face. She wore the calm, confident expression of a woman utterly secure in her man's love.

"So, how long have you known Cruz?" Lacey asked.

Again she didn't know how to answer that. Added up, she'd really only spent a month with him, but she felt as if she'd known him much longer. So this time she tried to explain in a different way.

"He's been coming to my inn every summer for a few years."

Lacey's brows rose. "So you're where he goes to?"

Kelsey colored. "Not me, the inn. It's a lovely setting, very peaceful."

Lacey looked at her assessingly, then glanced at Cruz, who was, Kelsey realized with a little shock, looking at her.

"I'll tell you," Lacey said, "if I wasn't so crazy about that stubborn Indian, I'd give you a run for your money with that one. He's a good man. The best. He's been with us through some tough times."

Kelsey's blush deepened. "I... We...we're not..."

Her voice trailed off awkwardly, and Lacey's smile widened. "Not yet, anyway," she said rather archly. Then she raised her voice. "Ryan? Come meet Kelsey."

The big man looked over at them. For a moment, Kelsey saw the same look of utter love and tenderness, a look that transformed his face. Then, as he started across the room toward them, he began to button his shirt, a modest gesture that made Kelsey smile inwardly. But when she realized Cruz was following Ryan, she felt a sudden tension begin to build anew inside her.

Ryan came to a halt beside his wife, slipping an arm around her. Lacey leaned into him in a movement that was clearly second nature to her. And to him. The sight of this big, powerful man so solicitously handling the much smaller woman warmed Kelsey.

She glanced at Cruz, remembering the rest of what he'd said about the Buckharts.

...behind the badge is just a man, a man who felt unbelievable pain when he and Lacey lost their first baby, a man whose divorce devastated him, because he never stopped loving his wife, so much so that he changed himself, his entire approach to life, to get her back....

Cruz's words echoed in her mind, and as she looked at the two of them, she saw not just the very striking couple they made, but two people who had fought hard for what they had now, two people who had earned this closeness that fairly radiated from them.

"Hello, Kelsey," Ryan said, studying her with an intensity that made her nervous.

"Hello," she said tentatively.

He just kept looking at her, studying her with those intense, dark eyes, until she shifted uncomfortably.

"Don't mind us," Lacey said with a laugh. "It's just that Cruz has never brought anyone for us to meet before."

Kelsey thought her cheeks must be the color of that deep red pillow on the sofa by now. She was afraid Cruz would instantly deny any connection between them of the kind Lacey obviously meant, and she tried to think of something neutral to say.

Before she could, Cruz spoke, in a mock-grumbling tone. "You sound like my parents."

Ryan chuckled. "Speaking of which, how are they?"

That diverted the conversation into safer territory and gave Kelsey a chance to recover. She wondered if Cruz had intended it that way, but decided that since he had—thankfully—no idea how people's seemingly persistent need to link them affected her, he probably had just wanted to avoid explaining again.

It was a moment before she had her nerves settled enough to pay attention to the conversation again.

"...have a great time, won't we, Sam?" Lacey was saying.

"'Course," the girl agreed. "We always do."

"Thanks again," Cruz said. "And about the animals... I should be there to feed—"

"We'll do fine," Lacey assured him. "It's not like your house is that far away. We can stop in every day so Sam can tend them."

"Hope you get this resolved," Ryan said to Cruz, making Kelsey wonder what Cruz had told them.

"I won't mess up your weekend plans to be alone with your wife," Cruz said, winking at Lacey.

"You'd best not," Lacey said with clearly mock severity. "It may be the last time we're alone for a long time."

"Yeah," Ryan said, moving his hand to rest it gently on the swell of his wife's belly. Then, reluctantly, he said, "I've got to get moving, or I'll be late."

"At least Robards won't chew on you for it," Cruz said.

Ryan laughed. "Thanks to my wife, he's been pretty much off my back."

It wasn't until they were back in his truck that Cruz explained. "Lacey caught the charming lieutenant acting…let's just say decidedly unheroically. She made a deal with him that as long as he left Ryan alone, she'd keep her mouth shut."

She thought of the man she'd seen in the hallway and the way Cruz had quickly gotten her out of sight. "Why was Robards on Ryan's back in the first place?"

Cruz started the engine and eased out onto the roadway. "Lots of reasons. Ryan's a damn good cop. He's tough and smart, and he stays on top of things. Everything Robards isn't." He slowed for the stop sign at the end of the Buckharts' quiet street. "But most of all, he hates him for the same reason he hates me."

Kelsey blinked. "What?"

Cruz held up his hand. Kelsey looked at it, then his face, not understanding. He reached out and grasped her wrist with his fingers. The heat of his touch sent her pulse rocketing, and all she could think of, inanely, was that he was surely going to know it, with his fingers right on her inner wrist like that.

She stared down at his hand, trying to think, to figure out what he was trying to say. And finally it struck her, as she at last noticed the contrast between her fair skin and his own golden tint. And remembered the contrast between Lacey's creamy complexion and Ryan's bronze.

Her gaze shot to Cruz's face. "He's one of those?"

"A bigot to the bone," he said. "And a sexist, and a few other not very nice things."

"Including a coward?" Kelsey asked, remember what he'd said about Lacey witnessing something that gave her a hold on the man.

"Including," Cruz agreed tightly. "More than once he's gotten some good men hurt. So far no one's died, but it's only been luck and their own guts and skill that have prevented it."

"My God," Kelsey breathed. "Then why is he still a cop?"

He looked at her then, at last releasing her wrist, letting her breathe normally again.

"I kind of got the idea you thought most cops were…that bad."

"I don't," she protested quickly. "I know it's an ugly job, and it has to be done, and all that. It's just that sometimes it seems like…the fact that people are hurting gets forgotten."

"Sometimes it does," Cruz admitted. "Sometimes you numb yourself so much that you forget what it's like to feel, so you don't think about what other people are feeling. It's an occupational hazard."

"Have you ever…?"

For a long moment, he didn't answer. He made the turn and drove on until she didn't think he was going to answer at all. Then, at last, he did.

"Once," he said, rather flatly. "Once I was so disconnected that I was just going through the motions. I didn't even realize it. It didn't show, nobody saw it. Except Yeager."

"Yeager?"

"Clay Yeager. He's…kind of a legend at Trinity West. The quintessential cop. Won three medals of valor. He was the one we all looked up to, the one we all wanted to be like. He was tough, never lost a fight…but he could handle a scared kid or a rape victim with a gentleness that would make you cry."

"Was?" she asked softly, dreading the answer.

Cruz's mouth tightened. "He…quit, a few years back. Some…awful things happened. All the help he gave everybody else, and he couldn't help himself. And none of us could, either. We could only stand by and watch his life fall apart."

There was such remembered pain in his voice that Kelsey couldn't bear to probe that wound any longer. So, instead of pursuing the mystery of Clay Yeager and what had happened to him, she asked, "He…helped you?"

Cruz nodded. "He recognized the signs. He took me aside, told me I had to deal with it or I was going to end up like Robards, not feeling anything for anyone but myself, and then

I'd really be lost. He kept after me, wouldn't let it drop, until I got help."

"Deal with…what?" she ventured, wondering if it had been the loss of his wife.

"I… It was back when I was in the patrol division. I'd only been on the department a couple of years. I went out on a 415 family. A domestic fight. I'd been out there before. They were both alcoholics, drunk most of the time, and they used to get in real knock-down-drag-out fights. We'd separate 'em, send one of them away for the night, and that'd be the end of it. Neither of them would ever press charges, and this was before the law was passed that said a report has to be made on any domestic violence incident, so the state can prosecute even if the victim won't."

"But…this time was different?"

"Not the call. Except this time, we got another call the next morning. A neighbor had found their little boy. In the backyard, lying in a bunch of broken glass and a pool of blood. He'd been thrown through a plate-glass window. And bled to death."

Kelsey sucked in a harsh breath, and a tiny sound of pained protest escaped her. Cruz went on, sounding dogged, as if he had to get through this, now that he'd begun.

"We never knew which of them did it. They'd both passed out and couldn't remember a thing. We thought it was him, for the strength it would have taken, but her clothes had blood on them. Crime lab found evidence on the child that could have come from either of them."

He was sounding like a man on a torture rack. "Cruz—"

"He was only five years old. Never had a chance to live. And I could have saved him. I was right there. In the house, and he was still alive."

Kelsey shuddered. She wished he would stop, this was too much, too painful to hear, too much like stories she'd heard, like the story she'd lived. But he kept on.

"Yeager told me it wasn't my fault. He made me see the department shrink. She told me, too. We never even knew they had a child. I'd been there at least three times before, and there'd been no sign, no toys around, no pictures, nothing.''

"If you didn't know, then what could you have done?''

"That's what they all said. But..."

He trailed off, that one final word saying volumes about the pain this man carried over that one long-ago incident.

It felt odd, defending a cop in that situation, but she could see that it was tearing him up, even after all this time. And she wondered, for the first time in her life, if the cops who had taken her back home had ever felt like this, had perhaps known they were sending her back into hell, but had been unable to do anything else. Had one of them gone home to his own family and hugged them tighter because of her? Were they still dealing with it, all these years later, maybe wondering what had ever become of that frightened little girl?

Was one of them haunted by her, as Cruz was haunted by a little boy who had died so horribly?

"Cruz," she said, suddenly, not sure why. And as she said it, she reached out and laid her hand atop his on the steering wheel, the first time she had ever dared to touch him of her own accord.

He tensed, and she started to pull her hand back, regretting that she'd done it. But before she could, he turned his own hand, capturing hers. He didn't look at her. He kept his eyes on the road, as if the traffic were twice as heavy as it really was, he didn't speak, but he held on, as if...

As if he wanted the contact. As if he liked the contact.

The thought made her shiver slightly. But she didn't pull away. Neither did Cruz. And she wished she was less of a fool, so that she wouldn't be reading more into it than there was. Because she was sure she must be, sure that he only needed some kind of human contact to help him fight off the ugly memories.

It wasn't because he...wanted anything more. Not from her. And thinking he might was as bad as any of the wishful thinking she'd done as a child, when she dreamed that if she just wished hard enough, if she was just good enough, her life would magically change.

She'd given up on miracles long ago. And she wasn't about to start believing in them again now.

Gage had been right, Cruz thought as he watched Kelsey talk to the two girls who'd been standing outside the coffee/latte store. They'd been wary at first, but once they realized who she was, they had, while casting wary glances at him, talked to her. He'd agreed to stay back, out of her way, and it hadn't taken him long to see the wisdom of that course of action.

It also hadn't taken him long to see that she knew exactly where to look. This place was two doors away from a bus station. Before this, they'd been at the video arcade—not, she said, because she thought this was Melissa's kind of place, but because somebody might have seen or heard something. Before that, they'd been to three houses near the beach, two of which Cruz already knew were frequent runaway crash pads. One he hadn't known, but he'd made a note to tell Gage about it. And before that, the Trinity West district's new shopping mall, where Cruz was a little startled at the number of kids who seemed to do nothing but hang out in small groups for hours on end.

They searched all day, and long into the night, in every likely place, up and down every likely street he or she could think of, until they couldn't find anyone moving who they hadn't already talked to. Cruz finally called a halt. Kelsey protested, but he insisted.

"It's nearly 1:00 a.m. We'll start again tomorrow."

"You don't want to…quit?" she said in some surprise.

"Yes, I want to. But I know you won't. So we'll start again tomorrow."

She gave a weary sigh as she sagged in the front seat of the four-wheel-drive. "I know it's probably hopeless, but I'm scared for her. If she wasn't pregnant, maybe…maybe I could just walk away from it. She lied to me, after all."

"I was wondering if you'd forgotten that part," Cruz said mildly as he turned the truck toward home. It was an automatic thing. He hadn't asked her if she would stay again—in fact, hadn't even thought much about it. Probably because he didn't dare think about having her under his roof again without Sam there to chaperone.

"No, I haven't," she said, apparently too tired to even rise to the bait. "But I also realize she thought she had reason."

"Don't they all?"

She sat up sharply. "If that's the way you feel, then why are you bothering?"

"Good question," Cruz said softly. "Why don't you think about it and see if you can come up with an answer?"

She stared at him for a long moment, then gave a little shake of her head, as if she were discarding an answer she'd come up with as impossible.

"Kelsey," he began softly.

"I can't give up," she said, turning away from both him and the subject. "It's not just Melissa, there's a baby involved. And now that...awful boyfriend of hers. I don't know what she might do if she got scared enough."

"Then we keep looking," he said, feeling a bit cowardly for being inwardly glad to dodge the subject she'd avoided.

But an hour later, when, after a quick meal of salad and a couple of steaks he'd thrown on the grill, Kelsey curled up on the sofa and promptly went to sleep, Cruz was left with little to think about but that subject.

For a long time, he sat there, watching her sleep. She was curled up, her hands tucked beneath her cheek, her knees drawn up almost to her elbows. It could have been because she was on the sofa, but Cruz had a feeling she slept that way normally, curled in on herself. Not, as Sam did, for warmth, but for protection.

He wasn't sure what made him think that, but he instinctively knew he was right.

What he didn't know was why it was making him feel so...odd. He felt a twinge of the same protectiveness he felt for Sam, wondering what Kelsey felt she needed refuge from, and why. At the same time, he found himself wondering what it would take to get her to uncurl, to allow herself to be vulnerable. Would she do it for a man's touch? His touch?

He clenched his jaw against a sudden, hot burst of need. This was crazy, he thought. He wanted to protect her, but at the same time he wanted to caress her until she blossomed for him, until she opened like a flower blooming beneath his touch, beneath him, period.

"You're losing it, Gregerson," he muttered to himself.

The last part, at least, he understood; he'd known for a while now that he wanted Kelsey, wanted her fiercely. True, it had been a long time since he reacted that way to any woman, but that didn't mean he'd forgotten how it felt. Or that he could stop himself from envisioning her soft, curved body welcoming his. But flowers? Blossoms? He'd never been one to think in poetic terms. Ellie had once told him that his drawings were as close to poetry as he ever got.

She stirred, her lips parting slightly. He fought down another wave of heat as he thought about them parting for another reason, for the deep, hot kiss he'd been aching to give her for days. Since that day by the pond, when he watched her dabbling her toes in the water and then followed the long, curved line of her bare legs upward with greedy eyes.

He stifled a groan; he was working himself into a lather here, with no chance for relief in sight. Kelsey didn't trust him any more now than she had before, he was sure. Certainly not enough to let him close enough to do what he was thinking about. Not enough to even let him start.

He got up, painfully aware of his state of rigid arousal. For an instant, he wished he was the kind of man who could blithely try to seduce a woman simply because he was horny. But Elena and Frank Gregerson, if nothing else, had managed to raise a gentleman of sorts, he thought wryly.

He gently covered Kelsey with an afghan his mother had made, then forced himself to walk away.

It was going to be a very long night.

Chapter 14

She checked all the places a cop would have checked, given the time to devote to one single runaway, Cruz thought. And she came up with others that he most likely wouldn't have thought of: libraries, not because Melissa liked to read, but because they were a cool place for a pregnant girl to rest and get away from the summer heat; then, of all places, the local marinas, because, she said, they had showers and even washers and dryers you could use if you could con somebody out of a key. In those places, he was able to help, getting more cooperation with his badge than she might have gotten. But it was still fruitless; the only thing he'd gained was a growing certainty about Kelsey herself.

It was an old saw that if you wanted to catch a thief, you used a thief, or, failing that, at least made yourself think like one. Kelsey was thinking like a runaway. And he was becoming more sure than ever that this was the reason she was doing what she was at the inn: she'd been there herself. She'd been a runaway, at some point in her life.

And he had the sinking feeling that the reason she had been

a runaway was that some cop had taken her back to an intolerable situation, and that was the basis of her distrust.

He probably hadn't known how bad it was, that cop, Cruz thought. Just as he himself hadn't known there was a child who would pay the price for his parents' drunken rages.

Funny how neither excuse washed.

By late afternoon, when every last, desperate idea had been pursued, Kelsey was beginning to flag, discouragement showing in the slump of her normally straight shoulders, in the drawn expression on her face.

When they got back into the truck after checking the last marina with no results, no one who had seen anyone even faintly resembling Melissa, he looked at her.

"Where to?" he asked, reaching for the ignition.

"I don't know," she said wearily.

He let his hand drop and leaned back in the driver's seat. He said nothing more. She stared at her knees. Then out the window at the row upon row of expensive boats of all kinds, the towering masts of the sailboats looking like a denuded hydroponic forest of some kind. At last she looked up at him.

"Thank you, Cruz." Her voice was low, but vibrant with a tone he couldn't have named.

"You're welcome. But for what?"

She waved vaguely toward the water. "Everything. You didn't have to do this at all. Let alone for two whole days. And you certainly didn't have to be so patient. And so... tenacious."

He chuckled. "There are those who would call it stubborn."

"Sometimes stubborn is all that gets you through."

His chuckle died away. "Sometimes," he agreed quietly.

It was a moment of silent communication that could not be denied. Each of them had been in places where it would have been easier to give up than to go on, and they both knew it. Cruz felt it as surely as he'd ever felt anything. And he saw in her eyes that she knew it, too. Had they found common ground at last? Could she set aside her preconceptions and see him as a man, not just as a cop?

Did she even want to? Or had he imagined those moments when he thought he'd caught her watching him, much as he watched her, with all the curiosity of a man looking at the first woman to interest him in a long time, with all the hunger of a man who'd almost forgotten what it was like to need like this?

"Kelsey," he said softly, leaning toward her without even realizing what he was doing. She lifted her head to look at him. He could guess at what was showing in his face by the way her eyes widened. Then her lips parted, as if she needed more air. The memory of last night, when he'd sat watching her sleep, shot through him like a magnum round, tumbling, searing, expanding.

He couldn't stop himself from kissing her any more than he could have called back that round once it was fired.

Her lips were as soft and warm as he'd known they would be.

They sparked a heat in him that was unlike anything he'd ever known. A heat that blasted through him, a heat that sent what remnants of caution he'd tried to hang on to skittering before it, a heat that surged and grew rather than ebbed. His body tightened with a speed that would have shocked him if he was thinking clearly.

With an effort, remembering her wariness, he stopped himself from plundering the depths of her mouth. He traced her lips with the tip of his tongue, gently coaxing, trying to keep the heat at bay. Trying to rein in the urges that were boiling up in him, telling himself this was neither the time nor the place.

He managed. Until she parted her lips for him, just as he'd fantasized. One tiny sign of willingness, and the heat became an inferno that was out of control of caution or any other restraint. He probed forward, tasting the sweetness, tracing the even ridge of her teeth. When he felt the faint, tentative brush of her tongue over his, his body responded fiercely, swiftly, and he hardened in a rush of pouring heat that made him groan.

He grasped her shoulders and pulled her closer, suppressing

the shudder that went through him when he felt her arms go around his neck, felt her fingers tangle in the hair at his nape. She had moved from willingness to participation, and the realization rocked him. He deepened the kiss, and she let him, until his tongue was tasting the deepest honeyed warmth of her mouth, until his nerves were humming, until he forgot how to breathe. Until he felt like he was underwater.

In over his head.

Panic kicked through him. He wrenched his mouth away, expecting to feel relieved, instead feeling only cold and alone and bereft. He fought through the haze of arousal that had swamped him to see her staring at him, her eyes wide with shock, her mouth looking softer and warmer and more tempting than ever.

Slowly her hand stole upward, and she touched her lips. Tentatively, hesitantly, as if she were no longer certain they were her own. And Cruz knew in that instant that if he made one wrong move, if he said one wrong thing, she would bolt like a startled deer. And he wasn't at all sure that he didn't want to do exactly the same thing.

He didn't know what to say. Didn't even know what he was feeling, why he'd felt that sudden alarm. It had been a reaction so deep and instinctive, he didn't know its source.

He wasn't sure he had the breath to talk, anyway; he hadn't realized until he pulled back just how long it had been since he'd drawn in any air. He took a long, almost gulping inhalation. He turned back to sit normally in the driver's seat, shifting a bit uncomfortably in his effort to hide his body's obvious response to that hot, furious kiss; somehow he thought that if she guessed just how aroused he was, she would run from that, too. And again, he wasn't sure he wouldn't prefer it that way.

He let his head loll back against the headrest. He'd never been so torn between wanting something and wanting to retreat from it at the same time. He understood the wanting, but he didn't understand the rest. He'd withstood the nagging and matchmaking of his friends; he'd always figured that when the time came, when he was ready and a woman he liked came along, things would happen...naturally.

And now here she was. And he was the one running scared. He'd been thinking about her not trusting him, but he'd been the one to bolt. And he didn't understand why.

He could hear Kelsey's quickened breathing, could sense her tension, as if it were tangible. *Correction,* he amended silently. *We're both running scared.*

At least he knew what Kelsey's reservations were. He just wished he understood his own. And he wished he knew what the hell to do now.

Sometimes, he thought grimly, discretion was the wisest course. Sometimes retreat was. And once in while, both were.

When he was relatively sure his voice wouldn't sound as thick as Ryan's coffee, when he was fairly confident his words wouldn't descend into mindless blather, he at last spoke.

"Is there any place Melissa might go that we haven't checked yet?"

Not bad, he thought. Only a bit wobbly. You would never guess he was dying, aching beyond bearing, confused beyond comprehension.

"Not...not that I can think of."

The catch in her words stabbed at him, and the husky tone of her voice sent a ripple down his spine, as surely as if she'd trailed her fingers along that path. The thought made his body clench, and flesh that had begun to ebb surged to hot life again.

Damn, he cursed to himself, clenching his jaw and every other muscle he could. He should have known, he thought. His libido hadn't just nicely left him alone for so long, it had been saving up. And it wasn't listening to any reservations he had, understood or otherwise.

"It's almost dark, anyway," he said after an embarrassingly long time of trying to get himself back in control.

"I know."

"I don't see any point in searching until morning."

"No."

She sounded so disheartened that he wanted to hug her, console her, lighten the load she'd taken upon herself, a load few others would even consider carrying.

He also knew he didn't dare. Not now, not when it was taking every ounce of willpower he had to argue his aching body into submission. He didn't dare even look at her, not yet.

"I think I should take you home," he said.

She sighed. He looked at her then, and although she was staring straight ahead, he could still see that she looked nearly as weary as that sigh had sounded.

"I want to go home," she said.

"All right."

"I meant *my* home. The inn."

"That's what I meant."

Her head snapped around. He shrugged. "We're closer to there than we are to my place. I figured you have things to attend to, and that you might want to…sleep in your own bed for a change."

The look of gratitude she gave him was tinged with an uneasiness it took him a moment to figure out.

"Much as I'd like to suggest otherwise, I mean alone, Kelsey. I know you're not…ready for anything more." And I'm not sure I am, either, he added silently.

Color flooded her cheeks, visible even in the fading light of dusk. After a moment of carefully not looking at him, she asked "What about you? You're tired, too."

"I figure you'll either offer me a room or I'll just drive home."

"And you…don't care which?"

"I care," he said wryly. "I'm just not sure which way."

He started the truck and put it in gear before she could come up with an answer to that absurd statement.

"Definitely an improvement on the Chez Gregerson menu," he said as he finished the last bite of a slab of the lasagna that he'd told her had his mouth watering the minute she took it out of the oven.

"Thank Dolores," Kelsey said.

"Didn't I?" Cruz asked innocently.

Oh, he had, all right, Kelsey thought. He'd swept the woman into an engulfing hug and planted a noisy kiss on each of her cheeks. Dolores had laughed, blushing prettily, rattled something off in Spanish that made him laugh in turn, told him his room was ready, then taken her leave.

But not before she had watched them both speculatively long enough to make Kelsey edgy. Long enough to make Kelsey wonder if the memory of that kiss was somehow emblazoned on her forehead.

The way the memory of the way he had retreated was emblazoned on her heart.

She'd been dizzy, whirling in a maelstrom of heat and light she'd never felt before, but still she had felt it, that moment when he pulled away from her with a distinct jolt. As if he had suddenly realized what he was doing and didn't like it.

Or who he was kissing.

He picked up his glass of wine. "It's nice of her to look out for things here for you."

Obviously, Kelsey thought ruefully, she was the only one caught up in memories of that kiss.

"Yes. She's always been good about helping out," she said, trying for a tone as casual as his had been.

Cruz took a long sip, then looked at her over the rim of his glass. "How long have you known her?"

"A couple of years. I met her...through her son."

Nothing changed in his expression, but she thought he seemed suddenly intent. "Her son?"

"John. He...helped out around here for a while."

Something flashed in his eyes, and Kelsey's pulse took a leap. For an instant, she wondered if he knew, if somehow he had guessed. But he said nothing, only took another sip of wine.

She kept silent, as well, not having the slightest idea what to say. What had happened to the woman who, albeit nervously, had started so many conversations with him before? What had happened to the woman who found herself enjoying their long talks and was surprised when she realized how much time had passed? Had she somehow vanished, wiped out of existence by one simple kiss?

She nearly laughed at her own thought. One *simple* kiss? Whatever else that had been, it hadn't been simple. At least not for her. She wanted to ask him why he'd done it, but she was seized with the fear that he would just look at her blankly and say, "What?"

He finished his wine and set down the glass, then just looked at her for a moment. She wasn't looking back, but she could feel his gaze just the same. Finally he stood up.

"Let's clean this up and go for a walk."

She hesitated, but it seemed harmless enough. In a few minutes, they had loaded the dishes into the big heavy-duty dishwasher she'd installed with her first profits and were headed outside.

It was a beautiful summer night, the kind that made her thankful to be living here, warm enough for just the shorts and T-shirt she'd put on after her shower. She wasn't surprised when he headed up the hill toward the pond; he'd always had a liking for the place, second only to the big tree. And on a night like tonight, clear and warm, it was her favorite spot, as well.

But as she sat down, her back against the boulder that still held some of the sun's warmth, as she sat there looking at Cruz, who was sitting beside her staring at the mirrorlike surface of the pond, his dark hair gleaming in the light from the half-moon that was nicely centered in the big oval of water, she wondered if this was really such a wise idea. She'd never been one for torturing herself, and this certainly seemed to be that.

A breeze kicked up, rippling the surface of the pond until the moon's reflection looked corrugated, and ruffling Cruz's hair, pushing it down over his forehead. Her fingers curled with the need to reach out and push it back, not because she didn't like it where it was, because she did, but because she wanted more than anything to feel the soft thickness of it again. She remembered how it had felt, warm and silken.

There had been something incredibly and unexpectedly intimate about threading her fingers through his hair. She'd never felt such feelings before, had never thought of such an act as intimate before, but somehow, with Cruz, it had been.

Or maybe it was just that with Cruz, her erotic imagination seemed to be working overtime, she thought wryly.

Not that there had been anything she could imagine about that kiss that would make it any hotter than it had really been.

Slowly, as if aware of her gaze, he turned. Her instinct was to avert her eyes, but a new sense of recklessness made her keep looking at him. He was such an anachronism, the manner and solid goodness of the proverbial boy next door, wrapped in a package that played havoc with female senses. In the moonlight, she saw his eyes widen, saw his lips part as if for breath. Those lips that had been so firm, so warm, so incredibly coaxing, making her feel things she'd never felt, making her want to feel more.

She wondered if what she was thinking was showing in her face, because he swallowed visibly.

"Kelsey," he whispered, and the husky note in his voice as he said her name exactly matched the wild yearning that had sprung to life within her.

"Yes," she said. It was the only thing she *could* say.

And then she was in his arms, wondering that she'd felt the night warm enough; it felt no less than chilly now, compared to his heat. His mouth found hers quickly, and his kiss was urgent, as if he, too, had been haunted by memories of this afternoon.

She had thought knowing what to expect would lessen the impact, but she knew in the first instant his tongue traced her lips that it was in fact the opposite; as if trained now, her senses came to life even more swiftly. With a soft moan, she opened to him, knowing the fire that would leap through her, welcoming it, wanting the taste of him. When he probed forward, she met his tongue with her own, dancing, tasting. She trembled, feeling like the breeze-rippled pond, helpless to do anything but move before the onslaught.

And move she did, in a way she was barely conscious of,

pressing herself against him, grasping at his shoulders with fingers rigid with the effort to get closer. He shifted then, pulling her down to the soft grass beside the pond, still green here, by the water's edge. She didn't fight him, never even thought of resisting; how could she think, when every nerve in her body seemed to be crying out, "At last?"

They were such simple things, really, why had she never realized how wonderful they could be? The heat of two bodies in the night air, the softness of the grass beneath them, the feel of being held so tightly, the thrilling sensation of being pressed against a strong yet gentle man from head to toe... They were swamping her with sensations, so many at once that she could not sort them out, nor did she even want to try. They all added up to just one thing, anyway. Cruz.

It was he who made the difference, he who was making this happen. She knew that as surely as she knew no summer night had ever smelled this sweet, no summer grass had ever been so soft. Because no man had ever made her feel like this.

He shifted his weight then, leaning farther over her. He never broke the kiss, in fact, he deepened it. Then, to her dismay, he drew back, leaving her longing for more. He flicked his tongue over her lips, then drew back again. And then he did it again.

Belatedly she recognized the invitation. She hesitated, but her sense of loss overpowered her shyness, and tentatively she tasted his lips in turn. She felt him tense, as if waiting. She went further, tracing the even line of his teeth. Teasingly, he let the tip of his tongue brush lightly over hers, then drew back. She followed, without thought, aware only that the hot, male taste of him was intoxicating and she wanted more.

It went on and on, that hot, probing kiss, so consuming that Kelsey was barely aware of his hands sliding down her body and then back up with painful slowness, as if he were tracing her, as if he wanted to be able to recognize her in the dark.

That thought sent a little shock through her, but it was instantly vanquished by the heat that swelled from beneath his hand as he gently cupped her breast. Helplessly, she arched toward him, quivering at the feel of her own soft flesh pressing harder into his palm. She heard him make a low sound, not quite a groan.

His hand moved, his fingers shifting, brushing over her already taut nipple. A sudden, electric jolt shot through her, arcing from the instantly hardened peak he had caressed to some deep, hidden place inside her. She nearly cried out, and when he did it again, she did. She cried out his name in a voice she barely recognized as her own, it was so full of hunger and need.

Through the soft knit of her shirt he caught the rigid peak between his fingers, rolling it gently. Fire burst through her, careening downward inside her until it seemed to gather in that low, deep place. Her body seemed out of her control, shivering beneath his touch.

Breaking that burning kiss at last, he lowered his mouth to her throat, his lips nibbling gently. He muttered something that sounded like her name, and she felt the vibration of it against skin she had never before realized was so sensitive.

Vaguely she felt an odd tugging, but only when she felt the searing touch of his hand on the bare skin of her stomach did she realize he'd pulled her shirt loose to free her for a more direct caress. She thought maybe she should protest, maybe even stop him, but as he moved with delicate care upward, the thought of that strong, hot male hand on her breast made her gasp with anticipation instead.

The feel of his fingers stroking that soft curve made her choke off her gasp. When he slipped inside the lacy cup of her bra to let her nestle gently against his palm, she couldn't remember how to take in the air she suddenly needed so desperately. And when he pushed her shirt up to repeat the earlier caress of a nipple that was now achingly eager for it, when she felt the gentle tugging of his fingers directly on that tight, tingling flesh, she let out what little breath she had in a near-strangled sob.

He shifted again, over her this time, and when he settled down against her, she became vividly aware of two things:

that she very much liked the feel of his weight, and that he was utterly and completely aroused. Both thoughts barely had time to register, because Cruz gently lifted her breast free of her bra and lowered his mouth to her nipple.

Kelsey gasped, then cried out as he caught that now incredibly sensitized flesh between his lips and flicked at it with his tongue. She went rigid, then arched again, thrusting herself up to him, silently begging him for more. He acknowledged her plea by drawing her into his mouth and suckling deeply, until she was moaning aloud and clutching his head to her, fearing he would leave her, when she needed more, so much more.

She'd never had an experience like this. Her only two relationships that had lasted long enough to reach the point of sex—a length of time that had ended several others—had been…almost businesslike compared to this. Conservative. A discussion, a decision, a bed and lights-out. All the standard conventions.

And none of the wildness she was feeling now, outside, on the grass, in the moonlight, a sea breeze brushing over her naked skin, and a man's—no, *this* man's—mouth hot and wet upon her.

Involuntarily her hips shifted, pressing upward. She felt the swollen, hard pressure of him against her belly in the same moment she heard his breath hiss out in a rush. He moved in turn, pushing against her, his rigid flesh caught between them. She felt a shudder go through him and thrilled to it. She wasn't alone; no matter what the reason, in this moment he wanted her.

He shifted his weight once more, and she almost cried out at the loss when he left her breast. She felt a chill beyond expectation and realized it was the faint breeze on the wet, aching nipple he'd aroused to a tightness she'd never known. But a new heat rocketed through her when he took her hand and pulled it between them, pressing it against the swollen flesh behind the zipper of his jeans.

The denim was soft and worn, and she could feel the whole hot length and thickness of him, could feel every contour beneath the cloth. Tentatively, for her experience did not include this, either, she traced those contours, then, when his breathing quickened audibly and he pushed himself against her palm, she caressed him more confidently.

"Yes," he gasped out. "Don't stop, Kelsey. Please."

The sound of his husky words gave voice to the roiling sensations inside her. She caressed him again, feeling an echoing shudder in herself when she felt him respond.

And then his hands were moving again, pulling at her clothing, his fingers trembling in a way that made Kelsey feel an unaccustomed spurt of power; was it truly possible that *she* had made him feel this way?

He fumbled with her bra for a moment, and inanely she wondered if he would figure out the fastening. Silly, he'd been married, he had to know about women's underwear.

He'd been married.

Sooner or later, Cruz, you're going to have to deal with it. It may be in the past, but you haven't let go of it yet.

Kit's words, and Cruz's far-too-vehement reaction when she'd reminded him of them, echoed in her mind, clear in a way nothing had been since the moment he kissed her. And for the first time since he'd taken her in his arms here by the pond, her brain kicked in.

"Cruz, stop."

The catch on her bra let go in that instant, and he cupped her breasts and buried his face between them, kissing her soft curves eagerly.

"Cruz," she repeated, more urgently this time, knowing that if she let him continue she would be lost, there was no way she could resist the kind of feelings he roused in her.

Slowly he lifted his head to look at her. She saw him try to slow his rapid panting, try to suppress a shiver.

"I..." She had to swallow before she could go on. "You said you knew...I wasn't ready...."

"I did." He shuddered. "Fool that I am, I even meant it."

"Good."

He winced. "Thanks."

Her eyes widened. "I didn't mean... I just..." She floundered, looking miserable. Then she tried again. "What Kit said... I think she was right. You have some things to deal with, about Ellen, and her leaving, before you...get involved with anyone else."

She saw his jaw tighten as he looked down at her. She could almost feel him decide to ignore the part of what she'd said that he didn't want to deal with. "Is that what I'm doing, Kelsey? Getting involved?"

It took all her nerve to do it, but she held his gaze.

"You're...dodging the issue."

He went very still. Slowly the passionate heat faded from his eyes. With sharp, jerky motions utterly unlike his usual grace, he rolled off of her. He scrambled to his feet and walked away without a word.

Chapter 15

"Tell me something, Cruz."

Her voice stopped him in his tracks, although he didn't turn around to look at her. He didn't dare; he was still achingly hard, and just looking at her, there in the moonlight, her lips swollen from his kisses, her breast still wet from his mouth, would be more than he could walk away from.

"How can a man brave enough to risk his life to disarm a bomb to save total strangers be so afraid of his own feelings?"

He went rigid.

"How long are you going to hide from it? How long are you going to let it fester?"

He whirled on her then. She'd pulled her T-shirt down and risen to her feet. He glared at her. He'd heard all this before. The department shrink had said it. Kit had said it. Even Chief de los Reyes had told him, in the most tactful of ways.

But somehow, it had never stung like this. It had never felt so much like a goad, like a jab so pointed he couldn't ignore it any longer.

It had never come from Kelsey before.

"You don't know the first damn thing about it." He ground out the words.

"No," she admitted, walking toward him; he had to make a conscious effort not to back away, a fact that only added to his agitation. She came to a halt before him. "But I know about loss and pain, and about being hurt by the people you should be able to trust most. And I know about being helpless, Cruz. And that that's how you must have felt, with no one to really blame for the destruction of your life."

"It wasn't anyone's fault," he said, wondering how many times he'd said it and thought it in the past six years.

"That doesn't take away the need to blame somebody or something, even if it's only fate. Because if you can't do that, then the only thing left is to blame yourself."

"It wasn't anyone's fault." He was starting to sound like an idiot, chanting those stupid words over and over.

She looked up at him, her gaze level and unwavering. "Are you saying you never wanted to blame someone, you never shouted at God for letting it happen, you never screamed at the fate that took your own life out of your hands and shattered it?"

He'd wanted to do all those things. Every last one of them. And it had nearly killed him not to.

"Sam," he whispered. "I couldn't... I didn't want Sam to hate her own mother."

"Of course not. But what about you, Cruz? When you were alone, did you ever let it out? Did you ever give yourself permission to be angry?"

"At who?" It exploded from him in a shout. "At Ellie? Because she nearly died and got scared into feeling like she had missed out on life, being a wife and mother so young? How the hell do you blame someone for that?"

"Hating the decision someone makes doesn't mean you hate the person."

She said it so quietly, so reasonably, that it prodded him over the edge.

"What are you, some kind of armchair psychologist? Do

you get a kick out of probing old scars to see if you can make them bleed?''

"Scars mean the wound has healed," Kelsey said, standing up to his anger unflinchingly, the only sign that she was even aware he was yelling a slight tightness around her mouth and eyes. "Yours never have, Cruz. Because you never allowed yourself what you had every right to. Anger. Your life was snatched away, through no fault of your own, and you couldn't do a thing to stop it. Why on earth *shouldn't* you be angry?"

You amaze me, Cruz. I'd be furious, but you're so... accepting. Lacey Buckhart's words, spoken long ago.

It's just not natural, Gregerson. I know you loved her. You can't be that blasé about it. Kit Walker, with her too-perceptive observations.

Until you face the loss, it will always be with you. Chief de los Reyes, speaking from painful personal knowledge; the whole department knew how devastated he'd been when his beloved wife died several years ago.

Kelsey's words weren't so different, were they? *Did you ever give yourself permission to be angry? Your life was snatched away, through no fault of your own, and you couldn't do a thing to stop it. Why on earth shouldn't you be angry?*

But her words were different, somehow. In all their attempts to console him, or counsel him, no one had ever made the simple statement that he had a right, a need, to be angry. His friends had wondered why he wasn't, although they'd all said they understood how he felt, agreed that it was really no one's fault. Some had even praised him for his generous, level outlook. A few who weren't really friends but felt compelled to stick their noses in anyway marveled—some in an almost accusatory manner—that he hadn't, as was typical with too many cops, plunged into a binge of drinking and carousing.

But no one had ever simply suggested that he *should* be angry, that it was a permission he should have granted himself. Just the idea was causing an odd turmoil within him. He'd felt something like it before, often, but he'd always written it off as just nagging, unpleasant memories. But now, in the wake of Kelsey's quiet words, he began to realize it was more in the nature of unfinished business.

"You held it in to protect Sam," Kelsey said softly, "and that's a good thing. She'd already lost a parent, and I know…that's traumatic. You needed to be strong, for her sake. But that doesn't make it go away. Sooner or later, it has to come out."

"You're sure of a lot of things," Cruz said, his voice tight under the pressure of resurgent memories.

"I'm sorry," Kelsey said, sounding suddenly very weary. "You're right. It's none of my business. I'm going to bed."

As she started to walk past him, Cruz had the sudden thought that, considering what they'd almost done here tonight, it was perhaps more her business than anyone's except his own. His hand even moved, as if of its own volition, to reach out and stop her.

But he didn't. He couldn't, sensing that he was on the edge right now; one more bit of emotional strain and he would lose it. He never had, and he didn't want the first time to be here, in front of her.

So instead he stood there and watched her walk back to the inn. He watched until she stepped in through a small side door that he knew somewhat vaguely led to a storeroom of some sort, where she kept extra linens and cleaning supplies, and also gardening supplies, hence the outside and inside doors. She'd said something about the latch sticking, and he'd meant to look at it, he thought vaguely, knowing he was looking for a distraction.

He watched until a light came on in the downstairs corner room that he knew was hers. A few minutes later, it went out. And still he stood staring, until he realized what he was doing. Then he forced himself to turn away from the building, trying not to be touched by the fact that whatever had passed between them, she'd still thought to leave the outside light on for him so that he could get in easily when he came back.

He needed to talk to her about that, he thought, seizing on anything to keep from dealing with what was uppermost in his mind. She really wasn't as diligent about keeping things locked as she should be. True, she was secluded and somewhat isolated up here on the hill, but that didn't mean it was safe to leave the place open at night. Of course, she was running an inn, so he supposed she was used to leaving things open for her guests to come and go as they pleased.

Or maybe it was for the kids she was apparently running some sort of halfway house for? Maybe they were the reason she left doors open too often for his comfort? Once they heard about her via the runaways' rather effective grapevine, did those who were willing to abide by her rules just show up? Did she just wake up in the morning and find one sitting on the doorstep or in the kitchen? And then what did she do? Try to broker some kind of peace between the kids and whatever had driven them from home?

He stared at the reflection of the moon in the pond, watched as it dimpled when another bit of breeze rippled the surface.

He knew perfectly well that he was doing exactly what she'd said, hiding from the real issue. He didn't like admitting it, but his grabbing at anything else to think about was too obvious to deny.

He turned on his heel and started walking, not sure where he was going, but choosing the uphill path because it would require more effort.

Still looking for distractions, eh, Gregerson? he muttered to himself.

He walked on anyway, hating the fact that although he was physically weary, his mind just wouldn't shut down. He'd thought he'd perfected the knack of shoving some thoughts aside; it was something cops had to learn or they would go nuts in the first year. But the talent had certainly vanished now; no matter how he tried, he couldn't shove this aside.

About a hundred feet past the pond, he reached a level spot, where a gravel road that came in from the south led farther up the hill, to a luxurious home that no doubt had been built by some wealthy refugee from the big city; it had that look. Cruz turned his back on it, the gravel crunching beneath his feet as he moved, much preferring the view across the pond to the tidy, much smaller and cozier Oak Tree. Whatever else was going on, Kelsey had made a good place here.

The pond looked like an oval mirror from here, polished and smooth now, reflecting that half-moon. There was enough light for him to make out the boulder…and the grassy patch where, just minutes before, he and Kelsey had lain.

Heat bubbled up in him, and he groaned; he couldn't take this roller-coaster ride much longer.

Without really thinking about it, he bent and picked up a piece of gravel from the road. He tossed it in the air and caught it a couple of times, staring at the pond. He gauged the distance, the trajectory and then the weight of the stone. Maybe, he thought. He gave a half shrug and threw the stone.

It fell short. He picked up another stone and tried again, giving it more power this time. Still short.

A heavier stone this time, and a little more oomph. And the satisfaction of hitting the edge of the water, hearing the faint plop and seeing the ripples spread.

Not quite a bull's-eye, which would be the moon's reflection, he thought, but a start. He bent for another stone.

And then another. And another. And another.

He didn't know at what point it ceased to be some silly game, at what moment hitting that silver half disk was no longer the point. He only knew that suddenly it had nothing to do with distractions or games or hitting some stupid target and had everything to do with the very thing he'd been avoiding, the very thing that had been building inside him, relentless and painful.

His motions quickened, the movement of picking up the rocks secondary to putting everything he had into the throw. He was sweating now, breathing hard, yet he didn't slacken, even when his throws became wilder. It didn't matter; he wasn't paying any attention to where the stones were landing or to the again-smooth surface of the pond. All that mattered was the throwing, the fierce exertion, the release of that awful pressure.…

And then he realized he was swearing, low and harsh and angry, with each throw. He tried to stop, but he couldn't. With every fierce motion, every cycle of putting his entire body into the effort of propelling that stone as far as possible, he swore, at the driver of the car that had caused the accident, at Ellie for not finding him and Sam to be enough and then for dying before he could tell her how angry and hurt he was, and then at fate and God for letting it happen, and finally at himself for being so damned helpless to do anything, he who had always, *always,* been able to do *something.*

Finally, exhausted, he dropped to his knees, fists clenched and pounding on the muscles of his thighs, his head turned up to that half-moon. In that moment he felt a primitive kinship to the animals who howled at night and wished he could howl out his loneliness and pain.

And it wasn't until the breeze kicked up once more, sending cooling tendrils across his wet cheeks, that he realized he was crying.

She'd expected him to look a bit weary; she'd heard him come back in, long after she left him by the pond. In fact, she hadn't been at all sure he would still be there, except that they'd left her car at his house, and she knew he wouldn't leave her stranded without it. She hadn't been surprised when it was late morning before he came into the kitchen, rubbing at eyes that probably felt as weary as they looked.

She wondered what she'd started with her impulsive words last night. After she left him, she'd heard some odd plopping sounds that had made her sit up in bed, wondering. She'd gone to her window and seen him up on the hill. It had taken a moment for her to figure out what he was doing, but when she did, she'd smiled. Until the intensity, the fierceness, of his movements got through to her, and her amusement was replaced by concern.

After a minute or two, she'd thought about going out to make sure he was all right. Then she'd heard the low, harsh string of curses and thought better of it. She'd felt a twinge of guilt for having prodded him into what appeared to be a fury of some sort and crept back to bed, wishing she'd kept her mouth shut.

She didn't know what had possessed her to talk to him like that, anyway. She had treated him like one of the kids, who not only needed help to understand their own feelings, but who needed help in confronting the fact that they even had them. Cruz was many things, but he was not a kid. He was a man, with a man's pride, and a man's emotions...and a man's passions.

She suppressed a shiver. And now, looking at the dark circles that shadowed his eyes, she wished even more that she'd kept out of it, that she'd kept her ridiculous urge to save him from himself under control.

She poured him a cup of coffee, and he took it with a brusque "Thank you" that made her cringe inwardly. She really had trespassed, trod upon things she had no right to even touch. She thought about apologizing, but had the sinking feeling it would only make things worse.

"I thought I'd go see Melissa's parents this afternoon," he said mildly, as if last night hadn't happened at all, "since I'm already an hour closer to them here."

Kelsey didn't know whether to feel relieved or upset that not only was he apparently not going to bring up her ill-advised attempts at counseling, but he was avoiding what had passed between them before as well. She told herself that she should be grateful, she didn't really want to talk about how close they had come to doing something neither of them was ready for, but she wasn't sure she was convinced.

Cruz, on the other hand, seemed to have made the decision easily; he was going to ignore it. And he clearly intended to go on with the search as if those passionate moments on the grass by the pond had never happened.

Or as if they meant nothing.

Maybe they didn't—to him. But it would be a very long time before she ever forgot the feel of his arms around her, the taste of his kiss, the sensation of his mouth at her breast....

She set her own coffee cup down with a thud.

"I gather," she said, doing some hasty collecting of her thoughts as she spoke, "that you got their address from the report your friend got?"

He nodded, taking a sip of the steaming coffee as calmly as if those wild moments of hurling stones and cursing to the skies had been merely a bad dream. "They live just north of Oxnard. It'll be a long drive, but I might learn something that'll help."

"All right." She managed to keep her voice even, as if she were no more thinking about last night—any of it—than he was. She should simply be glad he wasn't giving up on Melissa because of her own imprudent interference in his personal life. "We can leave as soon as I call Dolores—"

"Not we. Me."

Kelsey paled. Apparently he *was* thinking about last night. And she'd been right to think she'd trespassed.

"Look, I know I...offended you last night, but—"

"This has nothing to do with that."

Blast him, how could he sound so calm, when her insides were churning madly? She fought to hang on to an even tone. "Then I'm coming with you."

His jaw tightened a fraction, and for the first time she wondered if perhaps he wasn't quite as calm as she'd thought.

"It would be better if I did this alone."

"Melissa came to *me* for help. I'm responsible."

He looked at her for a long, silent moment before saying softly, "You can't save them all, Kelsey."

She flushed; that was too close to her earlier thoughts for her own comfort.

"I'm still going with you," she said, resorting to the stubbornness that had sometimes gotten her through when all else failed.

"Kelsey, I'm trying to keep you out of this, but—"

The way he cut off his own words bothered her as much as the words themselves. He was trying to keep her out of this? She searched his face, looking for some sign that he knew what was going on at Oak Tree. Some sign that he knew that Melissa was only the latest—

Her own thought was cut off by a memory.

Did she tell you she ripped off her folks when she left?

His biting question echoed in her mind. Was that what he

meant, that she'd known Melissa had committed a theft and
helped her anyway? That had to be it. Although she'd never
really admitted she'd known about the things Melissa had
stolen, Cruz was too adept at such things not to have seen
the knowledge in her face. Harboring a runaway was one
thing, but a thief was something else, she supposed. At least
to a cop, who no doubt wouldn't care that Melissa had had
reasons for what she did. That, he would say, is not the business of the police.

But she couldn't quite believe it of him, that he would be
so coldhearted about a frightened, pregnant girl. But then his
answer to her own question came back to her.

*Sometimes you wish you could do more, but the laws won't
let you. Sometimes you wish you didn't have to do something,
but the laws won't let you not do it.*

She bit her lip, looking away from him. Would he really?
If they found Melissa, would he just hand her back, to vanish
into the convoluted, unwieldy and sometimes apathetic juvenile justice system?

And then it hit her, the other significance of what he'd said.
He was trying to keep her out of it? He knew that she knew
what Melissa had done, yet he was still trying to…protect
her? Even, perhaps, risking trouble for himself?

The thought made her eyes widen, and her gaze shot back
to his face. For an instant, she thought she saw something
there, some warmth, even a memory of the heat they'd shared
last night. She wanted to ask, but the heart that hadn't risked
in so long quailed at the thought of what his answer would
be, of how humiliated she would feel if she was being, as she
must be, an utter fool to even think he might be doing it
because he…cared. Not that she didn't believe Cruz more
than capable of caring, five minutes of watching him with his
little girl proved that. It was the idea that he would care
enough about *her* to risk some kind of reprimand or censure
that was ridiculous.

No, she couldn't ask. But she could make sure that censure
didn't happen in another way, without giving away her fool-

ish thoughts, and all she had to do was insist on what she wanted to do anyway.

"That doesn't matter," she said firmly. "All I can think about is how scared she must be. I have to keep looking for her."

"Even though she lied to you?"

"She did," Kelsey said, "but that baby didn't."

She knew she saw it then, some sort of softness and warmth in his eyes. Very slowly, he nodded. "Good point, Ms. Hall. Let's go."

She was a little bewildered by how quickly he'd relented; she was used to having to fight much harder, and not always winning. But a few minutes later she was again in the passenger seat of his big four-wheel-drive and they were headed north.

She sat in silence for a long time, trying to think about what to say to Melissa's parents, wondering if there was any point in trying to communicate with the couple the girl had described as cruel and narrow-minded. But at the same time, she was all too aware of the man behind the wheel, and all too full of whirling memories of the passion he had evoked in her.

"Kelsey?"

She nearly jumped; he'd been as silent as she for miles, allowing her to sink deeper and deeper into memories that were too strong to fight off, although she had tried, cursing herself for a fool for every moment she spent dwelling on them. She glanced at him; he seemed intent on the road, and it was easier for her to answer because he wasn't looking at her.

"Yes?" she managed after a moment.

"Last night," he began, and her breath caught. He was going to say it had been a mistake, he never should have kissed her, let alone anything else. He was going to take those hot, erotic memories she'd been swimming in and douse them with the icy water of retreat. And suddenly the memories she'd been fighting against became precious to her; she searched for the words to stop him, but before she could think of a thing, he went on.

"You didn't offend me. I'm sorry I…yelled. I… You were right."

"I…was?"

"Yes. I needed to…be angry. I *was* angry. I just never…let it out. Until last night."

She let out a long, slow breath. She supposed, of the things he could have brought up about last night, this was the less dangerous. To her, at least. She studied his profile for a moment, thinking that never had two races blended so beautifully as they had in Cruz Gregerson.

"I'm…glad you're not angry with me," she said finally. "I know I…overstepped."

"No." He said it quickly, but without heat. "With all the advice I got when she left, all the people who…tried to help, nobody ever told me I had…the right to be angry. Even though it wasn't anyone's fault."

"Anger is usually…a fairly directed emotion. When there's no one thing or person to direct it at, it's worse. It becomes sort of wild, going in all directions. And that's scary."

He glanced at her. "You're…a wise woman, Kelsey."

She nearly laughed. Wise? Her? Sometimes she felt as if she barely knew anything, especially when trying to deal with a kid like Melissa.

"I had people always telling me I was…handling it so well," Cruz went on, "when really I wasn't handling it at all. I told myself I kept it buried for Sam's sake, but maybe I just didn't want to face it. Even though I understood why, at the time it…hurt that Sam and I weren't enough for her."

Kelsey felt a painful tug deep inside at the quiet admission of pain, even long ago. "Maybe…" she began tentatively, hesitant to say anymore than she already had, yet not able to just let it go. "Maybe nothing would have been enough."

"I know that." He gave her a quick sideways look before turning his attention back to the road. "I knew it even then."

"But it still hurt. Both of you."

"I tried to keep it from affecting Sam too much." His

mouth quirked. "But she's so...solemn, sometimes, so serious. Especially about her animals. She seems...driven or something."

"She's a very bright child," Kelsey said. "And she cares a great deal about things."

"I know. That was part of the problem. I knew she understood more than some people gave her credit for, when Ellen left, even though she was only four. So I tried to make her feel...as secure as I could manage. But I think I went a bit too far."

"Too far?"

He shrugged. "I let her get away with too much, back then, because I hated fighting with her. I think I was...afraid of losing her, too."

It was such a simple yet poignant admission of parental love that Kelsey felt a rush of emotions, a tangle she couldn't quite sort out. Then she chastised herself silently; she might not have known the kind of love Cruz and Samantha had, but she'd learned something else just as valuable; that that kind of love didn't necessarily have to involve blood ties.

"You'll never lose her, Cruz. Not completely. She'll grow up and away, naturally, but you'll never lose her."

"I hope you're right." He gave her another sideways glance. "I don't ever want to be doing this for her."

"Just keep talking to her," she said softly. "But more important, don't ever stop listening. And believing in what she tells you."

He glanced at the road, then back at her. "Is that what happened to you, Kelsey?" he asked softly. "You talked, but nobody believed you?"

She felt herself pale, felt the rush of a chill sweep over her. *He's a cop,* she told herself. *He's a cop, and he's smart. He's just making a lucky guess. He doesn't know anything.*

"Let's just deal with Melissa," she said, refusing to meet his gaze.

She was afraid he would push, and he had every right to, as much as he'd shared with her, but he said nothing. And she was seized with the irrational urge to pour it all out to him, the whole ugly story, something she'd never done in her life.

Cruz Gregerson had a dangerous effect on her, she thought, in more ways than one.

But she couldn't quite quash the thought that if she was to let it all out, he would understand.

And that, perhaps, was the most dangerous effect of all.

Chapter 16

"It's all our fault," Mrs. Bargman wailed. "If we hadn't—"

"Stop it, Connie," her husband said sharply. "Melissa is as much to blame as we are. More. She's the one who kept seeing that punk after I ordered her not to. And look what happened."

"But she's just a child—"

"She's old enough to let herself get pregnant, isn't she?"

Last time he'd checked, Cruz thought, it took two to manage that. But he kept his thoughts to himself; further annoying the already aggravated man would accomplish nothing. Not that they were accomplishing anything, anyway; these people knew so little about their own child that it was grimly depressing. They didn't know who her friends were, what her interests were, beyond "damn loud music," had no idea where she might have gone.

He leaned against the back of the chair, thinking he was going to be paying for days for that excess of exertion he'd indulged in last night.

"Edward, please, don't. We've been through all this."

"I said that she could come home, didn't I? But she can't keep the brat. That's out of the question. I've been embarrassed enough as it is, without having to put up with that."

"Surely that doesn't matter now?" Kelsey suggested gently. "The main thing is to find Melissa safe and sound, and then the rest can be dealt with."

They had told the Bargmans the minimum, a variation on the truth, that Kelsey had seen the girl and Cruz had offered to help. They didn't ask why a Trinity West cop would be involved, and Cruz hadn't volunteered an explanation. He wasn't sure he knew, anyway.

"Easy for you to say," Bargman said to Kelsey, his voice quivering with indignation. "You didn't have that punk busting into your house, waving around a knife and threatening you."

Cruz straightened up. "When did this happen?"

"Just this morning. He accused us of hiding her."

"What happened?"

Bargman's mouth tightened. "He searched the house. When he saw she wasn't here, he left. I called the police, and they came, but they weren't much use," he said, giving Cruz a pointed look.

He could imagine, Cruz thought. Domestic problems were the bane of a cop's existence. Everyone expected the police to magically solve in ten minutes family problems that had been years in the building. But at least this explained the man's attitude; it was a common result of having your home invaded and being helpless to stop it. It was frightening, and many men didn't take too well to that, hiding it behind a wall of outrage.

"What else did he say? Where he was going? Where he thought she might be?"

"He just screamed cuss words over and over. Typical. Then he drove off in that yellow car of his, screeching tires and waking up all the neighbors."

Cruz didn't bother to ask for a description of the vehicle; it had been on the supplemental report.

"Anything else?" he asked instead.

"He...threatened Melissa," Mrs. Bargman said quietly. "Said he was going to find her and kill her, so we'd better not try to hide her or help her."

"Bastard." Bargman spit the single word out. "Punk like that won't stop me from taking care of my own daughter."

So there *was* parental concern there, under the anger and the arrogance, Cruz thought. But it was buried deep, and he understood why Melissa hadn't thought it was there at all.

"Please," Mrs. Bargman said, "you're the only ones who have seen her since she ran away. You have to find her."

"We'll do our best," Cruz said.

"If we find her," Kelsey said, "there's no guarantee she'll want to come home. She was...very upset."

Mrs. Bargman sighed. "I'm sure she is. We were just so...shocked when she told us she was pregnant."

"She was always a good girl," Bargman insisted, "until she met this dope freak."

"Please," Mrs. Bargman begged, "bring her home. I'm so worried about her."

Cruz stood up. He was weary of this, and he'd only been here an hour; he could imagine how the girl had felt. "If we find her, we'll try to at least get her to talk to you. You might want to think about what you want to say, if you really want her to come home. I'd guess she'd take some persuading."

"But she's my daughter, and she's a minor," Bargman exclaimed. "You have to bring her back. It's your job!"

Cruz sensed, rather than saw, Kelsey stiffen. He glanced at her and saw that she'd gone very pale. He looked back at Bargman.

"It's not even my jurisdiction," he said, an edge in his voice that was due more to the look on Kelsey's face than to the man's belligerent attitude, even in the face of his daughter's possible danger. "Any agency that finds her can hold her for about six hours at the most."

"But the guy who took the report said if we filed charges against her for grand theft—"

"That," Cruz said, really irritated now, "is between you

and your conscience. Kelsey?'' He gestured toward her, indicating the door. She stood up, still a little white.

''I still want to know why you didn't call the police when you saw her,'' Bargman said, with a suspicious look at Kelsey.

''She'd never seen Melissa before,'' Cruz interjected smoothly. ''How was she to know she was a runaway? And then she was gone again, anyway.''

It wasn't exactly a lie, and at this point he wasn't sure he cared whether he lied to this blustering man or not. Right now, he just wanted Kelsey out of here.

She said nothing as they got in his truck, and nothing as he drove away from this house that was the picture of Middle America on the outside—neatly mowed lawn, flowers in the flower beds, windows glinting in the California sunset—and chaos inside.

When they were out of sight, he let out a pent-up breath. ''Well, they're not quite the monsters you said Melissa painted them as, but they're no prize, either.''

Kelsey said nothing.

''It never stops amazing me how little some parents know about their own kids. Don't they ever listen? I'd like to hear Melissa's version of what happened.''

The silence continued. Kelsey stared at...nothing. Cruz was worried, but he didn't know what to do or say. Finally he decided to just let her alone to work it out; he wasn't sure anything he would say would help anyway.

But when they had been driving for nearly a half hour and Kelsey still hadn't spoken, he pulled off the road into a rest area. She didn't even seem to notice. He turned in his seat and reached out to take her hands; they were like ice.

''Kelsey? Are you all right?''

She stared down at their hands, then, slowly, lifted her gaze to his face. She was staring at him as if she'd never seen him before. Or as if she'd slipped back to another time, a time in which he didn't exist, when nothing existed except the pain that shadowed her eyes.

''God, honey, stop it!'' he exclaimed, fear kicking through

him. "It's all right. He's just a jerk, that's all. And he's not *your* jerk. You don't have to deal with him."

It sounded silly even to him, but her eyes seemed to focus then, just a little.

"He...said that. Those same words. Just like he did."

It took him a second to sort out the pronouns and realize which two *he*s she was talking about. He swore silently, stung by her pain. He didn't know enough, and she didn't trust him enough to tell him the source of her fears. And that hurt in a way he'd never quite known before; somewhere in the past two weeks, Kelsey had become more important to him than he'd realized.

"Kelsey," he whispered, tightening his grip on her hands. "It's all right. You're safe."

He didn't know what else to say. But it seemed to be enough; after a moment she seemed to come back to herself. He felt a spark of admiration when she drew herself up and shook off the ugly memories that had seized her.

"I'm sorry," she began, but he hushed her with a gentle finger across her lips. A bad decision on his part, for the feel of her just reminded him of the well of hot imaginings he'd been living in of late, and of the moments beside the pond when those imaginings had nearly become reality, but when she lowered her eyes in grateful acceptance, he was glad he'd stopped an apology that was hardly necessary.

She drew a deep, long breath, and he saw her shiver as she let it out. He couldn't help himself, he reached out and pulled her against him. To his surprise, she came without resisting, sagging against him, as if too weary to protest.

They sat there for a long time as the last of the sunlight faded and the sky went from pink-and-orange-streaked blue to black.

"That...hasn't happened in a long time," she said at last.

"It's all right," he repeated. Then, trying for a lighter tone, "I can see where he'd bring it on. He's a real...peach."

He couldn't see her face—and he wasn't about to move her from where she was resting her cheek on his shoulder—but he thought he felt her smile.

"Thank you," she said.

"For a weak joke?"

"No. For…getting angry at him. For Melissa."

He opened his mouth, realized what he'd been about to say, and shut it again. Then, as she shifted slightly, resting more of her warm weight against him, he rather recklessly said it anyway.

"If I was mad, it was more about you than about Melissa."

She went very still. "Me?"

"He upset you, and I didn't like it. Or him, at that point. You didn't need that."

"That's…one of the nicest things anyone's ever said to me," she said quietly.

He gave her a swift, hard hug. "If that's true, then you need to hang around better people."

She leaned back then and, for the first time since they'd left the house, met his eyes. "I am," she said.

Cruz blinked. Then, incredibly, he felt himself blush, something that hadn't happened in years.

"I… That was quite a leap for somebody who hated the very thought of cops not too long ago."

"I never really hated cops, only what they…sometimes have to do."

"Even the cops who took you back home?" he asked gently.

"I…"

She shivered and pulled away from him. He hated to let her go, but he sensed this wasn't the time to hold her closer than she wanted to be. He didn't push, didn't speak at all, and after a silent moment a rush of words came from her, not the denial he'd expected but an admission he hadn't dared hope for.

"I did hate them. For a long time I hated them. But I grew up. I saw it wasn't their fault." She shook her head then. "At least, I thought I had. But apparently I was carrying around more of those old feelings than I realized."

Cruz tried not to read too much into the fact that she had

used the past tense, but at the same time he felt a burgeoning of hope deep inside him.

"Things have changed, Kelsey," he said. "Kids have more rights than they used to, and while the system is a long way from perfect, it's a lot more aware that sometimes...home isn't always sweet home."

She sighed wearily. "Mine is. Now. And I'd like to be there."

"Yes, ma'am," he said smartly, snapping off a salute that made her smile, albeit rather weakly.

She lapsed into a silence that lasted the rest of the trip back to the inn, but it wasn't the same; he didn't sense that aura of emotional shock he'd felt from her before.

It was quiet and dark when they arrived back at the inn. Since her car was at his house, at her indication he pulled the truck into the garage. Unlike last night, the evening was chilly, for a California summer, anyway, with a touch of unseasonable fog, and when he offered to start the fire that was already neatly laid on the hearth—Dolores had been here, it seemed, and busy as usual—she nodded silently before disappearing into the kitchen.

When she came back, she was holding two steaming cups. He got up to take one, although he wasn't sure he wanted coffee this late; his sleep had been restless enough lately. Then he smiled when he saw it was hot chocolate. Complete with marshmallow.

"Perfect. Thanks."

"You're welcome."

They were the first words she'd spoken in a long time, and he didn't want her to stop now. She curled up on the sofa, pulling her legs beneath her. He sat down beside her, but not too close, for his own sake as much as for hers.

"Everything all right?" he asked.

She avoided the real intent of his question, choosing to take it much more literally. "That storeroom latch finally broke," she said. "Dolores left a note saying the side door won't lock."

"I'll wedge it shut with something later, and we'll get it fixed in the morning."

Kelsey nodded; then, suddenly, her eyes widened, as if she had only just realized how...domestic that exchange sounded. For a moment she just stared at him, and he could see the flames reflected in her eyes and wished heartily that they were burning on the inside, as well. She looked away from him hastily, toward the fire, and lapsed once more into silence.

For a long time, she just stared at the fire. He sipped at the warming chocolate, watching her, aware of a matching heat from a different source building inside him.

Finally, she looked up at him. "What...do we do now?"

He thought of all the possible answers to that question and quickly decided that the first three that leaped to mind would probably not be advisable to voice right now. She seemed to read the nature of those answers in his face, because he heard her take a quick breath.

"I mean...about Melissa," she stammered.

"I was afraid of that," he muttered under his breath. Then, with a shake of his head, "I don't know how much longer I can keep the lid on this. It may already be blown off, after that stunt Sutter pulled this morning. Mr. Personality may not think he was taken seriously enough, but if the local cops have a brain stem, they'll be taking it very seriously."

"What will happen now?"

His mouth twisted. "The whole thing has shifted. Now they're dealing with a violent offender who's losing his grip. Maybe his crack use is getting worse, which makes him even more unpredictable. They're going to know they need to stop him before he spirals out of control. And since he's looking for Melissa, it's only logical that they'll be hot after her, too."

She was silent for a moment, then, her eyes troubled, she asked, "What will they do when they find out you...knew something and didn't tell them?"

He shrugged. "Depends."

He saw worry creep over her face. "You could...get in trouble, couldn't you?"

Her concern warmed him, but concern wasn't exactly what

he wanted from her right now. "Maybe. Not too much, because at the time I had no idea who the boyfriend was, or how far he'd gone."

"But you knew Melissa had...committed a crime. So did I."

"Running away?" He shook his head. "Not much of a crime, not anymore."

"I meant...the things she stole."

"Oh." He shrugged. "I'm not too worried. Under these circumstances, it's close enough to civil, being family property, crime of opportunity, all that stuff."

"But I thought..." She let her voice trail off.

"You thought what?" he asked softly. "That I'd arrest Melissa and drag her home, and then maybe arrest you as an accessory or something?" She flushed brightly, telling him the accuracy of his guess. "Your ideas about cops are from the child you were, Kelsey. Give me a break, all right?"

She stared up at him, wonder dawning in her eyes. "You should have told the sheriff's office everything right away, but you didn't."

"Letter of the law? Yes, I should have." He lifted one shoulder in a half shrug as he set down his now empty mug beside hers on the coffee table. "But as long as somebody rounds up Sutter before he hurts anybody, I'll be okay. And they probably will, now that they know how far over the line he is."

"Why?"

"Because if they don't, and he hurts somebody—"

"I meant...why didn't you...tell?"

He looked straight at her then. He knew the answer, and maybe it was time she knew, too. "You asked me not to."

"But I didn't even...tell you why."

"I know."

"But you still..."

"Yes."

"Why?" she repeated.

He reached out then, tilting her head back with a gentle finger under her chin. "I think you know why, Kelsey."

He saw her eyes widen again, her lips part, then close again as she bit the lower one, as if to hold back words. He wanted to tell her to say it, whatever it was she was holding back, but he couldn't seem to find enough air to speak. Or the words to say.

So he kissed her instead.

He leaned down and took that soft, warm lower lip she'd been nibbling on and nibbled on it himself, much more gently, salving the mock wounds with a stroke of his tongue. To his surprise, she rose to his kiss urgently, taking his mouth as if she'd been hungering for it as he'd been hungering for hers. It shocked him, thrilled him, sent a blast of heat rocketing through him, so hot and fierce and sudden that he groaned under its strength.

He leaned into her, pressing her back against the cushions of the sofa. She didn't resist, didn't protest, and he felt her uncurl her legs to stretch out beneath him, felt the tingling begin as she was once more pressed full length against him.

He probed deeply with his tongue, savoring the sweetness of her, loving the taste and feel of the intimacy, feeling his body tighten and surge to fullness at the thought of the intimacy that it had been denied for so long. And her welcome only stoked the fires higher and hotter; when she sighed and let her tongue dance with his in a twirling, stroking movement, he felt the shiver down to his toes.

He threaded his fingers through her hair, cupping her head and holding it as he deepened the kiss even more, feeling his pulse kick up one more notch as she seemed to undulate beneath him, her curved, warm body stroking his in one rippling motion. Convulsively he pressed his hips downward, increasing the pressure of his arousal against her belly, and when she lifted herself in response, he nearly gasped aloud.

Then he felt her hands sliding down his back, felt her fingers pressing against his hips, as if to urge him even closer. He shuddered, wishing more than anything to have her do that when they were both naked and he was buried deep inside her.

He did gasp aloud at that thought, and his fingers flexed

involuntarily. As if he'd only now remembered what else they could be doing, he reached to cup her breasts, lifting them slightly, then lowering himself to feel them against his chest. She rewarded him with a tiny sound of pleasure and an arching of her back that pushed her harder against him and made him groan anew. She rubbed herself against him; he felt the softness of her breasts against his chest and filling his hands, and his own flesh hardened even more.

He wanted more, more of those soft little sounds she made. He raised himself slightly, just enough so that his fingers could find her nipples. They were already tight and hard, and this evidence of her arousal made him feel primitively masculine in a way he'd never known before. Perhaps because he knew she was so wary, the fact that she was responding in spite of it fired him beyond resisting.

He plucked at the taut peaks until she made that sound again, and then again, and again. And still it was not enough. He wanted more, he wanted her as hot and needy as he was feeling, wanted to touch and stroke and taste every inch of her, and to have her do it in turn to him, until nothing else mattered.

He'd wanted before, he thought vaguely through the blazing heat, even since Ellie, but it had been a general awareness of need, not this fierce, aching wanting for one single woman. He'd wanted before, but that was a pale, inadequate word for what he was feeling now.

And stopping would be pure hell. But in mere moments it would be even worse. With an effort, he lifted his head.

"Kelsey," he whispered, all too aware of his own rigid flesh caught between them, pressing against her, knowing she had to be aware of it, too. The truth was, he was so hard that if she touched him again right now, even through his jeans, as she had last night, he was sure he would go off like some hormonally poisoned sixteen-year-old.

"If we're stopping, tell me now." His voice was a rasping, harsh sound, but he couldn't help it. "I'm already half out of my mind."

"Stopping?"

She said it thickly, as if she were in the same heated, mind-fogging place he was in. And as if it were the last thing on earth she wanted to do.

And it was certainly the last thing he wanted, yet he felt compelled to make sure, cursing himself all the while for not simply taking her implied answer and granting his body's sole wish.

"You walked away last night." He ground it out. "If you feel the same way—"

"But you're not the same man you were last night," she said softly.

He stared at her. She was looking at him as if she knew exactly what he'd been through last night, as if she knew every step of the battle he'd fought to come to terms with what he'd denied was festering just below the surface for so long. Had she really guessed so much from what little he'd said when he so stumblingly tried to apologize to her for the way he'd shouted and ended up instead spilling things he'd never told anyone?

Or was it simply that she had once walked a similar path herself?

"And I don't think I'm the same woman," she added softly. "You were right. What I thought... I had some old...childhood ideas I was lugging around. I'm sorry I hung them on you. That wasn't fair."

"And now?" he asked, his throat tight.

She smiled, a soft curving of her mouth that managed to be ancient and brand-new, alluring and innocent, welcoming and shy, all at the same time.

"Now," she whispered, "there's nothing at all childlike about what I'm feeling. And I want to go on feeling it."

Cruz closed his eyes and let out a harsh breath of relief.

Then he felt her hands cupping his face, and he opened them again. She was looking up at him, the firelight dancing again in her eyes. But this time it was matched by a glow from within.

Chapter 17

Had she known? Kelsey wondered dazedly. Had her body somehow known it would be like this? Was that why she had been drawn to this man from the first time she saw him, even though she'd never dared act on the feelings?

Somehow she had gotten the idea, from her few brief encounters, that when it came to sex, men were rather...limited in their approach. If they didn't go at it rather wildly, in what she'd always thought a parody of passion, they went at it mechanically, concerned only about their own release. Or if they cared anything about their partner's pleasure, it was almost as mechanical, a sort of duty they felt they had to accomplish before they could move on to their real goal, their own pleasure.

But it had taken only a few minutes with Cruz to convince her that she'd been wrong. Very wrong.

He was tender, unfailingly gentle and considerate. Things she knew little about. But mixed with that was an undeniable edge, an intensity that made her feel, when he looked down at her now, not just as if she were the only woman in the world, but as if it didn't matter that there were millions who were more attractive than she was, that it wouldn't matter if they were lining up at his door, he would still be looking at her in the same way.

She didn't really know when she'd gotten out of her clothes. She was hardly aware of her own nudity, except for the heat that blazed in his eyes when he looked at her, warming her as much as the fire crackling on the hearth. But she was very much aware of his as he stood beside the sofa and shoved off his jeans and briefs. She wished she had the courage to ask him to simply let her look at him; she didn't think she'd ever seen anything quite so beautiful.

And he'd never hesitated when, with a shyness that was almost painful, she mentioned the condoms she kept on hand for when she encountered a runaway whose education in that area had been sadly neglected. He'd simply gone to retrieve the box and then apologized for not thinking of it himself, saying with a sincerity that made her quiver inside that he was long out of practice, words that only thrilled her more; she'd sensed somehow that he was not a man for casual sex, and this proof only made her more certain that she'd chosen the right man to end her own loneliness.

She watched him come back, watched him cross the room in steady, even strides. She'd always known he was strong, known there was great power coiled in his body, but now that she'd glimpsed how beautifully he was put together, how one muscular plane blended so flawlessly into the next, how every part of him melded together to form a tightly knit, perfect whole, she wished she was an artist like him, so that she could capture those strong, powerful lines on paper. All of them, including the most male parts, fully aroused and incredibly potent-looking. For her. That was the most wondrous thing of all, that a man like this wanted her.

But then that body was beside her again, those fine artist's hands moving over her, and she couldn't think at all. He was touching her in ways she'd never been touched, erasing the memories of other, less caring touches. He was caressing her with his hands, then his mouth, in ways that made her see all her past experience for what it was, blind fumbling with men who had been wrong simply because they weren't Cruz.

But the thing that affected her most, the thing that sent her heart racing nearly out of control, that set the blood to hammering in her ears and the heat pooling low and deep and golden inside her, was the barely restrained hunger with which he did it all, as if he'd been waiting as long as she had for this. As if he'd been waiting for her.

It was a heady sensation, and despite the lingering fear that she was a fool to believe in anything so ethereal as this, she cast her reservations aside and let herself dare the rapids; once in her life, she thought amid the whirling sensations, just once, she would take the prize without thought of what would happen tomorrow, without worrying about losing it, without thinking about the pain she would feel when it was gone.

Then his mouth was at her breast again, his tongue teasing her nipple with quick, hot flicks, until she felt as if he'd seared a pathway from that taut peak to the hot place inside her that was crying out its own emptiness. She shivered at the feeling. For her, sex had always been more about closeness than about physical pleasure; she had never literally ached to have a man inside her before. But now it was both; she ached for this man, and the fact thrilled her even as it frightened her.

When he moved over her at last, she barely held back a glad cry. She felt the hot probe of his body seeking hers and surprised herself yet again with the urge to reach down and guide him, to bring him home to her more quickly. But then he did it himself, and she felt the blunt, rigid flesh pressing into her.

He was going too slow, it was driving her mad, and she began to lift herself, to urge him on. But then he stopped altogether, his eyes closed, and a qualm of uncertainty struck her; had he not finally dealt with the ghost of his wife? Was he thinking of her even now?

"Cruz," she said, urgently, before she could stop herself.

His eyes came open. "I'm...sorry, Kelsey. It's just that... it's been a very long time for me, and I...want you so much...."

There was no trace of haunted memory in his eyes and nothing less than raging hunger in his voice. Joy surged through Kelsey in a swell that washed away her last remaining apprehensions.

"I want you, too," she whispered, letting her hands slide down his back, slowly, until she reached his narrow hips and exerted a gentle pressure, urging him closer, urging him to complete the joining her body was screaming for.

He groaned, and his head lolled back, the cords of his neck standing out strongly. "God, I've wanted you to do that, now, when we're like this...."

Then he pressed forward, sliding into her in one long, smooth motion, until his hips were tight against her. The ease of it told Kelsey just how ready she was, for it was an exquisitely tight fit, yet there was no pain, only a marvelous sensation of stretching and fullness. And the empty place she'd only now realized existed was filled, and she knew in that instant that only this man could ever fill it.

He began to move, slowly, measuring his length in her again and again. Kelsey rose to meet him, moaning his name when he surged into the depths of her and nearly crying out at the loss when he withdrew. When she realized, by the tension that strung his lean body wire-tight, by the sweat beading up on his forehead and the trembling in his arms as he braced himself over her, that he was forcing himself to go slowly, much more slowly than he wanted to, she clutched at him again.

In her urgency, her hands had slipped downward, and she realized her fingers were digging into the taut muscles of his buttocks. Embarrassed even as she realized that embarrassment in these circumstances was absurd, she started to move her hands. But in that same instant Cruz hissed out a "Yesss!" even as the muscles beneath her hands flexed as he drove himself deeper and harder into her, exactly what she'd wanted but been unable to voice.

She cried out his name, and he stopped. "No!" she protested.

"Not...too rough?" He ground out the question between harsh breaths.

"No," she panted. "More. Please."

She felt him shudder. "Ahhh, Kelsey," he said. And then he was moving, harder, faster, driving her upward with each stroke, sending sizzling fire along her every nerve, until she was marveling at their capacity to carry so much incredible sensation. She'd become someone she didn't know, a wild, wanting person, conscious only of her own body and the man who was causing such sweet havoc.

She fairly writhed beneath him, and the fact that her every move wrung a throttled groan of pleasure from him only fired her more, and she urged him closer and lifted herself to him eagerly, fervently, until she was no longer sure of the boundaries between them.

She heard an odd sound, a voice, pleading...and realized it was her own. She twisted her shoulders, her hips, tightened her arms, her legs around him, striving, reaching.

"Kelsey, I...can't... It's too much...."

He drove into her hard and deep, then went rigid in her arms. His body bowed back, every powerful muscle taut, sweat sheening his golden skin, his face taut with pleasure. Kelsey had a split second to look at him, to marvel at the sheer male beauty of him in that moment of racking intensity.

And then the last shift of his body, his hoarse cry of her name, sent her careening wildly over the edge. It burst through her, heat and light and pulses of pure, sweet sensation and a pleasure she'd never known before, of feeling her own body squeeze and caress the male flesh inside it, as if welcoming home a part of her that had been missing for so very long.

She moaned his name again and again as the spasms went on, and as her body clenched around him, so did her arms and her legs; she clung to him tightly as the blissful waves rocked her. Only when they at last began to ebb did she realize he was holding her just as tightly, his face buried in the curve of her neck, his breath coming in harsh, rapid pants against her ear.

She felt a shudder ripple through him, and it made her hold him even tighter, grateful in a way she didn't quite understand at this evidence that it had been as powerful for him as it had for her.

Gradually his breathing slowed, and Kelsey felt the hammering of her heart retreat to a more normal level. She didn't move, was afraid to speak; she wanted this moment, with his body still inside hers, with his weight atop her an oddly comforting thing, to go on forever. She didn't know what to say, anyway; words seemed inadequate for what had just happened.

Cruz didn't move, either, for several long, silent moments. Then, at last, he shifted slightly, as if to ease his weight to one side, off her. Instinctively she tightened her arms, trying to keep him where he was. He stayed. And at last he lifted his head.

"I...don't have anything clever to say," he said quietly, looking a little uneasy.

"Neither do I," Kelsey admitted with a shy smile.

The smile, or her words, seemed to assuage his unease, for he smiled back at her, slowly, like the sun coming up over the hills.

"I don't think there are...any words for what that was, anyway." He shook his head wonderingly. Then he lowered his head again, resting it on her shoulder, and tightened his arms around her as if he were afraid she would somehow slip away.

That small act tightened Kelsey's throat unbearably. She prayed she wouldn't start to cry, not now, not in front of him, but he was so tender, so gentle—traits she would have thought impossible in a man capable of the passionate wildness that they'd just experienced. The fact that it was possible for a man to be both amazed her; that such a man was here with her left her more than a little stunned.

After a while, still floating in the golden haze he'd created, she realized that for the first time she understood how girls got themselves into predicaments like Melissa's.

"If this is what it's like, no wonder kids get in trouble."

Cruz lifted his head. "Was that a compliment?"

Kelsey blushed furiously when she realized she'd said it out loud. But the lopsided grin he was giving her wiped away her embarrassment. At the same time, she sensed that there was an element of uncertainty there, as if his joking question hid a genuine one.

"I suppose it was," she said, giving him the smile she'd been smiling on the inside for a while now. "Want more? I could give you a list."

His grin widened. "Sure. I've got time."

It took all her nerve, she wasn't used to such intimate teasing, but she couldn't deny what had passed between them, either. She didn't know for sure if there truly was any uncertainty lurking beneath that very male grin, but if there was, she was going to get rid of it.

"It's never been like that for me," she said honestly. "Thank you. You were gentle and considerate when I needed you to be, but...wild when that was just what I wanted."

Cruz's eyes widened, and color tinged his cheeks. He swallowed tightly, and Kelsey knew he'd needed to hear it as much as she'd needed to say it.

"I... Wow. That's..."

He stopped, swallowed again, then shook his head, lowering his eyes, clearly at a loss now. Kelsey wanted to hug him all over again.

"Although," she said brightly, "I feel a little foolish to have reached the ancient age of thirty before finding out what all the shouting's about."

His gaze came back to her face. "I thought I *knew* what it was all about." He hesitated, then added, "I'm glad...you didn't end up in Melissa's situation."

She went very still. And very stiff.

"Don't, Kelsey," he said, slipping off her to one side and then pulling her close. "Don't close up on me. Not now."

The instinct to hide her past was strong, well honed after years of practice. But the gentle warmth of Cruz's embrace was lulling, soothing, and she couldn't find it in her to run this time. She'd trusted this man in the most intimate moments possible between two people, and he'd been everything she'd never thought any man could be. Surely she could trust him with this?

"How did you know?" she finally asked.

"I guessed," he said. "It wasn't too hard. Some things you said, and Melissa, how much you care and how hard you've been looking for her. And the way you looked for her. Like you'd been there yourself."

"I have been."

She couldn't go on; there were too many years of trying to forget, followed by too many years of trying to remember, so that she could help those in the same impossible position she'd been in. The two sometimes seemed at war inside her, and never more than now.

Cruz didn't prod, didn't push, and she was thankful for that. More than thankful, since he simply held her close against him, as if she were something precious. It was a feeling she'd known little enough of in her life, and never from a man. After a long time, after the tension had eased out of her, he spoke softly.

"It scares me to death to think of those kids. I keep thinking of Sam. It would kill me if she ever felt that running away from me was the only solution."

"Just the fact that you know that is the best insurance you can have that it won't happen," Kelsey said, picturing in her mind again the closeness between father and daughter. "It won't happen to you, Cruz. Not as long as you keep listening."

"But that isn't always enough."

"No. But it's a good start. A start too many parents don't even bother to make."

"Like yours?" he asked quietly.

She recoiled inwardly. She didn't want to talk about it, she never had. She never even thought about it, unless she had to to help one of her kids. But somehow it was suddenly all there, boiling up inside her, ready to burst free. She could feel it in the tightness in her chest, in the moisture stinging her eyes.

And the quiet, compassionate concern of this man was going to be the thing that breached the dam. She knew it. And when he tightened his arms just enough, as if he wanted to be certain she felt warm and safe, she felt the pressure let go, as if it were a physical thing. And the words began.

"My mother...never had the chance. She died when I was about eight. But I remember her. She was...kind and warm, and she smelled of vanilla. Like cookies. And she loved me. I always knew that. My...father was a cold, distant man. He always had been. But I knew she loved me."

Cruz said nothing, but he hugged her tighter.

"When she died, all the warmth went with her. My father remarried a couple of years later. He needed a hostess."

Cruz made a slight movement, as if he were wincing. "Nice reason to get married. Is she why you ran away?"

"No," Kelsey said instantly, vehemently. "That wasn't it at all. She wasn't...one of those stepmothers. I thought she was going to be, at first. She was pretty, and laughed a lot, and I thought she would try to take my mother's place. But she didn't. And she was the warmest, kindest person I'd met since my mother died. I came to love Cecelia Hall."

She sensed him make the connection. "Hall?"

"Yes. I took her name as mine. For a lot of reasons." Kelsey took a long, deep breath, steadied herself, then said it. With no exaggeration, the truth of it ringing in her voice. "She saved my life."

Cruz went still. "What?"

"Cecelia saved my life. And ruined her own to do it."

She shivered slightly; she had never really talked about this to anyone, except Cecelia. Cruz moved, and for a moment she feared he was pulling away, but instead he reached for the blanket throw that was folded over the back of the sofa and pulled it over them. Then he pulled her back against him, settling himself in a silent indication that she should go on. He was making this easier than she'd ever thought it could be, and she plunged ahead.

"My father was a very wealthy man. One of those pillar-of-the-community sorts. He could charm anyone. Even

Cecelia, and she was a smart woman. But one day…she found out he wasn't all he appeared to be. She found out that…those nights when she'd wake up and he was gone, when she thought he was…in his office downstairs, working…he was really…''

She stopped, gulping in air, wondering how she'd ever thought she could do this.

"Kelsey?" She shivered in his arms. "God, Kelsey, no. He was…with you?"

She heard the undertone in his voice, a mixture of hope and horror, hope that it wasn't true and horror that it was.

"He told her he was just…checking on me. Like any loving father."

"Right," he said acidly, and she realized he'd probably heard that line many times before. His anger comforted her somehow.

"He never…really molested me. Not like…some of them do. He never raped me, never really even touched me, but he got into bed with me and made me…touch him."

She felt a violent shudder rip through him, heard him swear, low and harsh and furious, consigning her father to the depths of eternal fire. His embrace tightened until she could barely breathe.

"That's what you meant?" he asked, his voice a harsh, pained thing. "When you talked about listening? You told, didn't you? And no one believed you."

He curled himself around her, held her as if he wanted to squeeze out all the bad memories, as if he could somehow protect her now from what had happened then. She'd never felt as safe as she did in that moment. She nearly cried at the wonder at it, and it was all she could do to go on.

"No one could believe it, not about my father. I ran away, whenever I could, but they…always found me and brought me back. And sympathized with my father for having such a troublesome child."

"God, Kelsey, I'm sorry."

"I don't know what I would have done if he hadn't married Cecelia. He was her husband, and he tried to talk his way out of it with her, but she said there was no hell hot enough for people who did such things to children. She believed me.'' The wonder of it still echoed in her voice. ''And she brought charges against him.''

In low, heartfelt tones, he blessed her stepmother as he had condemned her father.

''Yes,'' Kelsey said, leaving it at that. ''He bought his way out of it, of course, and had it all hushed up. They made me go back to him.''

''No wonder you have no faith in the system,'' he whispered.

''Neither did Cecelia. My father told her that she couldn't be made to testify against her husband, and that he would have her arrested on some trumped-up charge if she ever breathed another word. She knew he meant it, and that he could do it. He had the power, the money...''

''What did she do?''

''She was going to file for divorce. But...''

She shivered, feeling suddenly barely able to breathe, let alone talk. But when Cruz's arms tightened around her again, she found herself able to go on.

''My father got worse. As if winning made him feel... invincible. I think he...would have raped me then. But she saved me. When she caught him that time, she...hit him over the head with one of my model horses. Knocked him out. And then...we ran. She stole me away from him. I wasn't even her child, but she refused to abandon me to him.''

''Bless her,'' Cruz said, with a fervency that warmed Kelsey to the core.

''Yes,'' she said again. ''She gave up everything for me. But she never, ever made me feel responsible. She said she felt like a fool for being blinded by his charm, but that she finally understood it had happened for a reason.''

''You?'' he asked softly.

Kelsey nodded against his chest. ''She said the only thing that made sense, since she really wasn't normally a fool, was that she was supposed to help me.''

''She sounds like...quite a woman.''

"She saved my life," Kelsey repeated simply. "We lived on the run for four years, sometimes in cities, sometimes in small towns, but never staying in one place very long, because we knew he was looking for us."

"How?"

"We checked the newspapers at the library, wherever we were. My father was a big wheel, so it was in all the area papers. He told the police Cecelia had tried to kill him and then had kidnapped me for ransom."

"And they bought it? After what had happened before?" He sounded incredulous, and Kelsey went still. "Never mind," he said before she could say anything more. "You'd think I'd know by now that the rich really *are* different, and that they get treated that way. I see enough of it, even here."

She relaxed then, and with an odd feeling of checking something off on a list she hadn't even known she was keeping, she went on.

"He had to keep looking, as part of his image as the grief-stricken father. But I'm sure it was rage more than anything that drove him. He couldn't let me get away from him. Couldn't have me out of his control, where I might talk."

"Bastard," Cruz said succinctly, and his tone was so cold Kelsey conversely felt warmed.

"I was sixteen when he finally found us. And that was my fault, really. Cecelia didn't want me to have to restart high school every year, so we stayed too long in a small town where newcomers got noticed more. The private detectives my father hired were waiting for me at school one day. They called me into the office, and I saw them there. I knew instantly, and I ran, but they caught me before I could get home to warn Cecelia."

"What happened?"

"I knew she'd be in trouble, that my father could really do what he'd threatened, and she had hit him.... So I gave up. I went with them."

"God, Kelsey—"

"I made them let me go to the bathroom and sneaked to the phone instead. I called her and told her. She argued, but

I knew I was right. I'd heard them saying that they would hunt her down next, because my father wanted her put in jail. I couldn't let that happen, not after all she'd done for me. I told her…I could handle him now. Cecelia had made sure I talked to counselors, so I understood better what was happening, how to deal with it. And now I was bigger, older, so I could fight him, at least until I got away again. But there was no way Cecelia could fight what he'd do to her.''

He pulled her even tighter against him, tucking the blanket closer around her shoulders, as if he sensed the inner chill of long-ago memories. It helped her to finish it.

"So I went back. He hadn't changed. He was worse, angrier, more vicious. In public he was the perfect father, overjoyed at having his daughter back. In private, he made sure I knew that I'd pay for this the rest of my life. And that he'd hunt Cecelia down no matter where she went.''

"And you…ran away again?''

"Yes. This time for good. I'd learned a lot about getting by. I knew about fake ID, places to hide, low-profile ways to travel. I changed my name every time I stopped anywhere. I learned how to look older than I was. Finally I ended up out here.''

"And went to work for what became the Sunset Grill.''

"Yes. And you know the rest.''

"Cecelia?''

Kelsey gave a sad, forlorn sigh. "I don't know. I've been looking for her, but for so long I had to be careful, so that my father wouldn't find her, or me. Once I was eighteen I was safe, he couldn't make me go back, but I knew he'd never stop trying to punish her. So I couldn't do anything that might lead him to her, like running ads or anything. And I couldn't afford to do much else, like hire someone, not for a long time, and by then so much time had passed…''

"I'm sorry, Kelsey.''

"I'm more hopeful now.'' She smiled for the first time during the long, painful discourse and added with some satisfaction, "With some of that money I came into last year, I hired a firm that specializes in missing persons.''

There was a moment of silence. "That money," Cruz began slowly, "did that by chance...come from your father?"

"A beautiful irony, isn't it? I'd kept tabs on him as best I could without giving myself away, because I wanted to be sure he didn't somehow wind up with another child to torture. When he died in a car accident, he was in the middle of trying to break the trusts my mother had made him set up for me, but he hadn't succeeded when he was killed, so I got it anyway. It seems the perfect final answer to him, to use it to find Cecelia. And I will. I swear I will."

"I'm sure you will," he said quietly, his voice a comforting rumble against her ear. "I think you can do just about anything you set out to do, Kelsey."

The calm certainty in his voice warmed her all over again, as did the comforting feel of his arms around her. She felt warm and safe, and almost unbearably light, as if finally telling the whole sordid story had relieved a burden she hadn't realized the weight of until she shared it.

For a long time, she just lay there, savoring the feel of his closeness, the coziness of being so intimately entwined on the sofa, the warm glow of the remaining fire. She couldn't remember ever feeling so relaxed, so languid, so utterly peaceful.

"Cruz?" she said, smothering a sudden yawn.

"Mmm?"

"Thanks...for listening."

He kissed her in answer, a soft, gentle kiss just in front of her left ear. She sighed, drifting, warm, safe. And when sleep claimed her, it was deep and dreamless and soothing, and finally free of the nightmares that had haunted her for so long.

Thanks for listening.

Cruz blinked rapidly at the sting of moisture still pooled in his eyes at her gratitude for such a simple thing. Especially since his heart was clamoring out a thank-you of its own, to her, for finally trusting him enough to pour out that awful, beautiful story. A story she clearly had not told often, if ever.

No wonder she seemed so serene; her life here must seem like paradise compared to what she'd known.

When he felt her slip into sleep, it was all he could do not to clutch her so tightly to him that she would undoubtedly wake up again. He settled for kissing her again, softly.

He was so full of so many emotions that he couldn't begin to sort them out. He suspected he hadn't really absorbed the magnitude of what had happened here tonight. The unrestrained fire that had raged between them was enough in itself, requiring a stunning reevaluation of everything he'd ever thought, ever assumed, about sex and passion.

But to his surprise, the fact that she had gifted him with enough trust to tell him her story meant as much as the physical intimacy that she had granted him, and that rattled him. As did the realization that he felt a powerful sense of pride in what she'd done, in her courage and determination, a pride so strong he knew it could stem only from feelings he hadn't quite admitted to yet.

But as she slept in his arms, he knew he couldn't deny the pride he felt, or the gratification the simple gift of her trust gave him.

Thanks for listening.

They had shared a passion, an intimacy, like nothing he'd ever known in his life, yet she'd thanked him for the simple act of listening to her unburden herself. She had been so understanding, so right, when he told her about Ellie, she'd known exactly how he felt, and she'd helped him to finally face it, to finally deal with the anger he'd carried around for years...but she'd thanked him for simply listening.

He shook his head in wonder, at all of it, at her, at himself, at them together. And caught his breath at the surge of sudden emotion, half thrill, half wariness, that shot through him at that seemingly natural linking of them as a couple.

Was he ready for this? Could he really—

The noise that cut off his thoughts was short, sharp and loud. He went rigid. Immediately, instinctively, he started assessing. From his right. The side of the building. Not metallic, not glass...wood.

That sticky latch finally broke.

Kelsey's words—and his own neglected promise to wedge that door shut—whirled through his mind.

Another sound, softer, a muffled scraping. Movement. Eliminating the possibility that something had simply fallen. Movement meant something had to be there to move. Something alive. Or some*one*.

Damn, his gun was in the truck. Safely locked in the glove box. For a moment, he regretted the compromises he had to make for Sam's safety, but only for a moment. He tried to move without waking Kelsey, but they were so tangled up together it was impossible.

"Cruz?" she said sleepily. "Was that…?"

"Shhh. Stay here."

He moved more quickly then, rolling over her to get to his feet. He grabbed a poker from the fireplace set and started moving toward the sounds.

"Cruz?" She was awake now, sitting up, clutching the blanket to her naked breasts, her voice echoing with a concern he had the fleeting hope was for him. But he waved her to silence without speaking and kept moving.

He reached the inner door of the storeroom. He stood to one side, holding the poker as if it were a police baton, ready to move in any direction. Then he shoved the door open.

A small, rapidly moving shape barreled hard into him. They both hit the floor with a resounding thud.

Chapter 18

"**M**elissa!" Kelsey's voice rang with relief. "Thank God you're here."

The girl crouched in the corner where she'd sprawled after the collision. The blouse she wore was too small, and Cruz could see the swell of her belly now.

"I only came back because I thought you were gone," she said, her voice tight. "I was tired of sleeping in crash pads that smelled bad."

"I've been so worried," Kelsey said, kneeling beside the girl.

"Sure." Melissa sneered, pulling back as she eyed the blanket Kelsey was wrapped in. "I can see how worried you were."

Then her gaze flicked to Cruz, who stopped rubbing at his aching shoulder where it had hit the floor and suddenly realized he was stark naked. He didn't trust Melissa not to take off if he risked going back to the great room for his jeans, so instead he kept an eye on her over his shoulder and reached into the storeroom to grab a towel, hastily knotting it around his hips.

"So now what, cop?" Melissa said, in the tone of false bravado he'd heard so often from scared kids.

"Melissa," Kelsey said, "he's been helping me look for you."

"I'll bet he has."

"Listen to me, he's kept it unofficial, even though it could get him in trouble. He wants to hear your side of it."

Melissa looked at them both, and then, with a cynicism that should have been beyond her years, she said, "You're just saying that because you're sleeping with him. You had sex, so you decide you trust him. That's how you rationalize it. I've been there."

Cruz glanced at Kelsey, and his stomach knotted at the fleeting expression of doubt that crossed her face. He looked back at the teenager.

"You have it backwards, Melissa," he said softly. "It is and should always be the other way around. You only have sex with someone you trust."

She seemed startled, whether by the idea or by the fact that he'd said it at all, he couldn't tell.

"And I trust him," Kelsey said, with a certainty that eased his tension a notch. It wasn't all he wanted from her, but it was a start. "You can trust him, too."

Melissa hesitated, then shook her head. "No. He'll have to tell my folks, and he'll make me go back. Maybe you trust him, and I can even see why you slept with him, but he's still a cop."

Kelsey blushed at the implication, and Cruz found himself feeling a bit disconcerted as the girl eyed his bare chest and legs. But Kelsey quickly recovered and went on.

"They *want* you back, Melissa," she said. "We saw them this afternoon, and they're very worried."

"You...saw them? And they said that?"

She nodded. "Your mother is very anxious to have you home—"

"If you're going to try and tell me my father wants me back, you can forget it. I know better."

"He's..." Kelsey's words trailed away.

Cruz guessed she was hesitant about denigrating the girl's father, but Cruz had no such qualms. The story Kelsey had told him had pressed every hot button he had about parenting. There was no way he could undo any of the hell she'd gone through, but he could make sure it didn't happen all over again to Melissa. And in that instant he realized exactly why Kelsey was doing this, why she was so determined to help kids like she had once been.

"Your father," Cruz said flatly, "is a bully. He controls his little world by intimidating anyone he has any power over."

Melissa turned then, her eyes widening as she stared at Cruz. He guessed she'd never heard another adult speak of her father this way; maybe it was past time she did.

"Most bullies," he went on, "are that way because inside, they're afraid. They think this is the only way they can make people notice them, that the only way they can feel on top is to keep others down."

Melissa's mouth gaped open. Cruz pressed his advantage.

"He can't bully me. Meet with them, talk to them, but with Kelsey there on your side. And let me…mediate between you."

"Mediate?" She looked at them both doubtfully.

"Make sure it doesn't get ugly," Kelsey said.

"And make sure you get heard," Cruz said, and knew he'd hit a chord by the look that flickered in Melissa's troubled eyes.

Again the girl hesitated, but again she shook her head. "I can't go back there. It's… I just can't."

"I know," Kelsey said. "It's their turf, their power base, and you feel…less important there, because you always have been." The girl flashed Kelsey a look of gratitude for her understanding. "Do it here," Kelsey said. "On neutral ground."

For the first time, hope showed in Melissa's face. But it was clearly warring with doubt.

"I have a better idea," Cruz said. "Given your father's attitude, and his nature, I think it might have a…beneficial effect to do it on *my* turf. Make him come to Trinity West, my station. Very formal. Interrogation-type atmosphere. I can make it…very intimidating for him.''

"You'd…do that?'' Melissa whispered.

"With pleasure,'' Cruz muttered. "I hate bullies.''

"But wouldn't…I have to go home with them?''

"There are other solutions, Melissa,'' Cruz said gently. His gaze flicked to Kelsey. "It's not quite like it once was, where the parents' home is assumed to be the best place for any child to be. There are other options. We'll make sure you have a choice.''

The girl seemed stunned, for the moment beyond deciding or even speech.

"Tell you what,'' he said, pushing on while he had the chance, "let's go for a ride, and you think about it. I have to go get my little girl anyway.''

"Sam!'' Kelsey exclaimed, her head snapping around to look at the clock. "Cruz, I'm sorry, I completely—''

"So did I,'' Cruz said, giving her a swift grin that made her blush. "It's all right. Ryan and Lacey aren't leaving for their weekend away until morning.''

"You have a daughter?'' Melissa asked, apparently distracted from her own dilemma.

"I do,'' Cruz said, amazed yet again at the preconceptions people had; did they really think cops were automatons, not human beings with families and feelings? He knew the answer too well, but it still astonished him sometimes.

"And she's adorable,'' Kelsey said sincerely.

"When she's not being too smart for her own good, and mine,'' Cruz agreed. He saw the look that crossed Melissa's face then, and added quietly, "But even when she is, I love her beyond measure. She's the best thing I've ever done in this life.''

When he saw his point had registered with the girl, he went on. "So what do you say? Come with us? Sam's got to get home and feed her zoo. I'll feed the raccoon, the rabbits and the possum, but I will *not* feed that damned snake.''

Kelsey laughed. Melissa stared.

"Your little girl has...a zoo?" the teenager asked.

"That she does," Cruz said wryly. "And if I don't get her home, I'm going to get stuck with taking care of them."

"Well, maybe..." Melissa glanced at Kelsey. "If you're going too."

"It will give you time to think, to decide what you want to do," Kelsey said reassuringly.

Melissa gave Cruz one last uncertain look. "You...really won't make me go back if I don't want to?"

Cruz took a breath, wondering if he was going to get himself into real trouble before this was over. "If we can't resolve this with your folks, we'll find another way. Somehow."

The look Kelsey gave him then was more than enough payment for whatever minor professional risks he might be taking by making promises he wasn't sure how he would keep.

"I fed Frisbee," Cruz told Sam, "so just take care of the rest, okay?"

"Okay," Sam said cheerfully. Then she eyed Melissa. "Wanna help?"

Kelsey held her breath. The teenager looked intrigued, although she was clearly trying to fight it. When she first saw the menagerie, she'd turned to stare, not at Samantha, but at Cruz.

"You let her...do this?"

"I even pay for it," he'd quipped.

"But...even in the house?"

He'd become very serious then. "I love her," he said. "And this is what she loves doing most. Of course I let her."

Melissa had stared at him, the wonder in her face speaking worlds about how foreign this was to her. And Kelsey wondered herself if Cruz had any idea how special a father he was.

"Well," Melissa said now, in answer to Sam's question, "I guess I could help."

In a few moments, the teenager was cuddling a baby rabbit

and looking not much older than Sam as she fed it a lettuce-
leaf treat to go with the pellets Sam carefully measured out.

Kelsey glanced at Cruz, who was lounging with one shoulder against the doorjamb, watching his daughter. It was hard
to believe this was the same man who had, at the sound of
an intruder in her home, turned from tender lover into fierce
defender; she would not soon forget the image of him, no less
dangerous for his nakedness, moving without hesitation toward the threat.

She would not soon forget many images of him from last
night, she thought ruefully, and now that she knew just how
beautiful he was, she was having a hard time not picturing
him as he'd been then, naked, aroused, utterly male...and
wanting her.

His gaze flicked to her, and before she could look away
she saw the knowledge of what she was thinking flash in his
eyes. There was a sudden tautness around his mouth, a sudden
tension in his body, and his head came up like that of a wolf
scenting his mate.

She felt her cheeks heat at the wild thought and finally
managed to look away. At first, when Melissa intruded on
their intimacy, she'd been relieved that she wouldn't be facing
the typical morning-after awkwardness. But now, when she
realized she had no idea exactly how becoming lovers was
going to affect their relationship—if, indeed, there was such
a thing—she was beginning to see some value in whatever
they might have talked about.

Sam and Melissa had moved on to the next cage. "He's
cute!" the teenager exclaimed. "I thought they were ugly."

"It's the possum tail," Sam explained kindly. "Because it
looks like a rat's, people think they're like them."

They were chattering as if there were six months' difference between them, rather than six years. Partly because of
Sam's precociousness, no doubt, but also, Kelsey guessed,
partly because Melissa found the simple innocence of the
child and the animals very appealing. In any case, she was as
relaxed as Kelsey had ever seen her.

A shrill beep made them all jump, all except Cruz, who

calmly looked down at the beeper on his belt. Without any perceptible change in expression, he excused himself to make a call. When he came back, Kelsey saw a tightness in his jaw that made her pulse pick up.

"Why don't you check on Slither?" he said to Sam.

Sam lifted a brow in a very adult manner. "What happened to 'that darned snake'?"

"He still is that darned snake," Cruz said. "But as long as he's here, he gets taken care of."

"Does this mean he can come back inside?" the girl asked, reverting to ten-year-old pleading. "He's been in the garage all week."

"Maybe," Cruz said.

Kelsey smiled inwardly as Sam gave him a grin that would certainly have melted *her* resolve in an instant. Cruz was going to have his hands full in a few years, she thought. And felt a longing to be there to see Sam grow into the lovely, self-confident woman she just knew she would be, a longing that she feared was futile, and that she tried to suppress.

"That was Trinity West," he said abruptly when the child was out of earshot. He looked at Melissa. "They had a message from your parents. Sutter's apparently been watching the house, waiting for you to show up. He saw us there this afternoon, and a couple of hours ago he broke into the house and came after them with that knife of his again."

Melissa paled. "Oh, God. He didn't…hurt them, did he?"

So there was something beyond hatred there, Kelsey noted, but it was only a brief thought, as Cruz went on.

"No. But he scared them badly. Enough so that they told him who Kelsey and I were."

Melissa gave Kelsey a wide-eyed look of distress. She tried to reassure the girl, but inwardly her mind was racing, trying to remember everything that had been said that afternoon. And when the crucial memory registered, and her eyes shot to Cruz's face, she knew he'd remembered it, too.

"The inn," she breathed. "I told them the name, and where it was, when they asked where I'd seen Melissa."

"I know," Cruz said.

"But…we're not there," Melissa said, confused.

"But this address is," Cruz said grimly.

Kelsey bit back her own exclamation of distress; Doug Sutter clearly would not be above burglary, and not only was Cruz's registration card still in her office, it was sitting nicely out on the desk where she'd left it when she scribbled down his address to return the sketchbook. Sutter wouldn't even have to search.

Then Cruz began to speak swiftly, and Kelsey knew she was again seeing the cop in action. "We'd better get to Trinity West right now. It took some time for them to determine just how urgent the message was and to page me. He could have as much as three hours' start by now."

More than enough time for Sutter to get here, Kelsey thought.

"Oh, God," Melissa moaned. "I should have listened. My dad said Doug was trouble, but…I thought he loved me. He said he did, and he wanted to be with me, no one ever had before, and—"

"It's too late to worry about that now," Kelsey said, with a briskness she hoped would hide her own dismay. "We need to get you to the Trinity West station, where you'll be safe even from Doug. Let's get your—"

The scream that came from the garage froze them all for a split second.

"Sam," Cruz hissed. And in that split second Kelsey saw terror flash across Cruz's suddenly pale face. It was the mere blink of an eye before he whirled and was gone, so swiftly it left Kelsey feeling sluggish and slow, despite the fact that she was right on his heels.

She nearly collided with his back as she ran into the garage. She could feel the tension in him as if it were a tangible thing, could sense that he was barely leashed. And in the next moment she saw why.

It was every parent's nightmare. The wild-eyed young man from the mug shot had Sam by the hair, the sunny blond mass yanked back from her head so hard that Kelsey knew it had to be hurting. And an ugly knife was clenched in his right fist, the long, dirty blade pressed to Samantha's delicate throat.

Chapter 19

Kelsey suppressed the scream that rose to her throat. Samantha was silent, her eyes fastened on Cruz, and the utter faith in them made Kelsey quiver inside. Sam had absolutely no doubt that her father would save her.

"Melissa comes with me and I let the kid go," Doug said.

"You let her go," Cruz said, his voice so low and harsh Kelsey felt a shiver creep up her spine, "and then we'll talk."

"Not a chance, cop. Melissa comes with me or I'll slit the kid's throat right now."

"If you so much as leave a red mark on her," Cruz said with lethal intent, "I'll gut you with your own knife."

For an instant, Kelsey thought she saw fear in the glassy eyes, but bravado immediately took over.

"Big talk, pig. Without a gun, you're nothing but a stinking pig coward."

"Don't you call my daddy names!"

Sam's shout was punctuated by a solid kick delivered to her captor's shin. Sutter yelped, and Sam elbowed him sharply.

"You tell her to knock it off or I'll kill her right now!"

Kelsey felt the barely perceptible tremor that shook Cruz, but his voice was dead calm.

"And lose your only bargaining chip? I don't think so."

Inspired by her success, Sam continued to kick and claw and elbow, doing everything she could to get him to drop her. In a moment that seemed oddly slow-motion, Kelsey realized that the child was trying to get her feet on the ground, and she wondered if she would then neatly toss Doug over her shoulder in some kind of trick karate move. It seemed entirely possible.

She heard Melissa sob and couldn't help contrasting the weeping, shaking teenager to the intrepid Sam.

Cruz, she thought. He was the difference.

And she'd brought this down on him, him and his precious little girl. She had to *do* something.

"Let her go," she said suddenly. "Take me instead. I'll…cooperate."

She heard Cruz's sharp intake of breath, but she didn't look at him. She kept her eyes on Doug, praying, but he shook his head as he struggled to keep his hold on the feisty little girl.

"I want *her,* bitch." He waved the dirty blade at Melissa, who wailed in horror. "She's the one who's going to be gutted here. I'm going to slice that baby right out of her, teach her to think she can cheat on me and get away with it."

Melissa continued to wail loudly. Kelsey wished she would be quiet. There was obviously no point in an explanation of the failure rate of condoms. The boy was well beyond rational thought, if he'd ever been capable of it in the first place. There had to be something….

Cruz was moving.

Slowly, so slowly she hadn't even realized it until she noticed that the space between him and the workbench behind him had lessened. He had a plan, of some sort.

Maybe it *was* time for that condom lecture.

"It's your baby, Doug," she said.

"Like hell. I made sure. Didn't want no bitch coming after me, tryin' to make me give her money for some kid I don't want. Happened to a friend of mine, and he had to run or pay till the brat was eighteen.''

"Condoms fail, Doug. Are you going to kill your own baby?''

"It's not mine," he insisted. "She's a slut, and she's going to pay for it!''

Kelsey heard the faintest of sounds. At the very edge of her vision, she saw Cruz reach behind him.

"All right," she said suddenly. "If you let Sam go, you can have Melissa.''

"No!" Melissa shrieked.

Sutter looked at the panic-stricken girl. Kelsey moved sideways a half step, to shield Cruz's action. She heard a sharper noise. And then Cruz moved suddenly, quickly. He tossed something. Something that hit Sutter and then slid down his body, landing in a writhing black-and-white scroll at his feet.

Slither.

Sutter recoiled violently, shouting a pungent curse.

Cruz exploded. Heedless of the knife, heedless of the hated snake, he launched himself at the man who threatened his daughter's life. Kelsey stared, taken aback by the cold rage on his face; he was focused on only one thing, Sam's safety. She knew she was seeing the fury of a quiet man stirred to defend the one he loved, and there was no hesitation in him.

They careened into the front of the truck. Kelsey saw Cruz wrest Sam free with a powerful shove of his right arm. The girl stumbled to her knees, but quickly got to her feet. Kelsey saw her move, as if to jump into the fray to help her father, as the two men hit the garage floor.

Kelsey leaped forward, grabbing Sam and pulling her back. She heard a low, throttled grunt; she didn't know from whom. She heard the sound of blows, dull thuds as flesh hit flesh. She looked around wildly for something, anything, to use as a weapon. Hanging on to the protesting Sam, she desperately searched the workbench. She grabbed the best thing she could find, a heavy wrench. She took a step toward the entangled men. She raised her arm, ready to strike the first instant she could be sure she wouldn't hit Cruz.

It was over before she had the chance. Suddenly Cruz was on top and Sutter's head was pressed to the garage floor. His glassy eyes widened as the snake slithered past his face, headed for the more peaceful space beneath the workbench.

"Kelsey... Top drawer of the bench... Two of those plastic zip ties."

He sounded a bit breathless, natural after such a fight, she thought. She turned hastily, then stopped when Sam started to move toward her father.

"Not yet, Sam," she said sharply.

The child stopped, looked at Kelsey, then back at her father, considering. Then she nodded and stayed still. Gratified for a reason she didn't stop to analyze, Kelsey dug into the drawer Cruz had indicated until she found the narrow white plastic ties generally used to hold hoses on engines. She handed Cruz two, and he quickly fastened one around Sutter's left wrist, looped the second through the first and then around the right wrist, making a highly effective pair of makeshift handcuffs.

Sutter protested at the tightness, but quieted when Cruz said, "You just keep quiet and hope I don't think too much about what you almost did here."

Cruz straightened then, still astride Sutter. Sam started toward him. Cruz stopped her with a shake of his head. "Get the snake, honey. Before he hides someplace where we can't get at him."

Seeing the wisdom in that, Sam scampered to obey, seemingly unflustered by all the high drama. Melissa's wailing subsided to quiet weeping at last as she huddled near the door to the house.

Kelsey's brows lowered as she watched Cruz get slowly to his feet; there had been an edge in his voice that she didn't understand, now that it was over. She took a step toward him just as Sam, her mission successful, returned Slither to his cage. The girl again started toward her father, and again he stopped her.

"Go ahead and...take him inside. I think he's earned it."

Pleased with the pardoning of her reptilian friend, Sam smiled brightly. "Thanks, Daddy."

The "Daddy," Kelsey guessed, was a sign the girl was still feeling a bit shaken, but she disappeared inside with Slither's cage carefully clutched in her hands. The moment she was out of sight, Kelsey swiftly turned back to Cruz; his voice had been far too tight, too controlled. And he was holding his right hand over his side.

"Cruz?"

"Get me…the phone, will you? I have to—" he winced suddenly before finishing "—make some calls."

"Damn," Kelsey swore softly, moving toward him. "You're hurt."

"Nothing serious. I have to call Trinity West."

"Cruz!" It broke from her when she got close enough to see the blood seeping through his fingers. She pried his hand away. "That's why you wanted Sam out of here."

"It's just—"

"Don't you dare say it." Kelsey cut him off sharply as she inspected the ugly gash. "You've been hero enough for one day, throwing snakes when you hate to even be near them, fighting a knife bare-handed. Just shut up."

"Yes, ma'am," he said meekly.

"You…could have been killed." It was Melissa, speaking at last, in patent amazement, although still through gulping sobs.

Kelsey turned on the girl, about fed up with her whining. "Yes, he could have. But that's what parenting is all about, Melissa. Being willing to die for your child if necessary. I know neither one of us knows much about that kind of father, but we just had an object lesson. I hope you don't forget it."

I know I never will, she added to herself.

A couple of hours later, she was shaking her head in amazement. She had never seen anything like this. Cruz had made only two phone calls, one to Trinity West and one to Gage Butler at home, and yet the activity had yet to stop. Cops had an amazing grapevine, it seemed.

And Cruz had a lot of friends.

She had the feeling she was seeing the true reach of Cruz's generous spirit. Shortly after the uniformed officers had arrived to cart off Sutter, Ryan and Lacey, announcing they'd canceled their long-awaited weekend plans, arrived to take care of Sam. Kit, clad in sexy evening wear and chuckling about her not-too-reluctantly abandoned date, arrived, promising to take care of the zoo if necessary. Gage was on the heels of the paramedics he'd called, guessing Cruz was playing down his injury, and insisting he sit still and let them patch it up.

Others came, too, including an impressive tall lean man with patrician features, dark hair silvered at the temples, and light gray eyes that seemed to peer into her, probing far past the surface. She wasn't surprised when Cruz introduced him to her as Chief de los Reyes, but she was surprised when, instead of being angry at Cruz—at least publicly—for not going by the book, the man simply said he understood and appreciated that, with his officers, people and getting the job done came first.

Others called, and whoever was closest answered, assuring the caller that Cruz was alive and upright.

For Kelsey, who, since having to give up contact with her stepmother, had never depended on anyone but herself, it was a revelation. This was a man everyone trusted, she realized. And, she added to herself as she watched the group ebb and flow, a man everyone loved.

Including, she admitted at last, herself.

She loved him. God help her, she'd fallen in love with a cop. Not that it was surprising, she supposed. He was everything she'd never expected to find in one man; strong yet gentle, tender yet tough, steady yet passionate....

She shivered, shying away from heated memories she couldn't risk indulging in among this crowd of people. Better to concentrate on the impossibility of it than to dwell on how Cruz's undeniable courage and capacity for love had affected her.

And it *was* impossible. Wasn't it? After all, she'd spent years of time and lots of money trying to get around the very

system he represented. While he'd surprised her with his flex-
ibility when it came to Melissa, and she'd come to realize
things had changed since she was forced to go back to her
father's tender care, she doubted very much if he could
openly support what she was doing at the inn. It could get
him into trouble of all kinds, she supposed.

Although it could be academic; if word got out that there
was always a cop around, she doubted she would get many
kids willing to take that risk.

She sighed. There didn't seem to be any solution. Unless
she gave up her dream, unless she quit trying to help kids
like the kid she herself had been.

Of course, that was assuming Cruz wanted there to be a
solution in the first place. And that was an assumption she
didn't dare make.

He needed sleep, Cruz thought wearily as he moved the
truck into the right lane. His side was aching where the med-
ics had put him back together with a string of butterfly ban-
dages after he refused to go in for stitches—one look at Sam's
white face had convinced him; she'd never really seen him
hurt before, and he didn't want to add that to the burden she
was already carrying from tonight's events. They'd topped it
off with a tetanus shot, a suggestion that he see his own doctor immediately for antibiotics, judging from the state of that
blade, and a glum prediction that he was going to wish for
more than aspirin before morning.

Cruz didn't doubt it, but he knew he couldn't be doped up,
in case Sam woke up scared. He glanced at Kelsey, who had
insisted she go with him to pick Sam up from the Buckharts.
The child had gone unwillingly; only Ryan's coaxing promise
that he was almost through with a carving of her beloved
raccoon, and Cruz's promise that he really was all right and
would come get her as soon as things calmed down, had convinced her.

As if she'd felt his glance, Kelsey looked over at him. He
knew she knew he was hurting; it had been clear when she'd
eyed him with concern and said that she wished she could

use a stick-shift so he wouldn't have to drive. But all she said now was, "Do you think Melissa and her parents will work it out?"

"I don't know."

He wasn't sure he cared, either. Not right now. When everyone had finally cleared out, and after Chief de los Reyes's pointed observation that he sincerely hoped he wasn't going to be dealing with another cop who had a tendency to run alone, that curing Ryan Buckhart of the habit had been quite enough, all Cruz had wanted to do was crawl into bed and sleep for a week. Instead, he'd wound up at Trinity West, trying to broker a peace agreement between Melissa and her parents.

"Thank you for...dealing with it. I know you're tired and hurting, and the last thing you wanted to do was negotiate a truce between them."

He shrugged, regretting it when the movement tugged at the rather neat incision that Sutter had left him with along one rib. The blade might have been dirty, but it had also been razor-sharp.

"I promised her," he said.

"I know. But not everyone would have kept that promise, under the circumstances. Nobody would have blamed you if you hadn't."

There it was again. No one would blame you. No one to blame.

He felt his jaw tighten and forced himself to relax. He knew this was at the crux of his weariness, despite everything else that had happened. He knew that the pain in his side wasn't the real problem, it was the pain he was still staving off.

Sutter was in custody, charged with enough felonies to keep him under wraps for a long while. Melissa had, albeit warily, gone home with her mother and her finally chastened father. He was on his way to pick up Sam. In essence, it was over.

And that was what scared him. Foremost was the fear that now Kelsey would drop back out of his life, that they would be reduced to the week a year he spent at Oak Tree. If he could even bring himself to go back, if that was what happened.

He knew part of his fear was based on the fact that they hadn't had any chance to talk about what had happened between them. His instinct was to assume that they would simply go on from here and work out any problems as they came up. But watching Ryan and Lacey had also taught him the truth of something his father had tried to tell him long ago, that sometimes women needed the words, as well as the actions.

But he knew the fear went deeper than that. Even if she didn't disappear now, he didn't know what would happen. The harrowing story she'd told him had made him want to hold her, protect her, had made him proud of her courage and endurance, had made him admire her tenacity and strength...but now that he'd had time to think about it, he couldn't help wondering if Kelsey, like Ellen, would one day decide she'd never really had a youth of her own and take off to find it. Given her history, he wouldn't blame her.

And there it was again. No, he wouldn't, couldn't, blame her. But he knew now that this fear was at the core of his own retreat, the mixed feelings he hadn't been able to understand before. He also knew he couldn't go through that again. Nor would he put Sam through it again. The child already liked Kelsey; if she was to become truly attached to her, and then it went sour because of something they couldn't help...

And it was that bone-deep fear that kept him from bringing it up now, although it seemed to be hovering in the air between them. And then Ryan was handing him a sleepy Sam, a perfectly carved little replica of Bandit clutched in her hand, and the child's presence made the topic safely impossible.

Sam seemed content to snuggle on Kelsey's lap on the drive back home. And Kelsey seemed content to hold the child, cuddling her as gently as if she were her own. The picture they made caused something to tighten in Cruz, tighten until it hurt and he could barely breathe. He had to look away.

"Why do people run away," the child murmured into the silence, "and cause so much trouble?"

Cruz swallowed tightly, knowing words were beyond him now. He stared at the road, as if he could find the answer in those yards of pavement lit by the headlights. When he didn't say anything, Kelsey did, gently, quietly, hugging Sam as she spoke.

"Sometimes things go all wrong, honey, so wrong that it seems like it's the only thing to do. And sometimes it is. But some people are lucky, like you, and have somebody they can always tell the problem to, who will always love them and help them no matter what."

"You mean my dad?"

"Yes. There's nothing you could ever, ever do that would make him stop loving you. You know that, don't you?"

"Yes," Sam said simply.

Cruz felt his eyes begin to sting at Kelsey's heartfelt words. And at his little girl's immediate and confident response, his throat tightened until he could barely breathe.

"Will Melissa stay home now?" Sam asked.

"I don't know," Kelsey said honestly. "I hope she can. But it's not going to be easy, for any of them."

Sam shifted a little, looking up at Kelsey, and with that wisdom that was sometimes so uncanny, she asked, "Did you ever run away?"

Cruz held his breath, wondering what she would say. Then he realized he already knew. She would be honest; it wasn't in her to lie to the child.

"Yes," Kelsey said, proving him right. "I did. I had good reasons, but it was still awful. I should have been home, playing, enjoying just being a kid, but instead I was running, being scared all the time."

Cruz found his voice then, and before he could stop the question he didn't really want the answer to, it was out.

"So maybe someday you'll go looking for what you missed?"

He sensed her gaze switch to him, but he didn't, couldn't, look at her. He could feel her studying him, knew she was guessing at what was behind the words he hadn't been able to hold back. By the time she finally answered him, his stomach was knotted so badly he barely noticed the ache in his side.

"No," she said. "When I was…with my father I never felt safe, like a child should. Then I was on the run, never staying in one place long enough to really have friends, or feel like I had a home, until I was eighteen. Cecelia did her best, but there was always that feeling of…temporariness. When I bought Oak Tree, it was because I knew it would give me what I wanted more than anything else…a home. A place to always come back to. A place where I belonged, where I could stay, where I was safe."

Ignoring the twinge in his side, Cruz let out the breath he'd been holding, unaware of really doing it. What he *was* aware of was something he knew now he should have realized long ago; Kelsey's inner strength, the strength that had enabled her to survive such hell, even as a child, would never fail her. She was not the kind of woman who would try to go back, to recapture something she'd missed. She faced forward, accepted the past and went on, in the hopes of finding something even better.

"Safe is nice," Sam murmured as they pulled into the driveway, sounding more than half-asleep. Cruz stopped the truck but didn't shut off the motor, didn't move at all; he didn't want to do anything that would stop Kelsey's soft words.

"Yes," she said. "It is. It makes all the other good things you can feel possible. You can't be comfortable or happy or glad, you can't feel joy or love, unless you feel safe first. Like your father makes you feel."

"Uh-hmm." Sam's mumbled assent was clearly her last contribution before she went soundly to sleep in Kelsey's arms. Cruz knew she'd gone to sleep, and he knew Kelsey knew. So there was only one reason for what she whispered next.

"Like he makes *me* feel."

Cruz's hands clenched on the steering wheel. "God, Kelsey," he said, his voice hoarse.

"Let's get her inside," was all she said. "She's a tired little girl."

He was shaking, he realized as he walked around the truck. And he knew better than to think it was because of his injury; that was nothing compared to the shock Kelsey had just delivered.

"I've got her," Kelsey said when he moved to take the sleeping child. "If it's all right," she added cautiously.

"It is," he said, still sounding as hoarse as he had when she said those simple words that knocked the wind out of him more thoroughly than Sutter's knife had. He looked at Sam, sleeping trustingly against Kelsey's shoulder. "With...both of us, I think."

He wanted to watch as she put the child to bed, but he knew he needed a moment alone to get himself together. It had been a long, tiring night, but he wasn't about to postpone this until morning. Well, later this morning, anyway, he amended with a rueful glance at his watch, which read well after midnight. Something else would come up, some other interruption, and he wasn't willing to wait.

He went into the den, checked the cages—Slither's in particular, with a wry, halfhearted smile—and added the whimsical raccoon Ryan had carved to the collection. He heard Kelsey's light footsteps coming down the hall and marveled at the sudden tautness that came over him simply at her presence.

"She's out for the count. Thanks for...letting me do that."

I hope you get used to it, he thought, but held back the words this time.

"How's Slither?" she asked, coming to stand behind him.

"He seems fine."

"Still hate him?"

He managed a lopsided grin. "Let's just say I still hate the species, but this individual member I'll try to tolerate better."

He checked the latch on the snake's domain once more,

aware he was doing it simply for something to do with his hands.

"When Sam started school, she came home with the idea that her mother had left because she was too much trouble to take care of." He heard Kelsey's pained sigh, but he kept going. "I tried to explain to her that she had nothing to do with it, and I think she believed me, but sometimes I wonder if her need to take care of all these critters isn't...part of that somehow."

"Perhaps," Kelsey said softly. "Maybe in her mind it's a way to make things right where she can."

He turned to her then. "Like you?"

"Me?"

"Isn't that what you're trying to do?" He smiled, then lifted a brow at her. "But I think it might be better if you did it...officially. Maybe a halfway house, or a sanctioned shelter? Maybe I can even help you through the process. I'm sure the paperwork is a pain."

Kelsey gaped at him. "I... You know?"

"I have for a while. Gage told me that he'd heard from kids on the street about you, that you gave shelter with no questions asked as long as they played by your rules and agreed to at least talk about getting help after a couple of weeks of refuge."

"I...didn't think... I didn't tell you because..."

She stopped floundering, and Cruz reached out to grip her shoulders. "I know. You thought I'd...do something coplike. Shut you down or something."

"I did...at first. But not...anymore," she added, so urgently it warmed him, gave him the nerve to go on.

"You're not doing anything that could get you in real legal hot water, but without some official authorization, you're walking a mighty fine line. Especially if some parents ever wanted to get nasty and go after you for contributing to the delinquency of a minor."

"I...know."

"Besides," he said, keeping his tone conversational, despite the fact that his pulse had suddenly picked up, "it's not going to work that way anymore."

"What isn't?"

"I mean, once word gets out, kids are going to be wary. You're going to have to go official and have them sent to you, not just wander in off the street. But I can't think of any better use for the money your bastard of a father left you."

"Cruz, what are you—"

"A cop's wife can't be circumventing the system so blatantly, after all. But she can change it from the inside."

She stared at him, looking so stunned that Cruz felt a sudden qualm. Had he read her wrong? Panic made his voice a little ragged.

"I...love you, Kelsey. I know it's asking a lot, to take on a ready-made family, especially one of two-, four- and—" he gestured at Slither "—no-legged creatures, but—"

"No," she said, cutting him off breathlessly. "No, it's perfect. Your family is perfect, critters and all."

"No, it's not perfect. But it could be." He tightened his grip on her shoulders, staring down at her intently. "Kelsey?"

"Yes," she whispered. "Oh, yes."

He pulled her into his arms, and she came eagerly, hungrily, and Cruz nearly shuddered at the utter rightness of it.

The animals, immune to the foibles of human emotion, ignored them.

"I'm not I'm?"

Epilogue

"**Y**ou look gorgeous, girl!" Kit Walker said, reaching up to tuck in a stray flower from the small spray Kelsey had chosen to wear in her hair instead of a veil.

Kelsey smiled at the blonde; they'd become friends in the past two months, once Kelsey was certain the woman's delight that the man she'd once dated had fallen in love was sincere.

"I love Cruz," she'd assured Kelsey, "and I always will. But I'm not in love with him. And I'm delighted that he found you."

And she had meant it. Kelsey couldn't doubt it; there was too much genuine pleasure in the woman's eyes.

"Gorgeous." Ryan Buckhart agreed with Kit's assessment as he stood behind the chair his now very pregnant wife was sitting in, one hand protectively on her shoulder.

"Look who's talking," Kelsey said, eyeing the exotically handsome man, who looked even more so in the tux he was wearing as best man. Dolores, who was loving her role as Kelsey's matron of honor, had nearly passed out at the sight of him. Kelsey never would have thought herself able to tease the imposing Ryan, but she did it easily now, knowing he would simply grin back at her.

Laughing at the exchange, Lacey stood. "You need to get back to your best-man chores, while I find Caitlin and Quisto. I have a feeling there's something she and I need to talk about." She patted her swollen belly archly.

"Really?" Ryan looked startled. "You think she's...?"

"I think so," Lacey said.

"I hope so," Kelsey said, knowing Caitlin and Quisto truly wanted a baby. She'd only met the strawberry blonde and her lethally charming husband a few weeks ago, but she'd felt an instant kinship with the woman. Cruz had told her they had a lot in common, explaining about the Neutral Zone, the club Caitlin ran for street kids, and even suggesting that they might be able to work in concert. They were already making plans.

"And I have to go find Gage," Kit said. "It's my job to rescue him from Pam, before she can set him up with her bubbleheaded granddaughter."

Gage, Kelsey thought as Kit gave her a final hug. She'd come to know him better, too, this driven man with the young face and the too-old eyes. Or at least as much as he allowed. She'd never seen anyone who seemed so divided; he seemed to function normally on a day-to-day basis, but those eyes...

He looks like my animals do when they're hurt. They can't say it, so it shows in their eyes.

Sam's words, full of the simple wisdom of childhood, rang in her mind.

Sam. The bonus in this unexpected miracle, the little girl she already loved. Not only because she was so much a part of the man she loved beyond her wildest dreams, but for her own unique personality and charm. It wouldn't always be easy, she knew, but she would do her best. With Cruz's help, it would be enough.

Alone in what had once been her room but was now theirs, she thought of how it had all worked out. Sam had been delighted with her new room, and even more so with Kelsey's suggestion that the entire toolroom adjacent to the garage be remodeled for her animals. The child was settling in and was seemingly happy with the new arrangements.

She thought, too, of Cruz's parents, who were the kind, loving souls she'd known they would have to be to have produced a son like theirs, and who had welcomed her with joy for the simple reason that she had made that son willing to risk loving again, something they had feared he would never do.

She had more than she'd ever expected, and there was little room in her full heart for regrets. If only...

"Kelsey?" She turned, startled, as Cruz's voice came from the doorway. "I know this is...against tradition, I'm not supposed to see you, but I wanted to give you your present before we start."

"Present? Cruz, you gave me my necklace last night," she said, puzzled; the small golden oak tree he'd had made for her had already brought her to tears.

"That was just in case...this one didn't get here."

There was something decidedly odd about his expression, but before she could decipher it, he did something very strange.

"I love you," he said, and disappeared out of sight. She heard him whisper something, then someone else stepped into the doorway. A woman, tall, slender, dark hair still untouched by gray, and with the laughing brown eyes Kelsey had never forgotten, eyes that were now glowing with joy.

Kelsey stared at the woman, her own eyes widening, then filling with tears.

"Cecelia?" she whispered brokenly.

"Kelsey, honey!"

The older woman crossed the room quickly, and Kelsey was caught in the embrace she'd never thought to feel again. They both babbled somewhat wildly for a few moments, before Kelsey finally managed to ask a coherent question.

"How?"

Cecelia laughed, the silvery, lovely laugh that was one of Kelsey's fondest memories from a dark time. "Oh, Kels, I'd been trying to find you ever since I heard your father had been killed, but I couldn't afford to pay someone to look. Then that man of yours not only tracked me down up in Canada, he made sure everything was cleared up down here, and then sent me a plane ticket. You've done well, honey. He's a good man.''

"No," Kelsey whispered, "he's the very best."

They talked on, trying to make up for all the time lost, even though Cecelia assured her that they would have plenty of time.

And when the time came and she took her place beneath the spreading oak tree, it was Kelsey who cried at her wedding, when she stood looking into Cruz's loving face, full of wonder at her good fortune.

He's the very best, she repeated to herself.

And that night, when for the first time they went to their room as husband and wife, Kelsey made very sure he knew it.

* * * * *

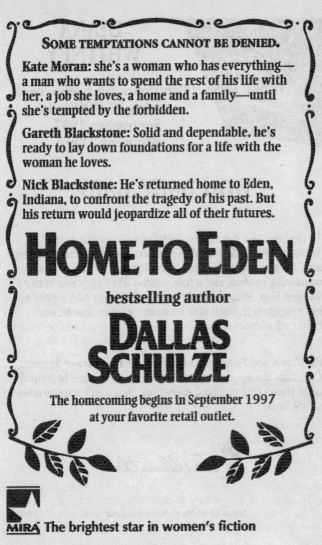

DIANA WHITNEY

Continues the twelve-book series 36 HOURS in September 1997 with Book Three

OOH BABY, BABY

In the back of a cab, in the midst of a disastrous storm, Travis Stockwell delivered Peggy Saxon's two precious babies and, for a moment, they felt like a family. But Travis was a wandering cowboy, and a fine woman like Peggy was better off without him. Still, she and her adorable twins had tugged on his heartstrings, until now he wasn't so sure that *he* was better off without *her.*

For Travis and Peggy and *all* the residents of Grand Springs, Colorado, the storm-induced blackout was just the beginning of 36 Hours that changed *everything!* You won't want to miss a single book.

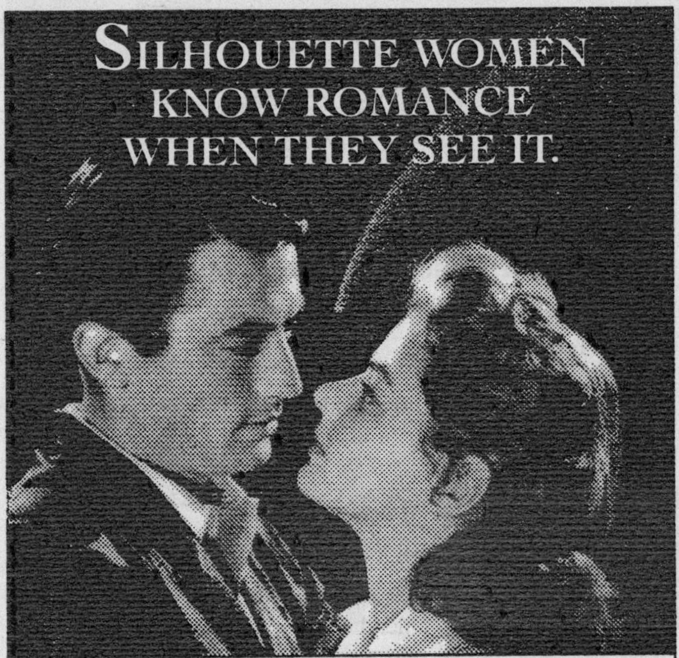
SILHOUETTE WOMEN
KNOW ROMANCE
WHEN THEY SEE IT.

1998

SUNDAY MONDAY TUESDAY WEDNESDAY THURSDAY FRIDAY SATURDAY

Keep track of important dates

Three beautiful and colorful calendars that celebrate some of the most popular trends in America today.

Look for:

Just Babies—a 16 month calendar that features a full year of absolutely adorable babies!

1998 CALENDAR

Just Babies

16 months of adorable bundles of joy!

Hometown Quilts
1998 Calendar

A 16 month quilting extravaganza!

Hometown Quilts—a 16 month calendar featuring quilted art squares, plus a short history on twelve different quilt patterns.

Inspirations—a 16 month calendar with inspiring pictures and quotations.

Inspirations

A 16 month calendar that will lift your spirits and gladden your heart

Steeple Hill™

❧ HARLEQUIN®

Value priced at $9.99 U.S./$11.99 CAN., these calendars make a perfect gift!

Available in retail outlets in August 1997.   CAL98

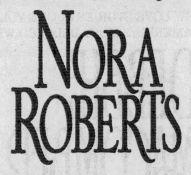

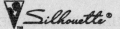

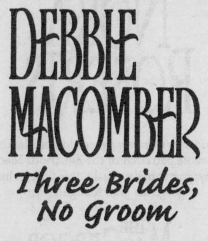